CEILINGS

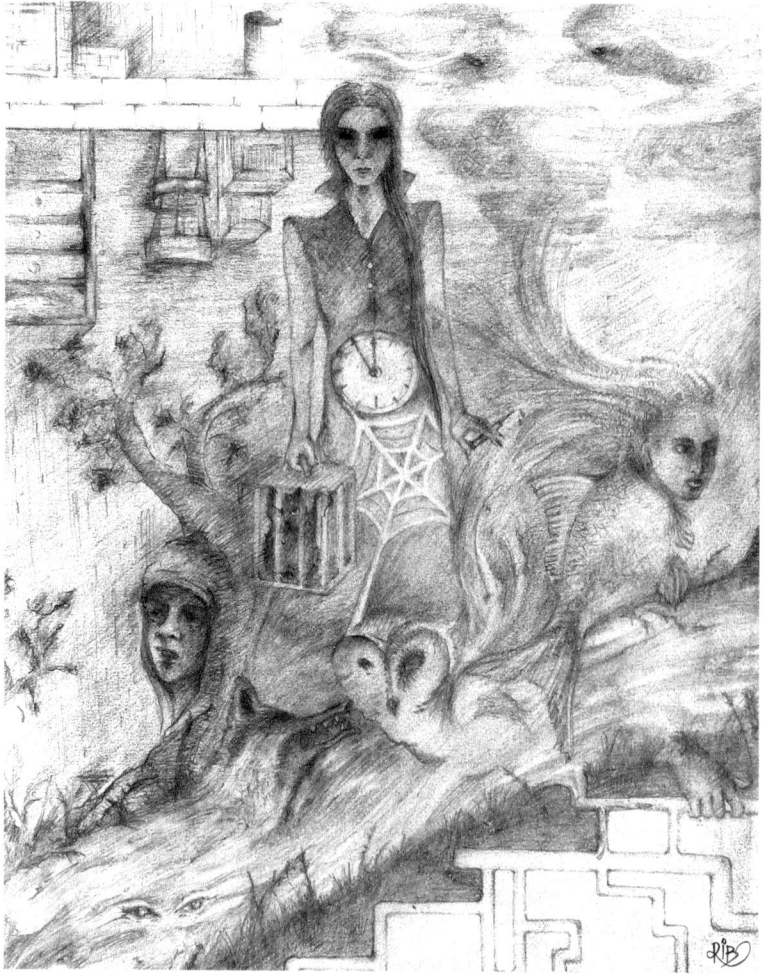

Zuzana Brabcová

CEILINGS

Translated from the Czech by
TEREZA VEVERKA NOVICKÁ

TWISTED SPOON PRESS
PRAGUE
2025

ISBN 978-80-88628-05-7
ISBN 978-80-88628-35-4 (E-BOOK)

This translation was made possible by a grant
from the Ministry of Culture of the Czech Republic.

MINISTERSTVO
KULTURY

For Sára

. . . the iceberg in my chest chafes
against the ceiling above the void.
— Ivan Diviš, *Psalms*

So now you know: certain realities flutter through the city for years and years, floundering, while others swiftly and immediately cling to the plaster, tree bark, or the skin of a stranger at a very specific point. Today, you know this, but back then, you thought they would all become static and disappear into the depths above the ceiling for good, into the yawning expanse of the universe.

But the goblin embraces you so intimately, for it was you trapped in the drum he was banging. If only he didn't lisp!

"No ekth-panth, no ekth-panth, there ith no ekth-panth!"

And because you are starved like an animal cowering for weeks and months within the scorched recesses of an island, unable to fathom its idealized outline, you'll consider yourself lucky to settle for the stale scraps of what you have experienced, the faded tableau and bare bones of the image.

•

Two paramedics in orange strap her to a stretcher and slam the door shut. "I'm like that frog," she tells the narrow space into which several years have contracted. "The well frog, whose head burst when it saw the ocean for the first time." They drive off across town, slowing down and accelerating at intersections. She's jostled on the stretcher with one palm pressed against the ambulance ceiling and looking up and through, a sky full of February clouds, made wild by the wind and rushing by in the opposite direction. Cracking and thundering iceberg clouds break off from the mass of ice and float off into an entirely different sky. Something erupts out of the movement, something that has a name, just need to remember what it is.

"Water . . . Please, some water . . ." She remembers now. Thirst is the name. She's never been this thirsty in her life.

A head of red hair turns to her as a naked lady tattooed on the back of a fat neck twists into abstraction.

"Don't have any, lady . . . Just chill, okay? We're almost there, you'll get somethin' to drink once we get there for sure . . ."

"Just a sip of water . . ." She pleads again as the redheaded paramedic in front takes a swig from a plastic bottle.

Wherever it is they're taking me, the only thing I have is this knapsack. I wonder if Rybka knows what a knapsack is? Or a haversack? Or a satchel? When I get back . . . And the flat roofs of skyscrapers merge with the clouds she's staring at, Siemens Microsoft Hewlett Packard.

She strains against the restraints in her desire for water. A single sip. To moisten parched lips. She tries to recall an expletive, any expletive. But after all those years with Dalibor she's forgotten them all. The fan of profanity has snapped shut.

"Look 'ere, lady, you'll get yours, don't worry 'bout it! Be there sooner than ya think! Don't go blamin' me, I'm just the little man here. It's them others that've gotta prescribe you water . . ."

What kind of patois is this? Maybe she's been unlucky enough to get stuck in the middle of a joke the redhead is getting tangled up in with the point nowhere in sight, and once the klutz finally delivers the punchline to the driver, it'll slip out of his mouth in a moment of awkward silence and head straight home.

Be there sooner than ya think. Where, exactly? The sheet of paper set on fire to get rid of the evidence is slowly turning to ash in the sink. And syllables, brittle and crackling and quiet, escape from parched lips, while old leaves and dry branches crackle underfoot and the sky covers her thirst and a mighty force conceals everything in sight: no longer is there a road and an ambulance traveling from point A to point B, no longer a knapsack at her side and the memory of Rybka: the thirst has curled her pinkies and cursed her liver, wrung her entire being dry and flung the rag into the desert.

Rybka, you have no idea all the things that had to be in our knapsack whenever we trekked through Šárka Park, into the Prokop Valley, or along the Berounka River on the yellow hiking trail past the cabin colonies, Botas sneakers on our feet. I've amassed a snowdrift of lies between myself and that bygone signpost, between myself and you, one that I'll never be able to clear away. Do they still even make them? Botas sneakers?

But now, my bag contains no band-aids, vaccination certificate, or salami sandwich, its smell always permeating everything. I should text you while there's still time, before you start to get worried and call all the nearby hospitals and ERs and morgues, terrified, but my restrained body has petrified into a monolith. I try to lift an arm: it's made of sandstone, granite, marble. It doesn't belong to me. It lies motionless alongside an unfamiliar body like the paw of the Sphinx.

The ride takes forever. She sees construction workers installing a neon ad on the roof of a glass building as they pass. She floats up to it, to the Staropramen sign of colored lightbulbs. She glides past and drinks the bitter, cold, glittering rust while her eyes fix on her slippers sticking up toward the clouds above the ambulance, suddenly fascinating to her, purple and fuzzy and clearly from the Vietnamese marketplace, a Christmas present from her mother. The redhead looks over his shoulder, eyebrows raised, at the woman now laughing like a lunatic, since she thinks something as tacky as these slippers on her feet must surely guarantee her a happy outcome.

To escape. To flee. To fly off, as soon as the ambulance bursts open like a white maggot.

"Where are you taking me?"

The female nude sprawled in the ginger brush hasn't budged, and the paramedic, having swallowed his dialect, has returned to silently staring at the road ahead. But now he starts to yawn so demonstratively that the supine lady suddenly shoots up and turns a shade of green. It might be from sipping an ice-cold Mojito. But it was she who ordered it! And that's her, sitting in the Cubist café with her mom, the waiter setting two glasses in front of them along with a cream puff. The cream puff is angular, of course — it is, after all, a Cubist café. A pianist takes a seat at the grand piano and the sound of all his knuckles cracking carries to their table as he wearily reaches for the keys.

"I wanted to talk to you, and now this . . ." Mom speaks over the first clamorous chords. And it's me, not the tattoo lady, who sips the Mojito and laughs, because: "Mom, do you recognize what he's playing?" And the pianist's worn vocal cords sentimentally rasp out a Russian folk song:

Black eyes, passionate eyes,
black eyes, beautiful eyes,
O how I love you,

how I fear you,
I chanced upon you
at the wrong time . . .

And Mom doesn't believe it's just a coincidence, that I didn't request the song, and she buries her spoon into the Cubist cream puff with gusto —

"Where are you taking me?" She doesn't scream. She holds it in. She masters her tone of voice so as to allow a completely normal, matter-of-fact, genuinely civil interpersonal conversation. But the neck-back has fallen silent. He's even stopped regaling his partner with jokes about gypsies and fags.

Without warning, the ambulance stops. The doors slam. Nothing happens for a long while.

I'm dreaming, not of a Mojito, I wouldn't dare: they're simply stopping for water and will give me a drink of it. They're not transporting an object. A slab of sandstone in slippers. They'll fill up a plastic bottle with water at a gas-station restroom and buy coffee from the vending machine, the driver with sugar, the paramedic without, and a sandwich and bacon-flavored crackers. A geyser's gushing out of the road ahead. A cloud above the city bursts and water streams straight into my mouth. At Můstek, three old chubby Italian women, laughing and chattering, bend over the water fountain on a hot summer day, July 16, 2008, at 1:15 p.m. Or was it some other time? Does it matter?

I place my hands palms-up under a stream originating somewhere high in the mountains. You are with me. I trail behind your bowed, delicate, girlish back, and your brisk, ungirly stride says: Damn it, stop lazing around in bed all day feeling blue all the time and get up and go outside, walk, strut, stride, tromp, march through the countryside and scramble up a hill, run down the hill, take deep breaths, as Mom used to say when you were a little girl, Jesus, you're gasping for air as if you're about to give birth, breathe! inhale the smells, look where the rustle of a tree is coming from, that animal, this rock, over there a dilapidated deer stand with porcini growing underneath it, when's the last time you found summer ceps? and the wind riffling the treetops and cobwebs between fingers as a mosquito sits on your shoulder in a droplet of blood.

And you let me drink from your cupped hands, clumsily, and I end up with a wet face. Feet blistered and still ten kilometers to go. The landscape in the valley below suddenly comes into view, lit by the setting sun. I embrace you as if for the last time. Where has this moment gone? Who could locate it within my body, now stiff as a statue? Where has this moment gone . . . Who could locate it . . . and your tongue in my mouth, the taste of blackberries, your saliva, life.

Finally. The redhead opens the ambulance door and slams it shut again. A guy in a leather jacket collapses into the seat next to her, square-rimmed plastic glasses protruding from his face and looking a bit like Andy Warhol.

"Got anything to drink? I'm so thirsty," she whispers as they start to move again.

He barely looks at her. He registers with little more than disinterest the strapped-down monolith adorned with purple slippers, an ancient knapsack on its stomach. In the rush, it was the only thing she found in Ash's box. He averts his eyes and says nothing.

I'll let them take me anywhere, Rybka, if only to make up for what I've caused you. I'll shuffle down hospital corridors, let them stick tubes down my throat, cover myself at night with the murmurs of sick old women and their children keeping vigil by the decrepit beds, children annoyed by the time wasted amid the foul hospital stench, I'll let the bottomless babbling of the world and the screeching of goblins permeate my brain as penance.

See how lifelessly and wearily I step into the prison yard, spilling sauce from my mess tin down my sweatshirt, and how the hungry hands of thieves grope me at night. I'll throw myself into prayer, icy as the Vltava in January, or freeze forever in a bubble of silence instead. And next, leaping, up-down, down-up, I'll walk around Mount Kailash with vultures circling above, at whose foot your granddad wished to be chopped into pieces and scattered when he died.

Anywhere but the Garden.

And they're off again, jolting along cobblestones and asphalt, stopping at traffic lights. At one point, Ema turns onto her side, straps permitting, and vomits. She vomits right at Andy Warhol's feet. A small jellyfish glistens on the ambulance floor, a speech bubble someone forgot to provide with text.

"You want to play the broken telephone game with me?" she asks. But Andy doesn't understand. And how could he? You need more than two people to play the telephone game. So she starts to play by herself, whispering and muttering, stuttering and passing the message along until she suddenly thinks, what if the game were reversed just this once? What if at the very end, what started as babble ended up as a distinct word: for instance —

The Garden. She sees it pulsating wildly as if it had sprung into existence just a second ago, a mockery of symmetry, a monstrous cosmos split into a triptych. In a dark landscape crisscrossed by streaks of light, naked riders on hogs gallop past a well into which clusters of dead birds rain down, sitting on an opulent throne, the devil-pope devours the damned only to defecate them, and in that moment an infernal band and that goblin with its drum imprisoning a toddler march past, and scorpions and a man crucified on a harp here while over there are two earlobes joined by a needle, a knife blade protruding from their midst.

"The devil-pope devours . . ." Four-eyes turns to her questioningly. "Do you know where they're taking us? You got anything to drink?" Surprisingly, Andy Warhol speaks. "No clue. You must be cold." And Andy Warhol takes off his leather jacket and drapes it over her, pulling it up to her chin.

The ambulance driver mutters something into his radio. Only now does she realize the siren isn't on. Luckily neither she nor Warhol are all that important. Not emergencies. She should've tried to leave the ER at the Motol Hospital on her own, just an empty wetsuit left behind in her stead, swum home and gone to sleep, finally without any pills, slept for twenty-four hours and then woken up, pulled up the blinds and off to work and to lunch with Rybka and in the evening lit candles and played Nico and waited for Dita to ring the doorbell . . . and talked with her and laughed and then made love all night long. Woken up. Pulled up the blinds. Gone to work. Called Rybka, invited Mom to the café for a Mojito and Cubist cream puff. Just moving within the safe belly of the everyday.

To sleep long, yet to be born, to fall asleep, finally, after all these years, without any pills. But could her body still manage that?

"Have you ever been under psychiatric care?"

She had been admitted to Motol Hospital three hours ago and was lying in urgent care, more poison dripping into her veins — on top of what she'd taken during the day and night. Next to her behind a partition screen, a doctor was loudly bringing a woman out of hypoglycemic shock: "Mrs. Voráčková, can you hear me? Blink if you can hear me!"

Ema heard his firm voice as it rose to the ceiling and fell back to the floor, over and over, a shamanic bouncing ball to awaken the dead. In the meantime, she had asked for the bedpan three times and a million times had wanted to get up, thank them for the care, and leave. But whenever she sat up, the room would spin wildly, moving upward in a spiral.

So she gave up. "For over a year . . . these pills are the only thing that makes me sleep and makes nothing hurt."

"Come on, Mrs. Voráčková! You're almost back! Can you hear me?"

"How many did you take today?"

She mumbled a number at random, not that it made any difference, it was a fail no matter what. Not a single muscle twitched in the doctor's face. She already knew everything, assumed everything, had seen it all before.

"You'll have to wait for transfer."

One hour, two hours, an eternity before two paramedics in orange strapped her to a stretcher and slammed the door shut. They drove off across town, the sky full of February clouds, rushing wildly in the opposite direction, the clouds split apart and grown heavy like icebergs.

And she spotted one more thing above Prague: two white sandals, unusually elegant, soaring and circling, disappearing and then reappearing out of the darkening clouds like two storks. She couldn't tear her eyes away from the sight. She tensely observed their graceful trajectories crossing, only to diverge again, leaving behind an ever more intricate tangle of lines across the sky, like airplane contrails. At one point they disappeared from her field of vision but soon reappeared, playing tag and chasing each other in the snowdrifts of sky. And yet this enthralling play of sandals had something disturbing and dismal about it, a splinter stuck under the skin. She suddenly realized what it was: in the throes of their baffling dance, one was irretrievably drifting away from the other.

It was their last day in Limni Keriou. They were waiting for the driver, their suitcases already in the bus. "Let's climb up the cliff one last time, to say goodbye. Who knows when we'll get to the sea again . . . The driver's not showing up anytime soon, time is quantified rather differently in this country." What Dalibor meant was that the driver had lost track of time while talking to the chatty cashier in the corner store.

They quickly scrambled up the cliff, which dropped abruptly into the bay. Every third, fifth, seventh wave shattered against the rocky mass, drenching them. "Look, there they go again!"

She spotted a tiny black dot in the sea at a considerable distance from the shore. The minuscule, barely discernible head of "their" swimmer. Each morning and evening, this endurance swimmer got lost somewhere in the ocean, and they knew them only as a dot disappearing and reemerging in the immensity — they never saw them getting in or out of the water, and had no idea who this person was or what they looked like. Man or woman, if the swimmer were to be submerged in the water for good, if they were to witness the swimmer's drowning at that unimaginable distance, they wouldn't be able to do a thing. Death, puny as a pinhead, would be a wholly insignificant, peripheral occurrence within the vast blue of indifferent, eternal motion, just another wave of countless waves. They would just climb down the cliff, get on the bus, buy one last Mythos beer at the airport, and fly back to Prague.

She decided to quit watching the endurance swimmer. On a whim, she slipped off her cork sandals, threw her arm back, and flung them into the sea. They disappeared in the foam; she wasn't sure they would reemerge. As she turned around to leave, Dalibor squeezed her wrist. The white sandals had surfaced and were now dancing wildly in the waves, but while one of them was being pulled toward the shore, the other was drifting out to sea. Sometimes a wave would bring them together, but the barrage of waves that followed inevitably pulled them apart.

"Why did you do that?"

She glanced at Dalibor in surprise. A straw hat, sunglasses, stubbled chin. He wasn't looking at her. He was watching the dance of the white sandals retreating into the distance, his sunburned nose as if wanting to free itself from his face and . . . and what? Perhaps fling itself off the cliff after them. It almost seemed as if . . . but no. Dalibor wouldn't . . . just because of some shoes . . . Surely just a spray of seawater.

"What's the matter? You know I need to buy new sandals . . . These were all worn and the strap was broken on the left one anyway and . . ."

She heard herself babbling, prattling on and on in sudden dread of the silence that threatened to lodge itself between them like an uncrossable rift. The inane stream of words kept gushing out of her, she didn't even know what she was talking about anymore, caught up in new summer shoe trends, and once they got back, she'd look for some . . . She really did need new sandals . . . She had a few stores in mind . . .

And while she despised herself, painfully disgusted with

herself like she hadn't been in a long time, while one white sandal became infinitesimal in the bay and the other disappeared for good, Dalibor, her husband, who as everyone knew never raised his voice, snapped at her. In fact, he yelled.

"Hush! Don't you get it? You should've connected them! Tied them together!"

Yes, she hadn't misheard. What he had shouted at her really had been "Hush!" He could've gone with "Shut up!" or "Zip it!" or "Cut the bullshit!" — but not even the greatest outrage could degrade his diction.

Dalibor filed for divorce nine months later. Oddly, there wasn't a single mention of white cork sandals.

Ema seemed to be willing now to settle for anything, any memory at all, she'd sink her teeth into old shoes, for what it's worth, just to avoid being in the here and now, just to escape the ambulance for a fraction of a second. But the ambulance was hermetically sealed like a bathyscaph: from that moment nothing could get in, and nothing could get out.

She was certain and under no illusion: if in some crumb-filled side pocket of her knapsack she'd actually forgotten to check, she might find a forgotten sleeping pill, she wouldn't hesitate for a second. Look away, Rybka, from the kinds of crazy your mom is up to. You're floating in her bloodstream toward her heart, and from her heart you sail in a rickety dinghy of pine bark. Look away, close your eyes, turn out the lights and off to bed, all the Grimm tales and the one about Koschei the Deathless long finished, just one last Stilnox, just one more hour of not knowing, not being.

But there was no forgotten pocket: Ema had already searched them all, every nook and cranny a million times over. In terrible tremors, she'd shaken out seventeen volumes of the classics, one after another, and countless other books that over the years she was in the habit of using to stash blister packs trimmed with manicure scissors. It had been ages since she last read any of these books, and yet she opened them with such eagerness that the sharp edges of the blister packs sometimes nicked her fingers. Thick novels worked best: who'd have the patience to thoroughly leaf through Volume II of *The Man Without Qualities* anyway?

No strays. Not even in the box of Kotex. Today she had polished off the last fifteen pills and that was it. Kaput. The end. Finito, and then just a vacuous cocoon, a wretched bug, a botched metamorphosis on the carpet. Not to think and to sleep. To sleep and more importantly not to think about what you'll feel like when you wake up.

Right then, a dazzling white bolt of lightning tore through the emptiness that was on the verge of engulfing her mind. She expected it to immediately dissipate within her, to again submerge into the darkness, but it remained motionless and quivered like a glistening trickle of saliva, illuminating the surrounding nothingness. The doormat! She'd forgotten about the doormat! There was one more hiding place, one she was especially proud of. But the pills — as if they didn't even belong to her when in the hallway! — had to be left in the box, otherwise the blister pack would crackle suspiciously and the contents get pulverized. She opened the door to her apartment and in a strange, hot vortex, dropped to all fours: nothing under the doormat but layers of dust.

And that's where a neighbor found her in the morning.

Sleep now, Rybka. Maybe everything will be reborn out of your name, little fish, like the water's surface blooming out of a single seed into a miraculous web of aquatic flora, and I will lean down to your sleeping form once again, to the fragrance of your hair. When you were young, you would insist on sleeping with your eyes open, like a fish.

She realized Warhol was observing her and tried to summon a grateful smile. For the leather jacket. He suddenly burst into hiccups, so hilariously, like a child, unstoppably, that his glasses started to bounce on the bridge of his nose. She didn't want to stare at him lest she make him feel embarrassed, so she turned away: and there, outside, on the wall, letters in motion . . . words . . . She kept repeating them in her head to figure out their meaning, "ústa v ní," literally, "mouth in her" . . . perhaps a fragment of a line of a love poem, or . . . "ústa v ní," "ústa v ní," "ústa-v-ní" — it finally clicked: this was no poem, but the name of a street: ÚSTAVNÍ, Institution Street.

They were at the Garden.

A doctor exited the admissions building and handed the redhead some papers. The ambulance slowly made its way along the asphalt roads and Ema forgot her thirst. They stopped. Detox — Addiction Treatment Center. I won't be getting out of here for at least three months. Possible side effects: reduced libido, hair loss, abnormal dreams.

"Well, lady, we're here!"

The jovial redhead yanked the ambulance door open and undid the straps. I handed Andy his jacket, picking up my knapsack with an air of nonchalance . . .

The paramedic wasn't expecting it, coming from such a wreck: all of a sudden, I dug my claws right into the back of his neck until the naked lady shrieked in pain, and taking advantage, in a sudden burst of strength, I shoved him, making him stumble, and made a run for it.

"Ruuun!" Warhol screamed somewhere behind me, a crazed exuberance lacing his voice, now cured of his hiccups.

So I ran. I knew full well where the exit was: I had been here before, once in the summer with Dita for *Mezi ploty*, the Between the Fences festival, where I'd bought a wicker basket for my sewing supplies. I had a stash in there too, under the needles, in a round mint container. And once, long ago, to visit Dalibor, who had taken refuge in the Garden to avoid conscription.

Naturally they ran after you. Mid-run, you pulled your phone out of your knapsack. "Rybka!" — "Mom? What is it? What's going on? Where are you? Why are you so out of breath?" — "Don't worry, I'll come back . . . They're gonna take my phone . . . ústa v ní . . . Detox!"

Some loon, wrapped head to toe in a swath of shawl, not unlike a mummy that had just clambered out of some forgotten fissure of time, stood on a bench and began cheering wildly, flapping his arms and yelling "Go, go, go! You can do it!" though it remained unclear whether his sympathies lay with the paramedics or the slippered woman. So what if those ridiculous house slippers her mom had given her for Christmas spoiled the whole action scene. So what if you lost one of the slippers — in your peripheral vision you could see the mummy jump off the bench and hurl himself at the trophy, snagging it like a sports fan snags a towel tossed by an athlete, tucking it quickly underneath the shawl with a triumphant expression on his face — so what: the other slipper will become a raft on which you will shoot the Garden's rapids straight into Dita's calm, soothing embrace. Into Mom's kitchen, the water for coffee already boiling. Two sugar cubes and an exhale later: "Mom, you wouldn't believe the awful dream I had today!"

She wasn't giving up just yet. If she managed to make it to that telephone booth over there, to run through the main building past the reception and then through the gate to the stairs, she'd find herself on the other side where she'd be, God knows why she thought so, untouchable. And mid-run, during her ridiculous, hobbly getaway, Ema made a vow: If I make it, I'll start over. I'll never touch that crap again as long as I live. I can do it. There was a time, damn it, when I didn't need the stuff at all. Back when . . . But now she couldn't recall a single such moment. She simply couldn't reach that point in time anymore when she hadn't needed it: It was too distant, and somewhere over the horizon it burst like an egg and spilled out formlessly across the Garden.

To capture a cloud and strangle it till it gushes a river.

The redhead caught her in a chokehold as the driver twisted her wrist behind her back. "Get a grip, lady!" he tried for a placating tone.

"You feckin' bitch," erupted the redhead, likely in retaliation for the spilled Mojito on his neck.

"I only have one slipper," she cried, as if that were a circumstance that could unequivocally forestall involuntary commitment in a secure ward.

But it was no longer the truth. For even the other slipper, the raft, in which she'd placed her last hopes, had capsized during the scuffle and disappeared somewhere in the chaos behind her.

The men supported her on each side, dragging her along as best they could, and she felt as if with the loss of her slippers she had lost her legs as well, as though her body from the waist down had turned into the useless fin of a giant fish. She was a fish, then, and a herd of hogs saddled with naked riders went hurtling past. Why not? In the Garden, anything was possible.

As the redhead rang the doorbell of Pavilion No. 8, in front of which the strange procession had halted, Ema, heart pounding, took one last look at the sky. Overcast, dreary, nothing special. But then: a piece of cloud broke off suddenly like an iceberg, with a terrible crack, and set off through space frozen solid.

Drink them up, swallow those clouds, gulp them down with all your might, because all you've got to look forward to now are ceilings.

A voice suddenly wailed down the length of the hall: "Admiiission!" The slam of a door. She squirmed helplessly in her socks in front of the nurses' station. She saw a kitchen right across from it, an enormous pot of spinach, a row of chairs underneath a wall-mounted telephone, a door leading to the canteen. Women were starting to amble out, at first lazy and apathetic, but once they noticed her, their eyes lit up, their lips parted, and the color returned to their pallid cheeks. At least *something* was happening. And that something looked even more wretched than they did — which was comforting in itself. The revived zombies discreetly came closer and moved away, as if apathetic, dipping into the canteen only to reappear, some of them missing a body, legs growing straight out of their heads like the tadpole people Rybka used to draw as a kid. The hallway began to disintegrate into a farrago of details: a toothless grin, a towel turban, a covetous wide-eyed stare, and a sharp whisper: "Got a cig? They won't let you smoke upstairs, you know."

Before Ema could reply, a massive woman with hair flowing down to her waist wrapped an arm around her shoulders: "Druggie or alkie?"

Ema didn't understand. She had no clue yet she would hear this question, used in place of a greeting, at least a hundred more times. She didn't understand, and thirst again buried her head deep into a sand dune. She swayed from side to side in a drowsy trance with the dull regularity of the metronome on the piano when Rybka used to play as a kid. A specter sidled up to her suddenly, her pale face full of piercings, and kissed her fiercely on the mouth before whispering wildly: *"Chaimo margiz duz!"*

Maybe she had misunderstood. She definitely wouldn't have been able to repeat what she'd just heard, yet the words seemed familiar, as if she used to know what they meant a long time ago, as if it had been her mother tongue in a previous lifetime — familiar, certainly more familiar than her own language right now, sentences which for months and years had been coiling tightly around her, wrapping her into a mummy like that loon's shawl.

The white specter's face still loomed mere inches from hers, a moonscape full of craters. A bit longer and Ema would've gotten lost in it for good. She awaited the next incantation, but the girl released a ferocious burp right in her face instead and let out a deranged cackle. Ema was assailed by a wave of stink. What on earth was that smell? Ah, yes, the smell of spinach, how could she ever forget! Mom, I'll go bananas in here, come get me, come pick me up right after lunchtime, don't leave me here!

And suddenly that green stench barreled into her like a murderer at the top of a staircase, and she fell, tumbling, clanging down stair by stair, and each one resonating like a piano key until the fall produced an off-key chord, one chord progression after another in a deranged, deafening atonal composition, she tumbled headfirst, icebergs breaking off in her mind, and

Rybka emerged from one of these crevasses, thank god I managed to call you in time, you'll be able to find me and maybe one day forgive me, you'll find me down there at the foot of the concrete stairway and you'll assemble the chaos of shards into a new shape, together we'll manage, but she'd already been falling for so long, the wind whistling in her ears, the air around her squeaking like a rubber toy, she'd been falling for ages — and just as she thought, what if the stairs are endless? what if whatever begins in the Garden never ends? she saw far below her, the bottom. A few more bloodied piano keys, somersaults, clangs, spat-out teeth, chords, tears, and curses before she finally sprawled out on the linoleum like a rag doll, before she plummeted into the kitchen of their old Smíchov apartment, before she landed right at her mother's feet.

•

"Emička, stop lazing around and go play with something! It's almost lunchtime."

She slowly picks herself off the floor; just a few welts and bruises, nothing drastic. She glances upward at the resonating stairway, but the mute ceiling of their kitchen is all she can see. She hears a strange thud, like when someone blows up a paper bag and pops it: the future has snapped the stairway shut like a fan.

"Mommy, do the voice!" She handed Mr. Mouse to her mother. Mom usually got into her role right off the bat, sometimes she even turned into Mr. Mouse, but this time, she just turned back to the stove where she was stirring something green, something that Ema knew for sure she wouldn't be able to stomach.

"Not right now, Emička. Later."

She pondered "later." It was strange, but "later" was in the future. As soon as Mom puts food on her plate, she'd try to say, "Not right now. Later."

After she'd given enough thought to "later" and climbed each "later" like steps back up the stairway, she spotted a strange specter, a phantom who sidled up to her familiarly and mumbled several odd, incomprehensible words. She found herself quickly sliding down the slide, luckily right next to the stairway, back into their kitchen.

She noticed that Mr. Mouse's belly was coming apart at the seams. The situation called for immediate anesthesia. She sharpened a pencil until it was thin as a needle and jabbed it in next to the plushie's open wound. The operation could begin. Focusing, she began to pull Mr. Mouse's entrails, dirty cotton, into the light, one centimeter at a time —

"Mom, does everybody die?" The question burst out of her almost involuntarily. She wasn't all that sure she'd be able to bring her patient back to life.

"Yes," Mom absent-mindedly shouted from the stove.

A lightning-quick intervention was called for — Ema abruptly tore open Mr. Mouse's entire belly, wanting to fill it with the cooked green stuff, but Mr. Mouse was no more — he had lost his form and synthetic matter had spilled out of his gut and his face had become warped beyond recognition.

"Not me." Not me! So nobody would notice her botched operation, she quickly tossed the torso into the trash.

She doodled on a piece of paper for a while, pretending to write an important letter, perhaps Mr. Mouse's death notice, but then she fearlessly pointed the rapier of her pencil at her mother to give her one more chance.

"Maybe everybody dies, sure, but not me."

"You too."

You-too, you-too, you-too — she began to sing, picturing an Eskimo floating away on an iceberg. You-too, you-too — and suddenly she remembered the day their turtle died and how she had stubbornly poked it across the floor with a ladle, pushing it all the way to the table, but it had made no difference.

Only now did the meaning of her mother's words click.

Their eyes met.

"Not me!" She gave her mother one last opportunity to set it right.

"You too, Emička, me too. We all die, that's how the world works." Mom must've had a bad night's sleep.

The little girl started to wail. "Not me! Don't lie! Lying is bad!"

She tried to hit her mother, to get her to see reason and stop spewing nonsense, but her little fist met emptiness as her mother began to recede rapidly though she stayed in place, standing by the stove even while disappearing into a thick, green swamp where Ema no longer recognized her.

Nothing was safe anymore. And after her mother threw cold water in her face to get her to stop screaming, Ema glimpsed a kind of fantastical crowd, figures and objects brightly colored like straight out of her English primer for preschoolers, a dog and a cat, a tiger and a lamb, a boy and a girl and a mailman with mailbag and a sailor in a striped shirt, a rocking horse and cradle and slippers and waterproof jacket and freshly baked bread and carrot bunch and jingling tram carrying all that through the city, and on top of that Grandad and Grandma and so many familiar beings, the line stretching on and winding and receding into the distance and one holding onto the other, the cat the dog, the dog the girl, the girl the grandad, the grandad the grandma, and they pulled and they pulled and pulled, and even though there was so many of them, they were unable to yank out that weight, its roots deep in the earth.

•

All around her hands in hyperactive motion, hands fluttering and flitting through a room too small to allow them to take flight, too small and getting even smaller, and if they didn't get out in time, the walls would close in on them and crush both her and the three unfamiliar women, who were like peas in a pod, crush them and their active hands, hurried but with intent and purpose, all these hands tasked with something, they pulled her sweater off over her head and removed her sweatpants and wrapped a rubber cuff around her bicep — "Look here, Mrs. Černá, don't fall asleep on us and give it a few good squeezes!" What nonsense, how could she possibly fall asleep amid this noisy swarm of hands! The bracelets on their wrists were clattering like chainsaws, their watches thundering like a mountain storm.

ID, cigarettes, lighter, cellphone, thank goodness I managed to . . . keys to the apartment . . . to call Rybka . . . disappeared in a locker. Fat fingers struggled to unfasten her earrings. She had four, slow work. Finally. She stood there naked, in just socks and underwear. Did she have any room left for astonishment? Yes: when a deft hand, riddled with eyes resembling warts, took a practiced look through her socks and patted down her crotch. Nothing? Nothing. Good.

Swaying in the doorway to the nurses' station was a wraith in a thin, washed-out nightie barely covering the butt. Ema was about to be dressed in an identical one. The wraith stared curiously, its face nothing but eyes. "Run along to your room, Gizela!"

"But I need . . ." she paused. "Nurse, I'm . . . psychotic."

For a moment, the harpy's sneer humanized her. "Aren't we all, dear?"

On the wall behind Gizela, a wall that once had been the horizon, a sudden gyration, a dance, thudding: an infernal band struck up a cheerful tune before vanishing into a giant well.

"But I'm having . . ." Gizela didn't give up. She raised one barefooted leg and propped the foot on her knee and stood in front of the door like a scrawny flamingo. "Hallucinations!" she blurted out triumphantly.

A pair of hands shot out from the nurses' station, grabbed Gizela by the shoulders, making her stagger, and led her off to her room. "Hallucinaaations!" It no longer sounded the least bit triumphant. A horrific, truly horrific, the most horrific howl filled the hallway and Ema saw claws sprouting out of the flesh of that howl, saw the claws trying to dig into the walls like hooks, yes, successfully here and there, but mostly slipping off, though without giving up and mulishly keeping up the effort, until the howl eventually scrambled up the wall to the ceiling where it stayed, hanging upside down like a bat.

Ema stepped off the scales. "Forty-seven kilos, Mrs. Černá, you're terribly thin! Are you eating?"

She wasn't quite all there yet. She was still with the howl up on the ceiling. Of course she eats! She eats and she drinks, and with relish! One banana and one nutridrink a day for almost a year now. And where that infernal band had been playing just a moment ago, a bulletin board was hanging on the hook of Gizela's howl, a cork board filled with pinups of beaming celebrities, each of their faces sliced in two by razor grins, looking quite terrifying, and it's plain as day that the cause of their joy was having survived their stint in rehab in good health, wearing nighties barely covering their butts and plunging necklines.

When the nurses finally tucked Ema into bed, time alarmingly contracted and liquified. In the distant past, she used to discuss the nature of time with Dalibor into the wee hours of the morning (up to the moment her theories began to disintegrate into animalistic yawns), but in the here and now, time — disdainfully dismissive of any dispute, compressed into a transparent plastic bag and resembling some inane liquid creature — dripped straight into her veins with brash intimacy, as if they'd been buddies at school, first infuriatingly slow, but then faster and faster. It pretended not to want anything from her, just here as an old friend, drip, drip, drip —

"Hey, my name's Gizela. Are you druggie or alkie?"

Hmm. Here we go again. The next morning, Rybka, I was black and blue all over from fighting it all night, from grappling all night long with the angel of time.

"Benzodiazepines." Surprisingly, she didn't stutter.

"Benzodiazepinesbenzodiazepinesbenzodiazepines," she tried to utter out loud three times in quick succession, not once tripping up. At the foot of her bed, the skinny eighteen-year-old Gypsy girl, Gizela, was hugging her knees, her arms and legs and neck riddled with scars, two of her front teeth missing. The girl giggled and attempted to say it as well, bez-die-ah, bez-die-ah, but she couldn't get it right, she was tongue-tied, we both started laughing like maniacs and the needle in my vein slipped out of place.

"So you're a junkie," Gizela concluded.

Only now did Ema notice the ceiling, awestruck. She'd been staring at it for some time already, she just hadn't been aware of it, like you're not aware of the screen in a cinema. The ceiling was towering — there was no other way to describe it — at an unimaginable height, and this height was simultaneously its depths, unfathomable because she had never seen such a high ceiling before. She tried to come up with a reasonable explanation. This pavilion must've been one of the oldest in the Garden, maybe from the turn of the last century as the year 1909 was etched above the entry gate to the grounds. The enormous wooden windows spanning one entire wall must date back to that time as well, windows riddled with loose panes, rattling in the February wind like dice in a cupped hand before being rolled. Maybe back then such towering ceilings had been all the rage in hospital architecture.

But she soon had to admit that she was missing a key to the ceiling. She opened her nightstand drawer — God knows what she was expecting to find in there — a pack of tissues thoroughly inspected by a nurse, an even more thoroughly inspected book, Rybka's letter, no visitors allowed, nicotine gum, which had almost made her hurl, no smoking allowed, a pen, and a checkered notebook. Why would a key be there?

And yet she still felt that in the space high above her she could make out lighter areas with the distinct marks of removed furniture. The outlines of a table and bookcase in the corner, someone had lived on the ceiling and had moved out in a hurry, and no wonder, with ever new batches of alcoholics in washed-out nighties and God knows who else gaping into the living room. If she could just manage to find that key, she could enter, settle in the spot where the rocking chair used to be, and rock away endlessly, hanging upside down like Gizela's howl.

Soon she realized that day and night did not alternate in here, despite the nurses doing their best. For instance, they would switch the lights on or off, and that signified something. Mornings were discernible by a poppyseed bread roll and a blood test, evenings were marked by a blood test and a poppy-seed bread roll and yogurt. For long hours, even days on end, the women would fall into a deep sleep or march from the giant windows to the door and back, spitting out crushed glass, parading before the tribunal of judges sitting in their own minds, and wring their hands (for the first time ever, Ema saw someone actually wring their hands, having believed until then that it was merely a figure of speech) or fold their arms behind their backs like wings, back and forth, forward march, over and over, like Irena, dubbed "the Lady."

Exactly twenty-three hours, forty-four minutes, and twenty-two seconds later — for time can be subdued only by the methodical recording of intervals between individual drips, so that night could be night again and day be day, for even on the ceiling in the abandoned apartment shone the pale round seal of the moon, which was actually the spot where the wall clock used to be — so right at the moment they laid Ema on the bed and hooked up her IV, a stately white chess queen, carved from a single piece of wood, strode into Room No. 1 in the company of the nurses.

"Greetings, miladies!"

The motionless cocoons didn't move a whit. Only Gizela spluttered, her eyes taking over her face like two targets. Oh, brother, brother of mine, who goes by the name of Ash, my brother whom I mustn't forget to mention in all these forms and background questionnaires and about whom I must talk during all those sessions and community talks and group therapies, whom it would be useful for me to incorporate into my collages during art therapy for the "my family" prompt, let no detail — no matter how seemingly trivial — escape my notice, for potential testimony, or just because, let not a single movement of the White Queen escape my notice, the way she cautiously advanced across the chessboard to her bed and then, after slight hesitation, stepped onto square c8 . . . how she gracefully placed her Louis Vuitton purse on the nightstand, as if she weren't just flopping into an aquarium wearing an absurdly tattered shift, but instead was entering the salon of a luxury liner in a gown with daring décolletage; I didn't want to lose it, it was my property now, I'd appropriate each and every expression, word, sigh, even the contour of her right eyebrow, which was now lifting and gesturing in my direction.

"How long have you been here, my dear? Alcohol? No? Oh, I see . . . pain, insomnia, I understand. Irena is my name, delighted, genuinely delighted, to make your acquaintance, Mrs. Černá . . ."

And out of nowhere, what at first was held back by the lid of a conversational tone began to boil, to roil, with each subsequent sentence to unstoppably surge across the room like in the fairy tale "The Magic Porridge Pot," until everyone had it up to their ankles. "This is a mistake, a fatal mistake, Mrs. Černá, an act of revenge of that . . . what to politely call that swine, that asshole! I'm not an alcoholic, damn it! To have me, *me* . . . locked up like some common . . . No offense . . . God forbid, Mrs. Černá, you're a different sort, an educated woman, it's clear as day . . . But that bastard has connections, you'd be surprised, he plays golf with the head physician! Those two on the golf course, me in the aquarium! For shame!"

In the aquarium? Gizela was howling with laughter and gumming her pillow with her toothless mouth. No matter, I am time. I am time and I drip, now noticeably faster, the intervals between individual drips getting shorter, still thirty-two minutes and thirty-one seconds to go before you get a bathroom break.

"This room is the worst room on the entire ward, you know. I kept hoping they'd put me somewhere else, if it came to this . . ." She nodded toward the door. No. Not the door, at the wall. Only now did Ema notice that it was glazed, a window giving onto a small nurses' station, and every so often a nurse would train her eyes on them. The aquarium.

"Me, here, of all places! Along with the scum of the earth, among filthy Gypsy drug addicts!"

I froze. Gizela's laughter shut off. The nurses might be able to see us, but they couldn't hear a thing. Fish mouths opening mutely, fish circling each other, the reflections of their quivering gills dappling the walls with gold. Here and there a fish glint floated up to the towering ceiling, bumping against it dully before sinking back to the bottom.

Gizela slowly sat up in bed. Gizela was sitting straight up in bed and slowly raised her arms, slowly spread her fingers, and Ema could see between them the coarse membrane of a dragon. She was poised to pounce on the Lady, sink her talons into her, wring the jabber out of her —

"Fuck her, Gizela."

Was it really you, Ema Černá, who uttered this out loud? Such a short time here and already talking like this? What would your ex-husband Dalibor say, that paragon of literary propriety?

And then, something remarkable happened: Irena approached my bed and shouted at me, "Now, Eva, that really wasn't nice of you, getting me pregnant twice and then leaving me for that floozy!"

"But . . ."

"I'll never forgive you for that!"

"But my name is Ema . . ."

The Lady dropped down on all fours and with the astonishing agility of a dog scurried over to a chair and began to stroke its armrest. "Come on, Markétka, just one more spoonful, you're so thin!" She continued to feed the chair a while longer, then abruptly stood up and went to the window, where the panes kept rattling gravely. She stared in silence for a long time, out into the darkness that pretended to have nothing to do with the Garden.

"Where am I?" she asked.

"Detox in the Bohnice psychiatric hospital, sweetheart," Gizela informed her with relish, keenly following Irena's every move.

But Irena objected. "Like hell this is Bohnice, you're wrong, dearie! I'd recognize my hometown of Čelákovice anywhere! Over there on the left is the town hall, next to the entrance is a bike rack, and I've been tied to it since 1989 when the Revolution won over our town."

"Gizela? What's gotten into her? All of a sudden?" One of the cocoons unraveled, followed immediately by another, and soon, all the women were watching Irena's odyssey through the room, the unpredictable moves of an utterly befuddled White Queen.

"This is what delirium tremens looks like, I read about it on the internet so I'd know what to expect," a disheveled head floating above its blanket laughed hoarsely.

"Crazy-ass DTs," Gizela nodded with an air of expertise.

All of us stared at the Lady. Eyes lit up, lips parted, the color returning to our pale cheeks. At least *something* was happening. And now that something was even worse off than we were, which was mildly comforting. Thirty-six minutes and five seconds ago Miss Irena had stepped into the room — and I was already giving in to it, too.

The White Queen slowly backed away from the window to her nightstand and gazed inquiringly at her purse. Sharp objects, manicure sets, cosmetic products containing alcohol, and pocket mirrors were not allowed in the ward. For a minute she kept turning the purse over in bafflement, sniffed at it, opened it, pulled out an imaginary lipstick, adjusting the mirror of her palm, and began to apply it to her lips with practiced movements. Gizela applauded her. When she was done with the makeup, she threw the purse over her shoulder and headed out to the hallway, her gait regal.

Then it was just voices from the hallway, "Miss Irena, go back to your room . . ."

"I'm leaving, I'm going back to Čelákovice!"

"Miss Irena . . ." Kicking and pounding on the door.

"Call me a taxi at once!" the White Queen yelled in a last-ditch attempt to extricate herself from the chessboard. "A taxiiii!" To break through the glass of the aquarium and return to the sea. Pushing, shoving, a melee that lasted but a moment: the door opened and three nurses dragged a defiant Irena to her bed. Like peas in a pod up to this point, only now did Ema begin to distinguish the nurses. One of them, whom she found out later was called Rambo and feared by all, had something wrapped around her torso. She conducted herself like a pro and with great, what's the word, brio. With practiced moves, they secured the Lady to the bed, her arms, then her legs, pulling tight, clicking shut, and done. Show's over.

No one said a word. Surprisingly, neither did the fettered queen, who by now was just wheezing away. The silence began to wrap them one by one back into cocoons; those whose beds lined the wall — oh, how great to have a bed by the wall! — turned their backs to the room. Ema tried to take deep breaths, like her mom used to tell her to do whenever they were in the woods, and later, Dita, too. She inhaled deeply and returned to the ceiling, which was the ceiling of the Tower of Babel, to the ceiling —

Oh, who was it that used to dwell at such heights, leaving for me just the pale moon of a removed clock as a memento? I'll never be able to fall asleep in here. I'll never be able to fall asleep again, period. For wherever night is canceled, the stream of consciousness will coil around the stalks and trunks of phenomena without end, until it bites its own tail.

And indeed: for the next several hours Miss Irena's soft, pleading voice did not cease for a single moment. "Eva, I beg you, loosen my chains! So many years, just imagine, I've been chained up since 1989, and for nothing! They're rubbing my wrists and ankles raw. Loosen them for heaven's sake! You must have the key somewhere, it's a tiny little thing, like for a mailbox or bike lock, I know you, you wouldn't have lost it, you're careful with this kind of stuff, you're an intelligent woman, that's clear as day . . . I'm not mad at you anymore, that you left me, just help me, for the love of God . . ."

Light streamed from the lookout the nurses were on

patrol Eva please the light settled on the ceiling traversed the room and the new tenant began to purposely reposition furniture loosen my chains after-Christmas sales in IKEA so, so many years and banana boxes lying around everywhere an empty one opened right above her head I'm chained here and for nothing she stared into the box and couldn't believe her eyes they're rubbing my wrists and ankles raw in the box was her cheerful childhood bedroom and she was lying in that room in bed with the cheerful kiddy bedcovers and she wasn't asleep just like now loosen them for heaven's sake and she wasn't asleep because she was puking Mom's cheerful spinach.

Mom couldn't carry out the bucketfuls quickly enough. She dashed from bedroom to bathroom and back again, faster and faster, back and forth, there and back, as if she were in a silent slapstick film, her slippers quickening on the parquet to the rhythm of "you-too-you-too" for so long it coalesced into an irreversible, unregurgitable blow of reality.

"Ah, so that's the way the cookie crumbles," Ema thought from within her box as the green torrent gushed out of her. The nurses evidently hadn't noticed anything amiss. It wasn't their job to monitor the ceiling. They were hunched over a screen in their lookout, bursting into laughter from time to time — probably some silly film.

"Look, maybe scissors will do the trick, I'm sure you keep a pair in your nightstand, they're not actually chains after all, just plain old fabric . . ."

If her mom knew — the little girl vomiting in the cardboard box wondered — that one day she would die too, why did she bring her into the world? Why do this to her? It was either out of stupidity or malice. And what about others — kids likely didn't have a clue, but the grownups?

And the awful sham caused the cheerful bedcovers on Ema to grow heavier and darker, lying on top of her like a tumulus, the snow of conspiracy shoveled onto her in piles of dirty slush.

Ema got up and not bothering with her slippers approached Irena's bed. She knelt down over her head. The Lady's hair still smelled like the shampoo and whatever else they dolled her up with in some fancy beauty salon.

"Forgive me, my Queen," Ema whispered, "but I can't. I have no scissors and no key." She noticed the skin on Irena's wrists was rubbed raw. "For heaven's sake, lie still and don't toss and turn so much. Tomorrow . . ."

The word abruptly jabbed under her fingernail like a thorn. "Tomorrow — wait, do you even know what happened to the little girl throwing up spinach above us on the ceiling?"

Irena tried to prop herself up on her elbows and perkily looked at Ema: "On the ceiling? My dear, that's remarkably intriguing! Tell me more!"

The rattle of windowpanes. The nurses' eyes fixed on the screen. An extraordinarily fat, old woman kicked off the covers, a deathly glow reflecting off her white thighs like off a fish's belly. The woman recited her shopping list in her sleep: six bread rolls, three-hundred grams of smoked salami, two containers of sour cream, a kilo of filleted pork rib —

"Imagine," Ema whispered, "that when they found themselves knee-deep in spinach, Mother gave up. It was like in that fairy tale 'The Magic Porridge Pot'! It gushed out of the little girl like the porridge did out of the pot and this pap surged through the room into the front hall and from the front hall into the hallway outside and surging and flowing down the stairway and elevator shaft, we lived on the top floor of an apartment building in Smíchov, several neighbors almost lost their lives, they fled the building, wringing their hands, by the way, have you ever seen anyone actually wring their hands? And then some lapdog appeared, curiously sniffing and biting into it, but was promptly swept away by the green wave, I didn't even feel sorry for it. What can I tell you: there was no stopping it, Mom even began to recite Hail Marys out of desperation, didn't help, probably because she wasn't very good at it, so she switched to Yiddish, what she recalled hearing from her father when she was a kid, but still nothing . . . Nothing seemed to work on the green sludge. She escaped the apartment at the very last minute, the poor thing soaked in it till her dying day . . . And although we saw each other every day for years, I haven't seen her again since."

The next day, Ema didn't open her eyes until after the ward rounds. The devil-pope, clad in an Adidas tracksuit, stood in the doorway, his cheeks crammed with lost souls as he cheerily splashed soapy water onto the linoleum floor.

•

Hey Mom,

I'm so glad you got to call me and let me know where you are. Or I'd probably be climbing the walls by now, maybe up to the ceiling, or even higher. I know it must be awful, but please hang in there. I left some stuff for you with a nurse, she looked pretty bitchy, those checkered slippers you asked for, they're hideous!!, soap, toothbrush, pen and paper and so on, blah blah, stuff you might need in there. Just keep writing! It doesn't matter what, silly shit even, because it isn't about the words anymore.

And even though it's not about the words, here's the text message Dita sent me: "Thanks! Thank God she's not staying silent like all those underwater monsters of hers. I'm sending a letter tomorrow, but she won't get it till Wednesday, hopefully they'll give it to her. Tell her not to panic. Nothing's changed, we were and will be together."

Your Rybka

•

"Černááá!"

Of course. She was determined to face the challenge. To cooperate. Not cause any problems. Accept the treatment plan. Get the most out of therapy, take advantage of supervised self-reflection sessions. Lay bare the evolution of her addiction, reveal its roots. And in the battle to come, soap would be her shield, a toothbrush her spear, the civilizational armor for those who wish to survive.

Cooperate. Toothbrush. Battle. Roots. She made a futile attempt to put on those slippers she so desired, but eventually gave up. Roots protruded from her feet every which way, evidently the roots of addiction, and her arms transformed into branches, from which sprouted more and more sprigs — they bumped against the walls, winding their way up them, and the bush she had now become simply would not budge. Luckily, Miss Marcelka knew what to do. She deftly chopped off whatever was in the way and sticking out and slid her out into the hallway.

Miss Marcelka was diminutive and round as was everything

about her: her mouth spewed out words like a stream of coins, her nails were like glittering fish scales, and her heart, her blessed little heart, surely must've been as round as a golf ball. Miss Marcelka squeezed Ema's elbow confidentially and lowered her already soft voice. Inadvertently, Ema shuddered in disgust: Christ, why does everybody keep touching me?! Were we schoolfriends or something? Is it some sort of new touch therapy, funded by an EU grant?

Marcelka knew everything. She could see into the bowels of the machine here as if the ripped-open belly of Mr. Mouse. And it made sense, since she had reached the milestone of her tenth treatment. This was her home, she was well-acquainted with the aquarium where she swam happily between the walls, beyond which the waters of an alien sea thundered ominously.

"Sweetie, Dr. Veselá wants to speak to you . . ." Right. Just let go of my elbow. "You better watch your step around her! Dr. Veselá is . . . a real sourpuss. She won't look you in the eye, she's never looked anybody here in the eye, but she sucks up to the deputy head physician. Watch what you say around her! It's not like she'll believe a word you say anyway, once an alcoholic always an alcoholic, and everything you say will be twisted and used against you. If you say you love your dad . . ."

"My dad's dead. And I'm a pillhead, not an alcoholic."

"Jesus, I didn't mean to hurt your feelings, hon! Just don't tell her you loved your father, or she'll make a note that your father abused you as a child and you've got repressed trauma! I checked *occasional alcohol consumption* in the questionnaire and bam! They had me on Antabuse by week's end!"

Dr. Veselá was sitting like a statue behind her computer and didn't even glance up. It occurred to Ema that if she had had such exemplary posture her whole life she could've avoided the IV drip, the icebergs, the February wind, the fettered Queen, and all those legless women who, like her, had sprouted a rather hideous sight from right under their nighties — massive fishtails.

Date of birth education profession medical family history mental health family history addiction family history marriages and divorces abortions and births — good God, and how dizzyingly fast her ten purple nails typed! Showing Ema a perfect profile on which one could unabashedly graze, the doctor hammered her life into the keyboard pell-mell until sparks were flying from underneath her nimble slender fingers and ignited a strip of gauze, which burst into flame that quickly consumed it as if it were a fuse, this couldn't end well, the door was ajar and the fuse spat and hissed like a fiery snake through the door into the hallway and Ema covered her ears in anticipation of the explosion, she wanted to yell "take cover!" but she wasn't such a nutcase to order around a statue, and then she heard a strange sound like a fire being extinguished, as the fuse sizzled its way straight into Room No. 1, into the aquarium, and sizzled for the last time and went out in the watery depths, only to coil in the sink, limp and slimy like kelp, until the janitor in the Adidas tracksuit disposed of it with disgust.

. . . on which one could unabashedly graze. But what grueling fare! Maybe the left side wasn't so bad, but the right side lacked any sort of feature or expression, as if poor Dr. Veselá had undergone some horrifically botched plastic surgery.

"Any allergies?"

"Spinach," Ema shot right back. Of course, no response. Not a keystroke nor bat of an eye.

"Husband?"

"Partner — female."

No reaction either.

Suddenly a shout from the hallway cut through the silence: "Lunchtiiime!" Ema pondered — and it was a dilemma straight out of the age of myth — which was more appealing: an extractive dialogue with a caryatid, or dumplings in the company of dual beings, half-women, half-fish. They sat around the table shoulder to shoulder, and Ema didn't need to be there to see it, because she would be sitting there with them for many more days, weeks, and months, and she didn't need to be there to see the damp gloom under the table where their tail fins were touching as they huddled over their plates.

"UBG again," Gizela gritted through the gap in her teeth.

"What's UBG? I'm happy to learn something new, dear ladies!" Miss Irena was back in fine form. With dignity, she sliced through the unsliceable, holding the flatware precisely as depicted in etiquette books. She didn't remember a single thing from her delirium episode, and she kept asking us to repeat it for her . . . Oh ladies, surely you must be exaggerating! It's outrageous! I said *what?* Čelákovice? I've never even stepped foot in that town! And feeding a chair! And I had kids with you, Mrs. Černá! Imagine that!

Dana, a retired prostitute who was glad for the food and roof over her head for a while and not having to squeeze through the basement window of a building in Žižkov for the night, rasped, "Who doesn't know UBG? It's . . ." but she was quickly cut off by Marcelka, whose ten stays at Pavilion No. 8 qualified her and her alone to hand down this piece of knowledge, and was simply not about to let anyone usurp that privilege.

"Why, sweetie," she graced Irena with an indulgent smile, "it's universal brown gravy, of course."

A reverent silence. Jaws danced, worked, crushed the provision of life.

Surprisingly, Dana ended up with the last word. "Lemme tell ya something. The stuff they served us in the Bory Prison in Plzeň wasn't half as bad as this grub."

A flock of birds with adhesive purple beaks circled above the keyboard and went still.

As if in condolence, the doctor's voice interrupted the tinkling of cutlery coming from the hallway. "You should know, Mrs. Černá, that you are here on what's called an involuntary commitment. Your conduct in the ambulance and during admission unfortunately indicates that you are a danger to yourself and others." Probably because, Ema vehemently nodded her head — pointlessly, as nobody was even looking at her — of how I ruffled the redhead's neck and roughed up the naked lady and knocked the Mojito out of her hands. She giggled.

"You're about to find out that it's not actually that funny, Mrs. Černá." Where did those Christmas slippers end up anyway? Maybe that loon, wrapped head to toe in that shawl, was skating across the Garden in them like a reanimated mummy.

Because unlike her — "You will receive the court ruling within the next fourteen days. In practice, this means you are not permitted any outdoor time, you are not allowed to attend therapy sessions outside Pavilion No. 8, and you cannot request to be discharged." — because unlike her, he was permitted outdoor time.

Instead of a nightie a sturdy, heavy-duty diving suit, straight out of a Jules Verne novel. Or: Ema submerged her head underwater, only her snorkel visible to Dalibor, and observed the paper-thin fish as they swam up to her, flipping their fins before disappearing again without touching her, just like the doctor's words. While she may have heard them, she didn't understand them, their meaning out of reach, as if someone were reading aloud to her the *Epic of Gilgamesh* in the original by mistake, instead of a well-known fairy tale.

So she decided to look elsewhere, through the statue and her words. Like in every nurses' station, glass cabinets holding medication lined the wall right across from her. Ema froze. She was going to miss out on today's dumplings. She was instantly seized by an uncontrollable tremor. The session seemed to be coming to an end. Look away. The roof of another pavilion outside the window. Her windows at home had iron bars too, so she was used to them. Focus on a sound, any sound, catch it and quickly ride its waves out of here. Focus on anything, anything at all, just look away. Because in that cabinet, right in front behind the glass, towering to the sky, were three even stacks of Zolpidem.

Ema couldn't control the tremor, she could taste the pills on the roof of her mouth. She never washed them down with water, no, she let them dissolve under her tongue like the Body of Christ. Look away — but it was too late now, they were everywhere she looked, flat packets stacked sky-high, one on top of the other, pillars supporting a cathedral's vaulting. Like a dog, her mouth suddenly filled with saliva, and craving clenched her entire body like a fist.

She raised her eyes to the vaulted ceiling until only their whites shone — a veritable martyr straight out of a Baroque painting. This ceiling was considerably different than the one in the aquarium, bearing no signs of settlement. Instead dozens, no, hundreds of boxes of Hypnogen and Stilnox were just lying there for no good reason — maybe an exaggeration, she also spotted some Oxazepam — and somebody's greedy fingers hastily ripped them open, popping the pills out of their blister packs and emptying them into their hands. The vaulted ceiling trembled, and a crack appeared in its center, a fissure just like the one she'd always desired. Through it she could fly out to the open skies! But when she finally managed to squeeze through the crack, she saw another vault above her, and another above that, and so on, without end —

And Ema right away knew beyond a doubt who had taken up residence on the ceiling in Room No. 1 and whom those half-unpacked boxes belonged to. "Ash!" Nope, not banana boxes! They were, in fact, Ash's notorious cardboard creations. She instantly latched onto one to stop her tremors and didn't let go.

"Doctor, I forgot to mention . . . don't turn off the computer just yet! It's really important. See, I have a brother! I really don't understand how it could've slipped my mind. I know you asked if I have any siblings. I have a brother and his name is Ash."

At that moment, Dr. Veselá turned her head toward Ema for the first time, ever so slightly, incredibly slowly — "It's a . . . how to put it . . . dark family history, a terrifying family drama, right out of an Edgar Allan Poe story . . ." — and as the doctor turned toward her, slowly and ominously, her neck creaked horribly, like the decrepit hinges of the House of Usher.

"That'll do. You'll get a chance to talk about your brother during individual and group therapy."

Ema staggered out to the hallway. Her plate sat waiting for

her on the otherwise cleared dining table. Dana was watching over it like a hawk. "Looked after it for ya, the girls woulda scarfed it down by now. That dumbass Květa's roomin' with might be an artist, so says she, a real Saudek in a skirt, bullshit! Whatever, she's bulimic, I got a nose for these things."

I stared at the dumplings as though it were the starry sky above the Sahara.

"So are you gonna . . . ?" Dana asked.

I shook my head and slid the plate over to her. She smiled gratefully, muttering a "thanks" before digging into the UBG.

•

I quickly pull the checkered notebook Rybka got me out of my nightstand. I'm in a hurry. Anything can happen in here at any given moment. I have to write down what I wasn't allowed to say out loud: that dicey situation Ash had to face so long ago. I don't know how I feel about him living right above me and that we'll be looking right into each other's beds. Ash was always a bit of a weirdo.

•

When I was a kid, I liked to make boxes out of cardboard. Some were pretty tiny, barely large enough for a Lego figure to lie in, others were the size of a dresser. I stored my toys and clothes in its drawers, everything in neat piles, and since I would always be — quiet and focused, tip of my tongue between my teeth — sticky, glue all over me, I'd stick to some surface, such as the underside of the kitchen table like a gob of chewing gum. That's why I didn't really register on my parents' radar until I was an adult; after all, they had enough problems of their own, times were tough, Father was fired for political reasons and it took a long time until he found a job as a watchman for the Motol Hospital parking lot, and Mother had plenty on her own plate, too, not least my sister, a year younger than me, who was forever causing some problem.

One time she hauled a dumpster all the way home and announced it was to store her duvets. As if it wouldn't have taken me three seconds to make her a much more hygienic cupboard out of cardboard. Sometimes she'd howl for days on end, banging on her guitar and saying she was Janis Joplin. Or she'd memorize Proust's endless sentences, not a single sensible word could be knocked out of her. But the worst was when she began to bring home her equally eccentric friends: they promenaded through the apartment as if it were an agora, guzzled down everything they could get their hands on, and rolled cigarettes with Drum tobacco, the ash . . . tapped . . . onto the carpet . . .

Ash. I soon realized I had a secret. As young as three I would stand for hours and hours wrapped in the curtains and stare down at the street. And why not; it was a busy Smíchov street with a tram stop, littered with people, shops, and cars. To be an eye and to see, unseen. But it was bad news when Mom wanted me to come down there, to speak, to be pulled into the game without being able to observe it.

I said to myself this secret of mine must be something like chickenpox; okay, in that case an autovaccine was needed to reduce the most visible traces to a minimum. So I decided to become a normal little boy, if that's what they wanted: I'd fight over toys in the sandbox and might even pee my pants in a temper tantrum, and I'd clap and giggle over my birthday cake; all this could be learned by observing other children. I methodically began to appropriate the behavior of others, their expressions, emotions, and gestures, and chose from this panoply the ones I considered useful, purposefully aping them. It was glorious: one by one, every sensation sunk into the hollowed-out nutshell of nothingness.

My rebirth every morning soon became routine, and I put on my face like a prosthesis. For instance, food, the need for sustenance, had always disgusted me. In ninth grade, I persuaded my dad, though he had completely different plans for me, to let me apprentice as a chef.

But my secret still lurked right behind my eyes, and this was dangerous. Mom was often close, and it was even worse with my sister; she didn't get as close, but sometimes when her eyes bore into me, making not the slightest attempt out of decency to conceal those two gleaming scalpels, my heart was in my throat. I said my eyesight was bad. Glasses helped a little, but not much.

Day and night I focused on my work until I finally achieved at least partial success. I managed to push my secret down, low enough to be beyond the sight of anyone's gaze, even my sister's.

Yet one time . . . In 1989, I was spending New Year's Eve at a schoolfriend's place in the Šumava Mountains. Everyone was having fun in the large room with a fireplace, pouring out punch from a huge bowl and laughing at the bad times everyone believed were now gone for good. The fire crackled and wisely, knowingly, and without any illusions devoured all their plans, projects, and dreams about which I, too, had my own ideas. Like them, my sister and I had stood on Wenceslas Square in the crowd of thousands beneath the balcony of the

Melantrich building, onto which paraded prominent persons to speak to the nation; my sister was clinging to me and all I remember of her from that day so long ago was her holey mitten. It's important not to overlook any detail, though it might seem insignificant at first. And then it happened. A duo appeared on the balcony and someone shouted into the microphone, "Karel and Karel!" The rally was coming to an end and it was capped by the two Karels, Kryl and Gott, launching into the national anthem, "Kde domov můj" . . . and a tone of all-embracing reconciliation flooded the square like . . . yes, I shouldn't flinch from saying it . . . like syrup. The whole square was abuzz amid the rocks, but by that point we'd already turned around and were pushing our way back through the crowd. My sister was clutching my forearm the whole time with such anger and force that her grip left a bruise for two weeks, changing into the hues of the national tricolor.

Yes, from that moment of truly historical import, I had my own ideas, which is why on that particular New Year's Eve I didn't join the rest of my classmates in making plans over punch, but chopped wood in the shed. I enjoyed it immensely. I'd never done it before. I could smell the wood's fragrance, and it was all the stronger as it didn't remind me of anything, and how could it, when I was nothing but an enormous vault with only the small gob of a secret stuck to its bottom. True, I was also helping myself to a bottle of Finnish vodka, my first time drinking it, because I had somehow figured vodka went marvelously well with the ax.

The wind drove flurries of snow through the open door of the shed. The palms of my hands, I noticed, were already blistered, and underneath the translucent skin of one of them I saw . . . What could it be? It looked a bit like some sort of miniature, filigree tableau with God knows whom . . . My sister's mittens would've come in handy here as flames began to erupt from my body, it must've been the firewater, and I didn't have the strength to stop. Again and again I raised the ax over my head and brought it down, and music blasted from the windows of the house and a girl's voice squealed, "Where's Ash? It's almost midnight . . . Get the champagne ready, and find Ash!"

Yes. The squeals fell damply into the sawdust, because Ash is my name.

And then it happened. A wolf stood on the doorstep of the shed, observing me. It looked very much like a wolf, but one of the partygoers must've brought her German shepherd. It stood there stock-still, as if a stuffed exhibit in a police museum, but its eyes were unusually lively, and those green eyes spoke savagely: "Don't trust me. Unlike you, I know what this smell means, and I lap up your ridiculously cherished secret with my daily chow. You poor wretch . . ."

The eyes were speaking but didn't finish. At the moment the champagne was popped, the ax split a piece of wood, and one half went flying across the shed and hit the dog right between the eyes.

Something tipped over inside me as I abruptly stooped down, and it all came rushing out, hot and uncontrollable, the secret, down the sides of the chopping block. I watched the dog out of the corner of my eye as it twitched and slowly, in slow motion, collapsed into the sawdust. In that moment I pleaded: let it just be a dream. I'll close my eyes and when I open them, just a flurry of snow will be lying on the doorstep. Deal? But the dog wasn't moving, and the snow fell on it as heavily and indifferently as my gaze.

I had to do something, cover my tracks, hide the body. Any moment now, they'd be coming to look for me. I moved. Something crunched underneath my foot. My glasses. They were useless to me anyway.

My secret slowly congealed on the chopping block like putty. A pair of work gloves lay on a shelf close by. I took a step toward them, hoping they'd make it easier to cover my tracks.

But it was too late. Ivana appeared in the doorway. Or was it Ilona? I really cannot recall her name. She'd been pursuing me at the time with excruciating tenacity, who knows why she decided I was . . . that I could be her . . . Maybe under different circumstances I would've had the courage to tell her that the desire for a relationship, the terrible effort it takes to wedge someone into your existence, was merely a manifestation of the inability to face your own secret, but she wouldn't have understood. I decided to give in to her. It didn't matter anyway. Nothing mattered, because the icy freedom of choice blew through the empty vault.

And as I looked at her goggle-eyed expression, it was a relief to realize that dating was likely no longer on the table. Partially covered in snow, the German shepherd lay dead in the blood-soaked sawdust at her feet. Her eyes met mine. I was standing at attention like a soldier by the chopping block sealed in the slime that had gushed out of my soul, if I ever had one. And suddenly a terrible silence descended. No more music, singing and shouting, no more firecrackers of popping cork or the crackling of fireworks. If I were to swing with all my might, I wouldn't even hack a splinter off that hardened silence.

Without thinking, I pulled on the oversized work gloves, and as I reached out my hand toward her in a desperate attempt for reconciliation, something like a smile must've warped my expression. "Happy New Year, Ivana."

"Ash," she whispered and began to back away into the yard. I suspected all the others were gathered somewhere behind her.

"Ash!" she suddenly yelped, and shrieked like a curse and her howl churned through the silence, churned through the entire village from one end to the other as if New Year ashcans or tin pails or brass urns were truly raining down from the sky —

I tried to oblige her. There was nothing more I desired anyway. I decided to disintegrate, and it was surprisingly easy. And when I had completely disintegrated, I began to drift down on the dog, the woodshed, the village in Šumava, the frozen fields, on that whole earthly paradise, impassively, coldly, and endlessly, just like the snow.

•

Ema wanted to set the notebook on her nightstand, but it slipped through her fingers and dropped on her slippers. An avalanche of fatigue the likes of which she'd never felt before suddenly overcame her. She couldn't even move her arm or lift her head, she couldn't take a breath, as if she really were pinned down by the tons of snow or ash into which her brother had once disintegrated in Šumava. She tried to speak, but her mouth was full of snow, too. She knew the taste well — once long ago she had talked Karolínka into betting on who could eat their snowman the fastest. So she wolfed it down, because naturally she had to win, bravely swallowing bites of the snowman that melted inside her for so long she — as if by some mysterious Eucharist — ultimately became one.

And Ema was no longer, just the snowman she'd transformed into, and even the snowman soon thawed, disappeared, evaporated into nothingness. Something was approaching. The dot in the distance grew and grew and suddenly, in what was once something, an enormous vulture with white head towered like a giant mountain. Its wings swept away the nothingness into the corner, and Ema fell into a deep sleep. She slept and slept, and even slept through the war that broke out in the aquarium and raged a meter from her: while Gizela was cold and kept closing and obsessively windproofing the lousy windows with rags, Miss Marcelka preferred the fresh air. As soon as one woman opened a window, another rushed to shut it, and vice versa, at first in silence and with a lag, then with increasingly shorter delays, accompanied by an exchange of abuse from both sides. The windows were slammed and the women screeched and even Miss Irena chimed in with her calming alto — "Quiet, miladies, quiet! Mrs. Černá has finally fallen asleep, and without having to resort to a sleeping pill! I beg you, please be considerate . . ."

Ema didn't care. She was off to grocery shop at Billa. Karolínka's mother stood by the mailboxes on the ground floor with an armful of coupons. "You're dressed mighty light, child!" She never addressed her in any other way, and now, at the age of fifty, it sounded really odd to Ema. "Today is particularly . . . chi-lly . . ." she lowered her voice and looked around, ". . . and there's this weird stink . . ."

She was right: Ema opened the front door and instead of the familiar smell of gasoline and wet dog fur her nose was assaulted by the smell of frankincense. And where's the newsstand with the fatso pressed inside? And Bistro Pivoňka with its permanent cluster of guys hoisting bottles of Braník beer? And the well-trodden shortcut across the grass to the tram stop —

Clutching the door handle tightly, she wasn't sure if she should step outside, as the front door didn't open onto her familiar street, but — and only now did she understand the "chilly" and "stink" from her neighbor — revealed the frigid space of a cathedral that extended in front of her like an immense skating rink. Tableaux of the Way of the Cross were adrift in the iridescent waves of light; it was impossible to distinguish what they depicted, and Jesus nailed to the Cross was so far away that from here he resembled an incomprehensible blowfly pinned down with a gold tack.

She gritted her teeth and stepped onto the ice.

"This must be some trap Dr. Veselá has concocted," she thought, but had to admit the trap was truly spectacular. If only it weren't so awfully cold here . . . and a nightie barely covering the butt was hardly the ideal outfit for church, let alone a skating rink. Mom would have put spinach-colored leg warmers on her, and solicitously wrapped her in an endless knitted shawl . . . Thankfully, the church was empty. And yet . . . the huddled figure of a man cowered in one of the pews farther in. She approached and touched his shoulder tentatively.

"Excuse me, sorry to bother you, but have you seen Rybka, my daughter, around here? Tall, thin, dreadlocks . . ." She became startled. Her voice began to echo a thousandfold, but the man didn't even budge. His head was buried in his hands, and he must've been praying.

"She lives in the Strašnice district, at Ve Studni 12," her whisper was barely audible. "But she's not at home and her friends don't know anything and she's not answering her phone . . . I'm really worried about her."

Nothing. Silence. No movement. He must've been petrified

on the spot in this unnatural position for some especially terrible sin. She bent over the man and heard at regular intervals a tinny, feeble, mouse-like squeaking. He was asleep.

She began to roughly shake the man — and realized he was dreaming, that she was only a part of his dream and unless she woke him up she would not wake either and never find Rybka. At once she started to panic: what if the man dies, or is already dead? Then Ema would never wake up and would stay trapped in this cathedral forever, merely a figment of someone else's imagination!

Snow shortly began its slow and silent descent onto the cathedral floor. A sky full of ice floes stretched across where the dome should have been. With unwarranted pride, she realized she might have finally smashed through the topmost ceiling, above it no other. She stood there, a diminished human variation of a temple, a billion snowflakes descending into her cracked skull.

Ceiling or no, she had to find Rybka. She began to ascend the wooden, spiral staircase to the pulpit, taking the stairs two at a time. The massive soles of Christ's feet, already half-covered in snow, loomed high above her — from this vantage point he looked like some monstrous showpiece from a museum of torture. She'd seen her share of Christs, but none had had six toes like this one — proof that this was all a dream. The difference between dream and reality, fiction and fact, and maybe life and death as well, was consequently nearly imperceptible, because it lay in that one single supernumerary toe.

Suddenly, music echoed through the cathedral where the snow kept falling. Of course the organ, of course a Bach fugue. The cliché of it all ruined her mood. It was enough of a struggle to accept that this bombastic cathedral had dislodged Bistro Pivoňka from her world, and now this . . . She finally made it to the top, out of breath. The registers of the organ made every stone, every atom, every cell reverberate, the splendor inescapable, so she tried to drown it out, yelling and yelling until her voice cracked, yelling furiously like a child being force-fed the fish oil of cultural values. And all at once she was shocked to hear her yells transform into words, against her will: "Mom, how could you do this to me? Why did you bring me into this world if you knew that one day I would also die? And how could I do the same to my Rybka?"

Where are you? Where are you hiding in this awful world? Will you ever forgive me? Or have I just forgotten where our home base used to be, but will soon remember? Surely she'll jump out at her, like so many times before, from behind this tiny door!

She grabbed the door handle and yanked the door open.

"Welcome aboard our Boeing 737," a flight attendant dressed in a chic blue uniform smiled at her, handing her the tabloid *Blesk*.

"Oh . . . This must be a mistake . . . I'm looking for my daughter, she lives in Strašnice, at Ve Studni 12 . . . I don't even have a ticket . . ."

But the flight attendant — her smile a tad wider now, so wide that the corners of her mouth disappeared somewhere underneath her earlobes — was already strapping her down into her seat using an elaborate system of seatbelts, just like Rambo had done to the White Queen when she wanted to leave to Čelákovice.

"We are truly thrilled you have chosen us as your travel agency," she said before handing Ema a leakproof sickbag full of something unpleasant which, once upon time in a kitchen somewhere, might have been considered spinach.

Only now did she notice the plane was full of passengers. Everyone's eyes gleamed with eager anticipation of the beginning of their vacation, except for one man, the one from the church pew, whose dream she embodied; naturally his head was tilted back and he was snoring up a storm.

"Yes, you've chosen our travel agency," the attendant continued, this time her grin splitting her face in two, "which is the only one to offer trips to the land of the *all*-possible."

"What does that mean — *all*-possible?" she asked as quietly as she could the elegant lady sitting right next to her, but isn't she . . . Miss Irena!

"Oh, dearie," she replied with a patronizing tone, "as we all know, a singular possibility in our land is only ever actualized at the expense of all the others. But in Strašmania . . ."

"You mean Strašnice?"

"Strašmania, Strašnice, does it matter, it's just a different transcription of the language of the dead, that is to say, rewritten using a different phonetic system, understand? So in Strašnice, as you call it, all possibilities can happen at once."

"Jesus Christ!"

She gave a cheer. "Exactly! I can see you get it! He has both died and hasn't."

"He redeemed and reproached," someone solicitously chimed in from the back.

"Yeah, saved and grazed!" Ema quipped, "I don't give a damn! I have to find my daughter, okay? And there's probably no chance of me doing that until that guy over there wakes up."

She noticed a woman coming down the aisle who didn't

look like a flight attendant in the slightest. She was attired all in black, skinny like Ema, but a good two heads taller, and looked like an Egyptian bird deity. For the life of her, Ema couldn't recall where she'd seen the woman before . . .

Thankfully the eyes of the sphinx, she'd hardly be able to endure their gaze, were staring right through her as if she were just air, nothing, a stranger's dream. And as if the woman were a mere figment of the dream as well, she dropped into Ema's lap in passing, as if accidentally or carelessly, a small scrap of paper folded into a square, and immediately vanished.

Ema opened the note in a way that Miss Irena couldn't see it, uttering the words in her head. "Chaimo margiz duz."

And she suddenly realized where the land of the all-possible lay: not only had she not lost Rybka there, so didn't need to search for her, but her own dad was buried there, in that soil, cremated, and — spotting flocks of white-headed vultures in the depths of the gaps between the clouds below the plane — chopped into pieces at the foot of Mount Kailash, as was his wish, and without ever having died.

•

She woke up. The sun was shining above her, and that came as a surprise. It could've equally been the moon or a hot air balloon, a wagon wheel or even a wheel of brie — God knows what it was.

"Come now, sweetie, sweetheart! Wake up! You keep shouting in your sleep, something about a little fish, "rybka" over and over. The aquarium must've made you go off the deep end!"

It was just Marcelka's round face.

"Where's the note?" Ema furiously began to look for it, searching underneath her blanket and bed. Someone had set her fallen notebook on her nightstand. She thumbed through it. A page about Ash, otherwise — nothing.

"What note, honey? You must've been dreaming. On the outside I never have any dreams, but the ones I have in here, they make me act up, too. Must be the stabilizers."

"It's not the stabilizers that are making you act up — it's the head physician! He's such an . . ." Miss Irena got a dreamy look in her eye, "irresistible, charismatic gentleman, and how refined . . ."

"But I can't remember those three words!"

"Go fuck yourself?" Gizela suggested helpfully.

"Emička . . ." Now Marcelka had gone too far. But she evidently liked the sound of it — "Emička, you're supposed to go straight to the nurses' station for medication, you know, the nurse . . ."

"The nurse?" Dana echoed. "You mean Rambo, right?"

"The nurse has to be sure you swallow it all down. Some of the girls in here have dealt meds, a barter system of sorts — five cigs for a xanny. One woman here saved up twenty-five and then polished 'em off in one go."

"Didn't really get much of a bang for her buck, eh?" Gizela smirked.

Ema shuffled to the door. Sink's over there, maybe a shred of fuse left in it, Gizela was banging out a beat on the nightstand, ta-ta-tadaaa-ta, Miss Irena was crocheting a doll in fast motion, a grotesque pantomime — knitting needles were not allowed in the ward — she'd managed to finish the head and neck — before it all abruptly and piercingly shrunk into a tiny ball, a tiny ball of infinite mass like the universe before its birth, and lodged itself right behind Ema's eyes. She barely managed to catch herself on the edge of the sink.

"Emička, are you alright?"

I'll smash it. That brie. If it touches me.

"It's nothing, just a headache." She heard behind her, "And don't bother asking for ibuprofen! They'll never give it to you! During the rounds I heard the head doc saying you have a habit of abusing painkillers!"

Rambo loomed in the nurses' station. Maybe in a parallel universe, Ema pondered, Rambo was stuck in an endless loop of strapping the Lady to the bed with practiced moves, the legs, the arms, pulling tight, clicking shut, this same scene, over and over again. But the universe wasn't merciful to her either: while Rambo was continually strapping down, Ema, on all fours like an animal, lifted up the doormat, over and over, nothing under it but layers of dust.

Rambo dumped two pills out of a paper cup into Ema's palm and didn't let her out of her sight. "What's up with you women? Everyone's moving like molasses today."

"What is this?"

"Five milligrams of diazepam and a stabilizer."

A baby dose. The Stabilizer 1, 2, 3 — a new action franchise.

"Where's your tea?"

"I don't wash pills down."

"You will here. Go get your tea!"

"What did I tell ya? Didn't give you any ibuprofen, did she?" Marcelka's round face was aglow and Ema couldn't remember for the life of her what she came back for. Gizela had fallen asleep. "I'm gonna air the room out a bit, it reeks in here."

Marcelka cautiously edged toward the window, pinning Gizela with a stare to her bed. "Rambo is a brute, you'll see for yourself once they transfer you to downstairs detox, Emička. Just look at the butch! I'd like to see what's between her legs. And she gets off on surprise inspections, that's her thing! You'll see for yourself, the way her eyes shine when the girls are standing at attention in the ward and she's rooting through their stuff. She goes through it all — and she's not above unscrewing the hollow hanger rods in the closet to check for any cigs stashed inside." She was unstoppable, hurtling words helter-skelter as if rolling flaming hoops.

Gizela suddenly sat up in bed. A trained poodle about to jump through one of the hoops froze in mid-air when it came face to face with Gizela. "Which idiot opened the window again?"

Oh, yeah. The tea. Rambo stood by the window, patting down the contents of two envelopes. "Your daughter dropped by, brought you some chocolate and nutridrinks. This letter's from her and this one's . . ." she scrunched her nose, "from your girlfriend."

My hands. For heaven's sake, please don't let them tremble right now. That other small head inside my head is throbbing furiously, threatening to spring into existence, threatening, in the here and now, at freezing point, to materialize. Who knows its meaning. Maybe then everything, Rambo and Marcelka, stabilizers and dreams, iron bars and ceilings with half-forgotten family members, the scarred body of the Gypsy woman also bearing the tattoos of my own lies, I can see and hear them, the bluish pallor of all those years full of lies right beneath my skin and the skin of others, years linked together from one snow-drift of lies to another, maybe everything then freezes into a single giant snowman I'd have to eat . . . I'd have to become and melt away.

I won't read them yet. Your letters. Only later, once I've managed to get down that first mouthful of snow.

•

Night. A brand-new kitchen unit has appeared on the ceiling.

"Hey, what're you looking forward to the most once you get out of here?"

And the women begin to dream, and dream out loud.

"My grandson! That I'll be allowed to babysit him again and they won't have to worry that I'll drink myself into a stupor and he'll disappear from the apartment, like last time, the front door downstairs was unlocked and the police eventually found him at the shopping mall inside a toy store."

"Pineapple pizza! The size of a wagon wheel!"

"The starry sky above the Sahara."

"A proper fuck!"

"A Shakira concert."

"The sea."

"A bubble bath."

"Seeing the girls and our gym teacher."

"Silence. Absolute silence!"

The game dies down. Now just occasionally from the throes of half-sleep: To laughing until the wee hours of the morning; to our shadows, walking ahead of us down some future street God knows where; to your bowed, delicate, girlish back and your brisk, ungirly stride; to a campfire; to how you hold a cup by the window in a stream of summer rays; to everything that is the opposite of thirst.

And then, after an endless silence, illuminated by nothing but the face of one of the nurses pressed against the aquarium glass, I hear Gizela's voice: "What I look forward to most is being able to lock myself in the bathroom again."

•

The next day, right after rounds, a petite blonde with a buzzcut breezed in, assumed the position of a meditating Buddha in the center of the room, and closed her eyes. Ema counted and recounted the blonde's fingers and toes just in case she had one extra. The creature abruptly jumped up and began to shriek, her eyes wide.

"DTs?"

"No. Dynamic meditation," Gizela said with disgust, turning over to face the wall.

The blonde was now inhaling deeply and exhaling. Inhale — "Hey, girls!" — exhale. "You don't mind if I practice the Five Tibetans in here, do you?" But instead of assuming the position of the First Tibetan, she walked up to my bed.

"Haven't seen you around here, sister."

I was positive she was going to hug me. Empathetically grasp my shoulder. Kiss my forehead. That's all the rage here.

"I'm Blanka," she shook my hand, "though you might be more familiar with my stage name, Karmela."

Oh, so this is the Saudek in a skirt that almost scarfed down my dumplings the other day.

"Ka-ra-me-la?" Miss Irena enunciated each syllable, perplexed.

Gizela snickered at the wall.

"Karmela, sister!" the blonde articulated as flawlessly and

precisely as if she were taking her entrance exams for drama school. In a sudden rapture, she exclaimed, "Sisters! We've hit rock bottom, the lowest point we can get as human beings, we've failed as mothers, wives, daughters, lovers . . ."

"Speak for yourself," Gizela hissed and began to scrawl something on the wall.

". . . and now here we are wandering through the vale of tears with an oh so heavy burden of guilt. But trust me, sisters, this is but a test . . ."

"Take it to the nurses!"

But Karmela didn't allow such pathetic inanity to sidetrack her. She was exquisite, majestic, growing larger with each word, higher and higher, until her head bumped against the ceiling.

"A test and a challenge, a challenge and . . ." she faltered, losing the thread after all.

"A test!" Miss Irena finished the sentence with her sense of symmetry.

"God loves you, sisters. He is with you every step of the way . . ."

"Sounds an awful lot like our head physician." A vulgar diamond shape appeared on the wall behind Gizela.

". . . and God will forgive your sins!"

She suddenly turned to me. "I heard you're a lesbian, sister. I can assure you that God loves even you."

She leaned down and I froze, expecting her to start kissing me, but she only placed something underneath my pillow.

"It's a picture of Mother Theresa. She was a great saint and is my role model. I wouldn't have made it here without her." She lowered her voice. "If you ever need anything, even just a shoulder to cry on, just remember I'm here for you."

I pondered what this creature's photographs might possibly depict. Dana had told me she was a photographer, but I couldn't come up with anything apart from porn.

"Vodseďálková!" Right as Blanka, alias Karmela, was contorting herself with remarkable flexibility into a breakneck asana, Rambo appeared. "Aren't you aware that visiting other wards is strictly forbidden?"

"Nurse, I do apologize. But my roommate, Květa, and her suffering, which I empathize with profoundly, was disturbing my concentration."

Finally, a momentary silence. I pulled out the picture from underneath my pillow and for a long time looked at the face of an old woman wearing a scarf, or whatever it was, wrapped around her head. When night came, I held the picture up to the ceiling. "Here you go, Brother . . . Something for your new pad."

For a while, nothing happened. All of a sudden, a small crack appeared, the ceiling opened up, and a hand emerged from the opening, grabbed the picture, and was gone.

Gizela's grating laughter sounded somewhere from within the room. "Christ on a bike! Karmela Vodseďálková!"

•

Dear Mom,

I came to visit today and left you some chocolate and nutridrinks and everything else you asked for. Just make sure to eat, please! You can't live off nutridrinks like some old granny. I walked through the garden for a while and circled Pavilion 8, trying to see if I could find your window, and I discovered something out of this world: outside your pavilion there's a statue of a gigantic athlete in boxer shorts — for real, boxer shorts! and upside down. What kind of nutjob decided to put it there! Pretty wild. I bet you're leaning out of a window having a secret smoke, tickling him on the soles of his feet, that'd be just like you. Dita came back from V., said she cut her way through half the forest there with her beloved chainsaw. I took her to our pub, where you always order the halušky. I can't wait for the three of us to go there for a beer, you have no idea. I stopped by your place to water the plants and feed the turtle, and while I was waiting for the bus at Na Knížecí, I watched the hustle and bustle there, those poor junkies wandering the place all day, hanging around for their next fix. It really got to me. I talked to your doctor and they'll be transferring you in a few days to downstairs detox, and you're allowed visits there. So hang in there, we'll be able to hug each other soon.

Your Rybka

P.S. I handed in your note of sick leave at work — your coworkers wish you a speedy recovery. Hah! They'll have something to write about for the blurb under that new cosmetic line they're pushing.

P.P.S. Oh and get this — I saw some dude on a bench in the garden, some loon wrapped head to toe in a shawl, and he was wearing slippers that looked exactly like those godawful ones Grandma gave you for Christmas!

•

"Mrs. Černá! This must be the fifth time already! You can't just promenade through the hallway at night!"

She really did say "promenade." "Promenade," such a lovely expression. Ema opened the door to the bathroom — something about Gizela's wish just made sense — which couldn't be locked. She nearly banged her head. What had she walked into? The ceiling was incredibly low, and she had to get down on all fours. At first she thought she'd suddenly grown, but the opposite was true, this wasn't . . . above her was a solid table-top, and reality in this unexpected space existed only from the waist down. So she made herself comfortable under the table and observed the two pairs of legs. One pair belonged to her mom, the other to their neighbor, Karolínka's mother. One was clad in leggings, the other covered by a skirt.

She poked at her pile of beans and started to line them up into rows of ten. The clattering and clanging of the beans against the floor tiles grated on the nerves, but a bean army had to be created with numerous firing positions against the massive calves, the mothers' fortifications.

"Emička refuses to eat spinach."

"Refuses or not, it's rich in iron."

"She throws it up every single time."

"Let her throw it up three, four times, the fifth time it'll stick."

"You know that turtle you brought us from Yugoslavia, well when it died, get this . . ."

"So it died on you, huh?"

"I didn't tell you? Well, when it died, Ema didn't shed a single tear . . . She's a bit . . . what's the word . . . aloof. Takes after her father."

Ema now heard a voice that didn't belong to the waist-up world above her, and it sounded hollow, as if someone were speaking into a cup. She pressed her ear to the table leg the voice was coming from: "Body and temple, like the universe and boxes of all sorts . . . These are all contained spaces. Only I am able to cut them open, to allow you the chance to breathe and soar."

The imprisoned creature might have been saying more, but for one, Ema couldn't understand a word, and for another, she heard above her: "That's not healthy at all, refusing to eat spinach and suppressing emotions like that. Can't she go play with Karolínka in the other room? The clatter of beans is driving me nuts . . ."

Ema looked up in disgust. Anything but that! Last time, when she'd refused to dress up the Barbies in nighties, Karolínka sunk her talons into her wrist and a slug fell out of her mouth. But it was inevitable; the mothers' gazes, swaying like pendulums, drove her out of the kitchen.

It seemed as if Karolínka didn't even register her presence: she kept turning the thin dolls over onto their stomachs in bed, one after another, and as they resisted, she vehemently explained to them that sleeping on their bellies was safer, or else they could inhale their barf in their sleep and choke to death. That caught Ema's attention. But just to be sure, she didn't take her eyes off Karolínka's nimble little fingers in case they wanted to sharpen into claws again. She decided to speak with her.

"Has your mom told you you're gonna die too?"

Karolínka froze. In that moment her eyes were even wider and brighter than usual, darting around the room like two small flashlights.

"It's true. And if she hasn't told you yet, I'm sure she will soon. As soon as . . ." She considered what would qualify as soon enough that would astonish the girl, "tomorrow morning at breakfast. And they'll also tell you there's nothing you can do about it and that we all have to die. But it's . . ."

Ema slowly approached Karolínka, and when she was within reach, she threw a handful of sandy truth straight into the girl's widened eyes. "It's a lie. Some people don't. Understand?"

"Who . . . who doesn't die?" Karolínka blurted out, confounded.

"When two people have a staring contest," Ema quickly replied, "then the one who doesn't look away won't die."

"Bull," Karolínka demurred, hesitant, her eyes immediately ready to take the bait. For either a second or eternity neither spoke, and their eyes suddenly clashed as they locked onto one another. Everything vanished as the girls tumbled into each other's gaze deeper and deeper, completely absorbed in the contest, which wasn't a fight to the death but rather a fight for immortality.

There were no witnesses. All the Barbies were lying face down on the bed. Ema tried not to blink. Time stood still, the mothers' pendulums frozen in mid-swing. The room transformed into Karolínka's enormous eye, a drop of water in the ocean, which Ema was now swimming across in her search for Karolínka, very likely cowering inconspicuously like a crustacean behind that coral reef, lost in the endless expanse of her own eye, as their tenacious staring caused fragments to transform into the whole and vice versa.

Tears were now streaming down their cheeks and their entire bodies were tingling, the beans on the kitchen floor had long since sprouted and grown over their apartment building, and their mothers, still conversing, had grown old, died, and turned to dust, yet neither girl relented in the contest.

When Ema was least expecting it, Karolínka began to slowly collapse onto her toys. She fought still to keep her lids from drooping a moment longer, but it was no use. She curled up into a ball on the carpet and fell asleep. Ema tucked her into bed, face down, so she wouldn't inhale her barf in her sleep.

•

They sat at the table eating lunch, today surprisingly in silence, all immersed in their own slop. Ema sopped up the last of the gravy on her plate with bread — she'd promised Rybka, and now herself, that she would eat. Karmela, who like an animal had long since devoured her portion, in a wholly unmeditative manner, was now nervously darting her pale eyes from plate to plate to see who'd leave what uneaten. Dana had been right: once Ema had forgotten to knock and after opening the bathroom door saw Mother Theresa — the name having stuck — hugging the bowl and puking up everything she'd just consumed.

A wave of pity washed over Ema, the emotion something she was suddenly powerless to control, as if it didn't belong to her, as if it hadn't sprung out of her own being — as if it had wandered to her side out of another lifetime, one that likely never even existed. She quickly shut the door. She didn't tell anyone, of course, but from that moment on, the photographer wouldn't take her eyes off her, and those eyes never ceased begging and bewitching and bribing her to keep quiet.

All of a sudden Mother Theresa's voice, thin and trembling like the thread of a spiderweb, cut through the silence of the canteen: "Ema, I have a favor to ask . . ."

Ema kept her eyes on her plate. To prolong for a few more seconds the illusion that I'm alone, that I'm about to put the dirty dishes into the sink and make myself coffee — drinking coffee was prohibited in the ward — and then head out to see Mom in Smíchov, where Mom will put on her Sunday best and be draped on my arm in the street like the fragile old lady she's become as we go to her favorite patisserie for a cream puff. And it doesn't even have to be angular, the Cubist ones are reserved for Sundays only. Just for a few more seconds.

"I'm trying to get through these trying times by making art," Karmela continued, her voice barely a whisper . . . Art? But cameras weren't allowed in here . . . "No, no, I've started to write, I've got fifteen pages already. An *essay*."

The word surprisingly resonated for a long time, quivering and undulating like air over a fire, and "essay" set sail, floating on the lightly rippled surface right to the lookout, where two nurses were changing shifts. Both paused and looked our way. One wanted to capture the word, raising her hand like a child reaching for a bubble, and "essay" burst in all directions.

Ema wondered which of the women bent over their plates even had an inkling of what that word meant, and she started cackling like crazy. And in the sudden blast, in the gaping emptiness of Gizela's missing teeth, she spotted a realm where all opposites had ceased to exist, where one phenomenon had absorbed the next, white absorbing black, knowledge ignorance, the words of a wise man the babble of a madman and vice versa, a realm where the bodies of all these women towered like ancient menhirs, stones vibrating with the incomprehensible word that was plowing its way through their midst, "essay" resembling a ship lost at sea.

Ema, taking the bait, found herself helplessly writing on the line. "Essay on what?"

"On suffering." Oh, that. "On suffering and its causes. Because . . ."

And Karmela was suddenly back in her element, back to being the fiery, fearless woman who'd seen the light, self-assured, standing firmly on ground her great theme had placed under her.

"Because suffering is punishment, because we suffer for the sins of others, just like others suffer for ours. Humankind is a single whole, a living organism, in which every cell, every tissue . . ."

Dana shot up and began to pile the cart with dirty dishes, damn near breaking them. One after the other, the women sauntered off to the ward, leaving me alone with her. Even Gizela, with her "shut up, dingus" only half-heartedly muttered at the threshold to the aquarium. With regal disdain she left those two prattling highbrows. And Ema painfully wished she could follow her, because in just a few days she'd become one of the pack, because to orient herself in here her instinct was needed more than her reason. She found Karmela's smell unbearable, even though they shared the same cultural language, but she'd follow Gizela's scent, the scent of a Gypsy junkie she didn't know, to the edge of the world. Curious: I don't trust her, but my blood does.

Everyone left. So none of them witnessed what followed, apart from round Marcelka.

When the two finally found themselves alone beneath the bulletin board of beaming celebrities, Ema heard soft singing coming from one of the rooms. And that plaintive, wavering voice was singing in Russian, just like her mom once had:

"City on the Kama, where no one knows us,
City on the Kama, mother of all rivers . . ."

Ema didn't dare move. She felt that if she got up, the song would not only immediately stop but would also cease to exist in her memory. She completely forgot about Karmela, unable to make sense of the incessant stream of her chatter, her litany on the topic of suffering. Karmela suddenly took a deep breath — inhale — and forcibly exhaled her trump card right in Ema's face: "For instance — the Holocaust."

That word coming out of her mouth had an extraordinary effect on Ema. Black spots appeared in front of her eyes and her body tensed as if she were about to pounce, and rusty barbed wire spikes sprang from each and every pore. And then — and then just blinding white light and darkness and the jangle of a bell.

"Mom, someone's at the door!"

She ran to the door, dragging Mr. Mouse behind her — whom Mom had rescued from the trash, stitched up, and breathed new life into. A tall lady in black stood at the door as she handed Mom a piece of fabric, quite small and round — "Good afternoon, my name is Mrs. Schwarzová, I live a floor down from you. I just wanted to ask if this is yours, it might have fallen from your balcony . . ."

The light disappeared and the darkness slipped away, just the small skullcap flitted and danced in the boundless space of the giant box as the woman leaned down to Ema, caressed her hair, and pressed a chocolate egg with a surprise inside into her hand. When she squeezed it open she found another chocolate egg inside, one egg containing an identical egg, only slightly smaller than the one before, ad infinitum, until she got bored of it and fell asleep.

She woke up with her arms and legs bound to the bed. She wanted to look up at the ceiling, that singing, that Russian song must've come from up there, but Marcelka obscured her view. "My, my, Emička, ya sure went off and lost the plot there! Such a beanpole like you, like just back from a concentration camp, but damned if I ever saw a brawl the likes of that! They couldn't rip the two of you apart! And just a moment before you'd been chatting away like the best of friends, educated women, the both of ya, that ain't hard to tell! And then outta nowhere, you . . ."

"Daaaaamn," Gizela stretched out the vowel as she yawned, shoving Marcelka out the way, "it was pretty hardcore. First you picked up a bowl of leftover soup, and then . . ."

Ema at once started to hum to block her ears as Gizela handed her the book that was lying on the nightstand. "Look, to hell with it. Sooner or later, they're gonna untie you again. Here, read me something, so I can get to be as smart as you."

It was a book from Rybka, one of those that Rybka was reading at the moment. Ema wanted to pick out a passage specially for Gizela, but this wasn't the time for such luxury and her bound limbs didn't allow her to flip through the pages anyway. So she let the book fall open at random and began to read out loud to the sound of Dana's inhuman snoring from the opposite corner of the room: "Take a sheet of paper, for instance. Everything is contained in this sheet of paper, not just pen and ink. The fact is that this sheet of paper is made up only of 'non-paper' elements. And if we return these non-paper elements to their sources, if we return the sunshine to the sun, the wood to the forest, the forest to the logger, the logger to his father and mother, and so on, then there can be no paper at all. Without non-paper elements, like mind, logger, and sunshine and so on, there will be no paper. It has no autonomous existence. It is made up only of non-self, non-paper elements. If we remove them, the paper is empty, the paper does not exist. It has to inter-be."

Ema fell silent and felt herself turning red, as if she had just finished reciting a poem in a school show. As if words, screams, cries, profanities, the thousandth variation of wretchedness held any meaning in here. As if she weren't dizzily free in here, where else if not here, as if she couldn't walk through walls and bust through the ceiling into her past and the past of others, into her future and of others however she saw fit, as if she couldn't read out loud whatever she wanted to, the Koran, or the Communist Manifesto, as if everything wasn't allowed in here. During the night, they brought in an unconscious Doctor Helga, who proceeded to defecate the bed until morning. To feel ashamed for a paragraph cast into nothingness, for words nobody was listening to?

And yet — the marble colossus of Doctor Veselá deliberately walked across the room, floating, drawing near — and yet, Gizela eventually yapped into the silence what Ema so wished to say: "What a load of crap, the fuck does that even mean?"

Doctor Veselá slightly tottered, but immediately stiffened in place and began to address the wall about fifteen centimeters above Ema's head. "Unfortunately, Mrs. Černá, due to today's incident . . . We were planning to transfer you to downstairs detox first thing tomorrow, but due to your overall instability and aggression, and due to today's incident . . ." She got a bit tongue-tied. Nobody wanted to hear the word "incident" for a third time, not even her. And that's why she sternly addressed the wall, whose faded patterns, painted over a hundred times since the late 19th century, gradually turned red under the weight of her words. After all, you had been determined to face the challenge. To cooperate. Not cause any problems. Accept the treatment plan. To lay bare the evolution of your addiction . . . To accept . . . Supervised self-reflection sessions . . . To polish your civilizational armor daily prior to roll call.

And now this. Who would've thought I'd have my first brawl at fifty. They soon unlocked me with one of those tiny keys for a mailbox or bike lock, they unlocked me as if incidentally, and the chains clattered to the linoleum floor and the nurse yelled, "Showertime, ladies!" and we were given towels and bars of soap and shampoo and we shed our nighties and stepped into the showers naked, all of us at once, shivering with cold in there as Gizela immediately drew a crude diamond shape on the steamed-up window, and then she cracked it open and lit up a cigarette, the others in a tizzy about it at first, then they stepped up to her to take a drag themselves, Gizela's scarred lithe body pressed against the glass, blowing out smoke into the dark, revoltingly indifferent Garden, women's bodies flashed by in the steam, slender and massive thighs, crotches, feet, a tattoo here and there, shrieks and curses and laughter amid torrents of water, and Ema finally gathered enough courage and, feeling thoroughly embarrassed, naked like them, the same as them, stepped toward them, even though at some point she'd become afraid to open any door, afraid where it might lead, and suddenly she lost her footing on the tiles and began to slide and fall down an icy slope until she eventually landed on a riverbank.

She stuck out her tongue and caught a snowflake. It was snowing heavily, and the river before her was rolling from side to side like a colossal white dream-being. Despite her nakedness, she didn't feel cold or ashamed, she felt nothing at all except for a terrific longing for Rybka. She got up to follow her daughter's tracks that might be preserved in the snow. But more and more of it was tumbling down from the sky, and Ema saw the opposite bank spun out of snowflakes as if it were an impressionist painting, and on that snowflake riverbank the composite hunched figure of a fisherman.

The man sat there motionless on a small camp stool. She didn't know anything about fishing, but thought it strange he'd be catching fish in winter on the river with icebergs floating past. A large tin can of bait sat at his feet. Bet it's teeming with worms, she thought, just like her mind was teeming with memories. "That fisherman over there is using my memories as bait," she said aloud and clearly, so the words would not escape the river's notice, "overfed and bloated." She crossed her arms over her chest and glanced at the opposite bank: the fisherman had just done the same as her. She slowly lifted her hand and flicked the edge of her imaginary hat, while the other, composed of snowflakes, parroted her gesture with hardly a lag.

It occurred to Ema that both riverbanks were identical, after all, the man was copying her as though he were just her reflection. It looked like the river was split down the middle by a mirror wall, reflecting back herself but in male form, imperfectly, faltering, only certain parts, to show her other possible variations of reality. She froze, realizing the fisherman on the opposite bank was her dead father.

By the time she realized this, it was too late. The gaping maw of bridge arches began to disgorge evening. Her father put away his fishing rod, shook out the tin can full of her memories into the river, and before getting into his car, before vanishing in the web of distinct points of death of which he was composed, just as a moment ago he had been a composite of countless snowflakes, he turned to her, facing the mirror, and waved goodbye. Ema returned the gesture.

She noticed a book lying on a nearby rock. She wiped snow off the soggy newspaper the book was wrapped in and opened it. "If we return these non-paper elements to their sources . . . the wood to the forest . . . the logger to his father and mother, and so on . . ." It was the same passage she'd read to Gizela today. But that means Rybka had been here, had sat in the exact same spot she was sitting in right now! What could her daughter have seen on the opposite bank?

Ema looked at the river one more time, but the river was no longer a river, the snow no longer snow, the book no longer a book: that terrible energy at the core of all things melted everything down into a homogeneous, pulsating mass, a medley of color, sound, and movement, purified and liberated of human perception.

She tried to scramble up the slope, but with the aid of just one hand, as the other was clutching the book — it was a struggle. She heard a strange panting and groaning and it took her a while to realize that the sounds were coming from her. Crawling on all fours, she finally latched onto a wire fence. She slowly pulled herself forward through the snowdrift. When she glanced at her hand, she noticed it wasn't blood streaming from it, as she'd thought, but the river, which she'd inadvertently taken with her. She was moving away from it, the river illuminated by a myriad of lights from an enormous boatel anchored on her father's side. She heard the rumbling of a freeway in the distance. Darkness tripped her feet and set pieces of wire and old flatboats and piles of empty canisters in her path, but she felt nothing, no pain, as her father's strong, invisible fishing line kept pulling her toward her daughter.

She climbed over a mountain, just a pile of frozen gravel, actually, and she climbed over several other ones like it, a pile of sawdust and sand and something that defied identification. Above her stretched a gray, duct-tape sky, the snowfall relentless, and suddenly somebody gripped her wrist.

"Turn off the light!" The mittened hand was crushing hers, but Ema didn't care. In the darkness, the outline of an old man took shape beside her, an ushanka on his head and entirely wrapped in a swath of shawl like a mummy.

"But I don't have the lights on! What's that on your feet? Those are my slippers I got for Christmas!"

"It's your eyes, they are shining light. Turn them off." She dutifully switched off her eyes. "Besides, aren't you going to the board meeting of the Society for the Preservation of Darkness?"

Mitten man held onto her like a vise and dragged her along the wall. They soon rounded a corner. As they stumbled across a courtyard, the man spoke to himself in two separate voices: "Forever and ever, the roots hold firm in the ground," he declared dramatically, only to derisively laugh at himself the very next moment: "You mean beetroot? The cat tugged at the dog, the dog at the girl, the girl at the grandad, the grandad at the grandma, and they pulled and they pulled . . ." "Quiet! It's the dead, the living, and the unborn who do the pulling, forever and ever . . ."

The old man's unrelenting grip was now pulling her behind him like some undressed, half-animated doll down a narrow hallway which stank of piss and God knows what else, and then — She found herself at the threshold to a vast space, evidently an old factory hall, since here and there she noticed the wreckage of machinery and motionless conveyor belts. Above her a draft swayed the metal hooks dully glinting on steel cables under the ceiling. In several places fires rose from the concrete floor, around which figures wrapped in sleeping bags swarmed like enormous bugs.

The swarming ceased the second the hard, cold eyes of the creatures locked onto the newcomers. A German shepherd ran up to Ema, a scar running down between its eyes, its claws clacking on the cement as though they were tapping out the rhythm of a New Year's Eve song which had long since fizzled out. But of course! She had no doubt where the animal had come from: the snowfall on the woodshed's doorstep stirred and suddenly came to life, the dog stood up on wobbly legs, shook off the snow, and ran into the yard. It ran up and down along the fence momentarily uncertain, but the gate was open, and the dog scurried down the driveway and dashed into the fields; it ran and ran and flew through the blizzard of all those years and the nasty weather of all those places until it arrived — Ash's canine greeting — at her feet.

She bent down to pet the dog. "Watch out, he bites!" Her hand froze in midair. The voice was familiar, where had she —

"Gizela, is that you?" she smiled, and went to her, one of the caterpillars undulating by a firepit. But Gizela just buried herself deeper into her sleeping bag and ignored Ema. Yes, they were the women from the aquarium. She saw Dana and the White Queen and the gray balloon of Marcelka's face peeking out of rags and also the large pale eyes of Mother Theresa, which pierced her through like the metal hooks above and dragged her through the hall and wouldn't release her, and many others. Everything they could get their hands on was crackling and snapping and sizzling in the flames, and in the suffocating smoke the remnants of their long-expired lives fluttered up to the ceiling.

Wine boxes and needles lay scattered all around them, and only now did Ema realize that they were all high, stoned, tripping, plastered, out of it. "Fuuuuck, that was a damn good hit!" Ema heard someone say, and she turned around, get out, get out of here quick, but while one Ema headed for the exit, the other one didn't budge, completely forgetting she had come here looking for Rybka, and she stepped toward the women. Because she was absolutely certain they had what she craved.

She noticed a pencil case lying on a fantastical heap of junk and grabbed it. It was all scuffed and torn, the cheery pictures of Mickey Mouse hardly recognizable anymore. She was absolutely positive what she would find inside. She yanked the zipper — a pencil sharpener, three colored pencils, and a barely legible class schedule — and her fingers closed over a shiny blister pack full of pills.

She was just about to empty them into her hand when someone twisted her wrist and wrested the treasure away. "Now wait a minute! What's the rush, lady?" The old man in the ushanka. She was surprised he was still here. This time, he borrowed a woman's voice. "Did you pay the admission fee?" Her anxious eyes stayed glued on the rattling pack of pills as he shoved it into his mitten.

Ah yes, she must chuck an offering into the fire. She had nothing on her, though, nothing at all, not even clothes! At once she realized she'd found Rybka's book down by the river. Where had she put it before they came in? Aha. Here it is. She quickly handed it to the old man.

"I won't get this . . ." he muttered as he thumbed through the book raptly. "Look!" he thrust it right in Ema's face, so she couldn't actually see anything. "One page after another. They're in sequence! A real-ass book should have pages that are layered one over the other, under and over and over and under, like a proper onion."

She didn't hear a word of what the man was babbling. Her eyes were fixed on his mitten. Finally, the old man swung his arm and tossed the book into the flames and fished out of his mitten the thing that had her in trembles. Ema's face collapsed, as if it were merely ash, holding shape out of sheer will alone. She had just exchanged non-paper for non-bliss.

But the first Ema was power walking through the smelly hall to get to the open air. She wanted to go back to the place she'd fallen from to here, to the showers with the women, under a stream of water, who didn't toss their essence into the flames. She walked off aimlessly, having no clue how to get there. And, too, wherever the book had been, Rybka must have also been.

She stumbled through the dark, it could've been in Podolí, but what use was it to her, what use was this utterly unfamiliar black stretch of space on the outskirts, seashore, land, this unknown black planet where the shower room of the upstairs detox ward had spat her out.

At once she found it unacceptable that she had been wandering around this entire time stark naked, and the freezing temperature made her curl up into a ball. The sky cracked open like an egg and light spilled out, and in that light an old hag appeared, just as curled up as she. She feared the old hag belonged to the women inside, but she had a genuine old-fashioned back basket hanging from her shoulders, and Ema was convinced, even in this space of the all-possible, that anyone walking around with a back basket could never be as bad off as they.

Ema realized that the back basket was here just for her, that she had to fill it up with age-old events, a tangle of notoriously predictable paths, even if she were sick of it a hundred times over.

"You there," she started, "did you happen to see Rybka pass by here?"

"Eh? You've got grass in your ear?"

"No, you don't understand, I'm asking if you've seen my daughter?"

"Eh? You want some water?"

"For heaven's sake, no! Daughter, I said!"

"Old bat, common sense is dead."

The hag turned to Ema and rustled her back basket as though it were a beetle's shell. "Might I interest you in some soup? Chicken broth? It's tasty, it'll get you back on your feet and maybe put some clothes on your back, too. There used to be a Chicken Paradise near here, and it was still pretty fresh when they threw it out."

Ema downed the entire steaming tin in one go. It tasted like window cleaner and pork punch and a killer's tears all mixed together in a concoction that ignited Ema's head and shot it straight back into the shower room.

Turning off the tap, she quickly dried herself off and slipped into her nightie. She reflected if she'd ever been so terribly cold as now. She could hear her teeth chattering loudly. Nurse Vendulka opened the shower room door and attempted to shout over their clamor and running water. "Alright, girls! Time's up!"

One by one the showers fell silent. Nurse Vendulka was just about to disappear into the hallway when she swiftly turned back and scrunched up her nose. "Ladies, come on, now.

Which of you's been smoking in here? I'm putting it in the report, and the head physician will be here for tomorrow's rounds."

I quickly ran across the hallway and lunged beneath the covers. To not exist, at least for a little while, a brief, merciful moment. And I didn't give a damn that a goblin was straddling my headboard and began to bang its drum with its imprisoned toddler.

•

And time was deaf and dragged on like that old hag with her back basket. For a long time, I stood by the window rattling in the wind and observed the Garden. Columns of rain were marching below, zigzagging from chestnut tree to chestnut tree, and a woman opened her umbrella as she and a little girl made a run for it. The child glanced back in awe at the naked riders galloping past on hogs, and looked up to the sky at the clusters of birds now raining down. Her mother seemed not to have noticed any of this, and the two figures soon disappeared from my view.

I thought I caught a glimpse of a green raincoat flash behind one of the trees.

"If I may?" Miss Irena gently pushed me out of her way so she could hang on the window handle her twelfth doll she had just finished crocheting. With a beatific smile, she decorated our aquarium with the dolls as if it weren't March but Christmas Eve.

Dita had that very same raincoat. I tried to focus my gaze, but beyond the gray watery veil, all the contours blurred and the Garden transformed into a collage of blots and shapes.

Nonsense, I reassured myself, but my heart was furiously pounding. Dita teaches in the mornings and then — in the pouring rain — behind a tree —

"Doesn't it just brighten up the place, ladies?" — this would be more like me than her. I can see her now, her ironic squint and her mandarin face, her wrinkles which I adore and which from up close look like parentheses, forever containing not only my chaos, but all the chaos of the world. No. Dita would never pointlessly stand at home base in a downpour if she knew I had cheated and stopped playing the game altogether.

The dolls were hanged from the window handles and they fluttered cheerfully in the draft. I can no longer imagine we'll ever embrace again. All it took were a few days, and I can no longer bring the blurry outlines of the outside world into focus. I touch you, and you dissolve and vanish, like in some terrible, irreversible game. And when you come to visit for the first time, if you gather the courage to do so and if the pain and mountains of lies I've piled between us permit it, don't forget to leave a trail of beans so you don't lose the way back home. Come in a Viking mask. Show up in the doorway holding a warrior's shield. Arrive as a cliff, flow in transformed into a raging river full of ice, the cracking deafening, emerge here on the surface in a diving suit, or at least in your green raincoat. Amen.

I once spent hour after hour stumbling behind that raincoat in the mountains, boots thoroughly drenched. We had gotten lost, and rain had been pouring all day long. There was no longer any point in consulting the map, it was getting dark, and you were blazing a trail for me through the brush. I wasn't worried, you were always the pathfinder who slung my backpack over your shoulder to rid me of any responsibility, like so many of my loved ones before you. Every time someone was there to take on the weight I was supposed to carry myself.

You flicked on the flashlight. A couple steps away, we'd almost missed it, a concrete bunker protruded out of the ground. We entered it. An oil lamp dangling from the low ceiling illuminated the space. Weapons were lying around everywhere, bandoliers with cartridges, rifles and a map of the region from 1938 hung on the walls. An ancient transmitter was sitting on the table. It appeared as if we had gotten lost in both time and space. A gas cooker with pyramids of tin cans were tucked into a small nook.

We heard someone grunting, clambering up a metal ladder from somewhere below. A soldier appeared before us wearing a uniform from bygone years, a pistol and knife sheath hanging from his belt. "Evening, ladies," he greeted us calmly, as though he'd been expecting us since the time of mobilization. "I'll heat up some beans and make tea."

The man spent his entire summers like this. Sometimes his friends came to visit, sometimes he showed kids from camp how to take apart and clean a machine gun and where the line of defense had been. He cosplayed a war that had never broken out.

He was amazed you had a firearms license. While you two talked about calibers, range, types of ammo, I climbed down below to the space with six bunks for a squad, two triple bunkbeds. I clambered up to one and crawled into the sleeping bag. The ceiling was so low that I just had to lift my head a bit for my forehead to touch the concrete. Using a burnt match, I scrawled a crooked heart with our initials.

You eventually came down to join me. "We'll blame it on the kids from camp," you said. The soldier hollered from above: "Good night, ladies! Sleep well! I'm gonna stay up here and try to get the transmitter working again."

And then nothing but your lips, your touch, clenched teeth instead of sighs, pleasure beneath that black smudge of a heart, while above us, a war was raging.

In the morning, the soldier stood in front of the bunker and for a long time, until we'd disappeared from his view into the trees, waved us goodbye. When I glanced back, it looked as if a concrete, moss-covered turtle shell was growing out of his back.

And yet, what if that's really you, hidden behind the chestnut tree, all your senses alert, my own personal sniper watching over and protecting me? What if that liquid green flutter in the Garden below is really you?

•

Something had happened. Apart from the dolls on the window, everyone was absolutely still. It was almost as if someone had cut off the oxygen supply to the aquarium and was now observing what would happen to the creatures within. The White Queen was gasping for air while an irregular wheeze came from Dana's bed. Only Gizela's raspy voice still carried across the room, though its tinfoil rustle paused more and more frequently.

I didn't listen to what she was saying. Only individual words reached me from a distance . . . The griffon vulture . . . the reptile pavilion . . . the giraffe sleeps only half an hour a day. It sounded as if she were leafing through a fauna atlas.

Above us, Ash was now cutting through thick cardboard with a handsaw; his fumbling fingers squeezed out too much glue and pieced together misfitted parts for so long that a malformed box took shape under his hands. I was pretty mad about it: just a moment ago I was feeling happy he had finally given up this rather peculiar hobby. Even without it, my brother was still quirky — not everyone would've been willing to help me look for Rybka, especially when it was my own fault that I had lost her, or would be willing to live on the ceiling.

Not even Marcelka's increasingly frequent ventilation operations could rid Room No. 1 of the awful stench of Petr Ash's glue. Only Gizela continued to talk, a recording no one had the strength to switch off; bizarre beasts leapt out of her toothless mouth and her fingers would occasionally curl like lizard tails. The lookout was swarming with activity — I didn't understand what was going on. The nurses, Dr. Veselá, the deputy head physician, even the head physician himself were closely observing a creature's behavior from behind the glass, exchanging their impressions one moment and looking at the computer monitor the next. The creature under observation was Gizela.

Brother, that dream, remember? It's come back, returned out of the blue, and I wasn't ready for it. It had avoided me for years, didn't dare to show its face, a coward, scared stiff of the benzodiazepines like a demon the cross. Bez-dia, bez-dia . . . repeat it three times quickly in a row! But Gizela was no longer laughing. Only now did I realize that she hadn't laughed in days.

"My boyfriend well ex by now I guess used to work as a zookeeper at the reptile pavilion." She spewed out words without pause, in a single key, scraps of sentences falling from the sewing machine to the floor, pierced by a needle. "One time we stayed there overnight in this dark corridor you got no friends when you're hooked on meth lit only by the terrariums and we took a hit was a little weak at first some of the monsters were staring at us really observing us but then what happened after and we were staring at them too all night I sat there nose pressed up against the glass staring into a snake's eyes and the snake staring into mine . . ."

It's come back after my body expelled, at least to some extent, the poisons that were competing with it. I'm in a room, I need to get out, I rise to the ceiling. I tear through it, relatively easily, because the walls and ceiling are made of cardboard, and find myself in another room. I escape through a chink into another room and so on and so forth, again and again, one room replaces another, always the ceiling, never the sky. But what if it's not the dream that's come back to me, but it's me who's come back to it? Maybe the waking life of Ema Černá is merely a sequence of pauses, brief interruptions of flight with no beginning and no end.

Today I no longer know what came first: if my brother's boxes brought on my recurring dream or the other way around, if I had told him about the dream and he then converted it into his shabby creations.

The sewing machine kept whirring. ". . . for hours and hours and right at dawn I had a wicked hallucination where for Chrissake under me the soft sand heats up open that window one more time cunt and I beat the shit out of you I was inside the terrarium and had no arms or legs all in snakeskin it looked damn good on me too and in the front of my mouth where I have no teeth I had two magnificent fangs."

Gizela showed us her gums. The head physician in the lookout had his eyes locked on her as he lightly took Dr. Veselá by the shoulders and muttered something into her beautiful, fair, undoubtedly nice-smelling hair.

This was all likely Gizela's invention, concocted from some ugly, expired piece of reality, this cock-and-bull story, this fantastical tale which was meant to sate her. What I couldn't understand was why she was telling it to us in the forced tone of a confession with a gun held to her head. We were all professional liars here, terrific braggarts, fiercely protecting and nurturing our inventory of situations that never happened and characters who never existed.

"In the morning an attendant found us and snitched on us and Tiny was sacked on the spot gonna freeze to death in here the radiator's stone-cold today and then he started working as an undertaker good times we had the cash for dope and a roof over our heads and so doing cold temperature and ice jet therapy now and Tiny looked real good in a black suit and white dress shirt nothing gave away he was a junkie apart from the tattoos he had everywhere once he showed me the coffins they're either celluloid with a zinc bottom or metal with a leakproof lining cremation takes ninety minutes tops he had a beautiful Statue of Liberty in color tattooed on his cock. And one time . . ."

Enough. I covered my ears. I didn't need to hear about the time they got high in a crematorium and come dawn Gizela had turned into a corpse. The snake was more than enough for me.

There was no space to move in Room No. 1. It was filled with the junk from Gizela's monologue. Coffins lay upright against the wall in between the beds, reptiles were crawling out of broken fluorescent terrariums, and smelly glue was dripping down on it all from above. I had a sudden powerful urge to flee. To escape, before I truly lost my mind in this place. This time, I wouldn't screw it up like before, when I broke out of the ambulance in my slippers! The animalistic desire to run through a peopleless space with no right angles had attached itself to my back like a hump, which from that point on I mulishly lugged around with me.

Gizela suddenly fell silent in mid-sentence. Inhale. To breathe in air that doesn't stink of disinfectant and hospital food and isn't full of drivel endlessly swirling. In a completely different tone, as if only now really her, as if only now she had found herself after a long wandering — it sounded like a prayer, a bone-chilling prayer — she pleaded: "Oh, my God. My God, I want . . ."

All those nighttime mute fish wishes: the sea, silence, bubble bath, pizza the size of a wagon wheel, your embrace.

". . . to get high again so bad."

I had to quickly get to the window for some air. I nearly killed myself tripping over Gizela's junk, that mountain of detritus she'd piled up here today. Go ahead and beat the shit out of me for opening the window. Don't worry, you'll get yours. It's because of the poorly oxygenated water. You'll do it as soon as you get out of here.

I stood at the open window and took gulps of the brisk, moist March air. When Marcelka saw that Gizela wasn't reacting, she merrily scuttled up to me; even Dana, whose wheezing was sounding more ominous, dug herself out from under the covers, and the White Queen joined us as well. This time there wasn't anything phantasmagorical happening below in the Garden: a cyclist sped by, wearing that gross skintight sportswear, and two grandpas wielding canes paused and looked up at us. One of them lifted his cane, and it wasn't clear whether it was a wave or a threat. We stood there, crammed against the open window, not saying anything and trembling with cold in our nighties barely covering our butts, and also waved and also threatened, long after the path was empty once more.

Gizela didn't even budge and just stared at the ceiling. No way she could see what I could, my lost-and-found brother, his hands and face crusted in glue. She was more than likely peering into an upside-down well, from whose bottom, if it had one, snakes were falling onto her bed. It seemed to me that her mouth was emitting an almost imperceptible hissing and the skin on her arms was turning coarse and changing color. What was now lying motionless on the bedding was no longer Gizela. Some new being, a caricature of the girl I had met a few days ago, was now blandly and disinterestedly, just to keep up appearances, impersonating her.

But before I could start to feel pity, a sudden spasm ran down the length of Gizela's body, which was no longer hers. She reared up on the bed like a cobra and slammed her new snake head into the wall with all her might. Over and over. All while a stream of shrieks and curses and foulness totally incomprehensible to me spewed from her mouth. I put her in a headlock, as I'd learned from the paramedic, but she slipped out of my hold and threw herself against the wall again. The White Queen ran out into the hallway as Marcelka shouted and gesticulated toward the lookout. After an eternity, a nurse ran in, while we were all holding down a writhing Gizela as best we could, and gave her a shot.

Her forehead was bloodied to a pulp. She had stopped moving. Only her teeth chattered faintly. I quickly closed the window and we all piled our blankets on top of her.

Mother Theresa stood in the doorway: "Oh, sisters, you didn't know? She wanted to hang herself from a toilet stall door handle last night."

Oh, Gizela: that very toilet stall couldn't be locked. You pinched some gauze from the nurses' station, waited until the coast was clear, and got to work. As if the coast could ever be clear in here! You probably mistook the gauze for a safety fuse like me and had actually wanted to blow the Garden to kingdom come. In reckless haste you unwound the gauze and wrapped it around the door handle and yourself and your fingers weren't cooperating and it wasn't going as planned, the gauze too stretchy, and so you helplessly floundered on the floor tiles until Mother Theresa appeared and grabbed the door handle and pulled you out of the trap, out of the cocoon that imprisoned you, freeing the ridiculously oversized white crocheted doll.

Miss Irena took her knitting needles and ball of yarn from her nightstand and set to work. Their clacking cut through the silence as if from afar.

"Mrs. Černá," the nurse acted as if nothing had just happened, and she wasn't wrong. "Pack your stuff, you're being moved to downstairs detox."

Right now? "Get a move on, we've got an incoming patient waiting in the hall!"

I quickly tossed the contents of my nightstand into a bag. Mainly letters from Rybka and Dita and postcards of animals from my mom, I guess she thought I was still at summer camp.

"Good for you, Mrs. Černá," Marcelka chirped roundly, "downstairs it's another story. They've got a TV and movies and you get to play nice games and then in a few days you'll get put on a treatment plan and you get to walk around in your own clothes, and that's sure to add a bit of pep to your step!"

I wanted to say goodbye to Gizela. Her unblinking serpent gaze was fixed on the ceiling. I stood over her, at a loss. "Bye."

Nothing. Could she even hear me? And so I leapt to Miss Irena's side, yanked the knitting needles out of her hands, and began to bang on Gizela's metal bedframe, singing off-key a song she and I used to sing in here:

"I ride around on a lame mare,
none other was left in my care,
let her, let her limp uphill
she's got courage, heart, and skill!"

Nothing. No reaction at all. She was in the terrarium for good, and no sounds could penetrate the glass.

The checkered notebook was last. And just as I was shoving it into my bag, it fell open. I skimmed the page and froze: my entry about Ash ended mid-page and continued in a handwriting that wasn't mine.

•

And then, in 1990, the year when everyone was coming back, I, Petr Ash, left. I only took a couple things with me that could fit in a shoulder bag, Rybka's childhood drawings of tadpole people, and my vocational certificate. With all due humility I must declare that if there is one thing in this world I know my way around, it's food. I did nearly fail in goulash in my junior year but that was still at a time when the dense matter of my secret would sometimes ensnare my fingers.

Mom gave me a few pieces of Grandma's jewelry for my journey, so I'd have something to keep me afloat in the beginning. I still have them — not that I'd been especially capable of taking care of myself, but I simply didn't need all that much. I didn't care where I slept and what I ate, and I didn't feel the cold.

Dad had been allowed to work as a journalist again and he was being honored left and right, he might not have even noticed I wasn't living with them anymore. I never understood why everyone was so obsessed with their parents, why for years and years they would crease and crumple some old postcard from their father, or enjoy imagining his death. The past of so many people had piled up in layers within my emptiness and had cost me so much effort that I didn't get why I should cherish my own. And then, I was secretly convinced I hadn't been born like everyone else, but that I had come into this world in some unusual way, through cloning or mitosis, or that I had even sprung into being out of a sound, barely exhaled by someone at death's door — why I was certain it was the sound Wuh is anyone's guess.

In the train, I kept rereading a news story in which I took an excessive interest: A woman from the Icelandic town of Hlynur can recall every single event in her life from the past 15 years. She is even able to remember exactly what she was doing, whom she met with, and what she had for lunch on any given day since 1975.

For years I knocked around Europe, making money any way I could: dishwashing in bars, cleaning international express trains in depots, picking up trash on beaches. And it was on one of these beaches that I realized something had changed. "Desire" would be too strong a word, but for the first time in my life I wanted something, something I hadn't prised from others and hadn't been drilled into me: to have, whether in front of me or behind, the sea within reach.

I eventually settled in a village on the French coast. In this restaurant, called Verdi for some unfathomable reason, I no longer mopped the floor, but prepared refined dishes for diners, and thankfully not one ordered goulash. I liked to stand behind the curtain, naturally in a way that allowed me to observe unseen, just like right now, the diners skewering forkfuls of my Terrine de coquilles Saint-Jacques or my Magret de canard, and as always I imagined that at that very moment a kind of transubstantiation was occurring, in which the meal transformed into the person who had prepared it, into the body and blood of Petr Ash. Apart from my wife — getting married an incomprehensible, monumental mistake — this was my only means of communication with others, only in this way, in their saliva, digestive juices, and intestines, was I able to experience a sense of communion with other human beings.

Two women sitting at a corner table ordered Lamb bourguignon. I got to work. The key to the art of cooking, as everyone knows, is a complete set of impeccably sharpened knives. I sank the blade into the meat and contemplated cannibalism under my breath. I could afford to — nobody here understood my mother tongue. And just as easily and without resistance as the steel penetrating the animal flesh did my thoughts and opinions — light and exchangeable, because I had picked them up somewhere, filched them from God knows whom, collected them on some beach who knows where — penetrate the huge dead body, of which I, too, was a part.

I also imagined it to be mother and daughter, the two women for whom I was preparing the lamb. It was very likely. It could've even been Ema and Rybka. After all, why shouldn't they one day enter the Verdi restaurant? I had written them countless times how much I'd like to see them, not quite true, but just one of those things you say.

Lamb, de l'agneau, agnus, Lamb of God. I took an onion, the largest one I had. You don't add chopped onion to Lamb bourguignon, instead you peel the onion, layer by layer. I placed the translucent onion layers one by one into a bowl and then — within the space where the onion ended and nothing began — Ema appeared.

We had taken a day trip once, Ema, Rybka, and I. Rybka must've been about two years old at the time. I had her in a carrier strapped to my back. We got lost in some village and found ourselves in the local cemetery, old and unkempt. We strolled among the tombstones as Ema read out the names of the departed and talked of death. How come, she said angrily, nobody teaches us how to die? How come we don't read out loud from guides to the dying, who are already on their way out? "O nobly born, with every thought of fear or terror or awe for all set aside, may you recognize whatever visions appear, as the reflections of your own consciousness; the radiance of thine own true nature . . ."

I wasn't really listening to her. Rybka was fidgeting on my back as she babbled and the topic didn't really concern me, since having never been born, logically speaking, I couldn't die. Feeling awkward, I recited to her a couple of recipes I'd tried out recently, but we switched tones: while I waxed lyrical about eggplant stuffed with ground mutton braised with white wine reduction, Ema kept talking about death as if she were reckoning the ingredients.

And then she read a funny name off a grave that I remember to this day: *Here lies Váša Šála.* The headstone was adorned with an oval-framed portrait of Váša, the face of a ten-year-old boy with Dumbo ears, permeated with a light from some distant time and place.

The sun was just setting behind the cemetery wall, an enormous crimson-gold sphere, a sheaf of golden stalks suddenly sprouting out of it. Both lights, the light of the instant when Váša Šála grinned at the camera and the sunlight, presently converged on the photo in his protruding earlobes. In that moment two needles wove a single glow, a single natural radiance, all the less fathomable as it belonged neither to me, nor to the sun, nor to the dead child.

My eyes were burning as I headed to the gate. "Wait, let me take a photo of this, are you seeing this?" Ema dragged me from one gravestone to another, pointing out the portraits of the deceased. The appearances were completely intact on some of them, while on others time had replaced parts of the face with a tangle of lines, so it was only possible to make out the likeness in places, as in a collage, the contours of a chin, an eye, a hair style. And then there were the last, oldest photographs: within the oval frames only lines remained, crisscrossing, weaving, branching in and out.

I didn't know what had gotten into her. She began running from gravestone to gravestone shooting photos in that dual light, sometimes exclaiming, "Get over here, you gotta see this!" or "Pure graphic art!" and I huffed and puffed my way to her with Rybka bouncing up and down on my back and giggling, because she thought it was a game.

Simply put, she was being obnoxious. I felt something — and the waft of a feeling, no matter what it was, always filled me with a sense of satisfaction — which probably remotely resembled anger. For one, I had long ago learned how people usually behave in a cemetery, and for another, it aggravated me how my sister was pretending to be a muse-possessed artist who could see more or something others couldn't. I suddenly realized that even the giggly little girl on my back would die one day, and it baffled me how Ema could have done this to her. Would she be willing to take a photo of her, too, transformed into "pure graphic art"?

She finally grew tired of it. We sat down on the stone rim of Váša Šála's final resting place and Ema fed Rybka applesauce as if it were normal. As we were leaving, she said: "There's only a single minority on Earth who ignores the majority and takes up space in its stead: the living." And then also: "My poor, cold-hearted baby brother, I love you so much. Promise me you'll finally stop gluing together those damn boxes of yours!"

I turned around. Above the gate was an inscription set in a semi-circle, of the kind commonly found in cemeteries: *What you are now, we once were. What we are now, you shall be.*

Not me.

Anatole, the restaurant's owner and my boss, was holding out to me a ringing cellphone. My wife. Who else. I shook my head. No, not now, I'm preparing a meal with utmost care and attention for my sister and niece. It's enough that today like any other day I have the usual night shift to look forward to. Why should anyone, and by that I meant myself, who has absolutely no appreciation for any sort of addiction, no matter how cleverly altered, why, I ask, should anyone have to be exposed to it on a daily basis for seventeen long years in its most vulgar form? I pitied myself, because self-pity is what's appropriate for people in such situations.

I scrupulously wrapped the phone in a dishcloth and covered it with a roasting pan.

I knew the routine by heart: like any other day, first the hiccups, then the reproaches, the insults, the tears, followed by a stare nailed to the wall like a hook. Then the jerky movements, the dance of a dragon. And when sleep finally replaces the dragon phase, I clean up the vomit, throw my wife's clothes in the wash, and set my alarm for three in the morning. Exactly at 3:20 a.m. my wife would wake up, appear by my bed screaming, and begin to tear the sheets off of me, leaving bloody scratches on my arms. I told Anatole that we'd gotten a cat. Then the anxiety phase. The direction of the scratches is clear, she being the one who determines them; she pulls me toward her and wants me to follow her even further, to throw myself alongside her into a depth breaking through which to the surface can only be achieved with a burst head from a lack of oxygen.

"I don't want to die, Pete, do something, can't you see I'm dying?"

I struggle my way out of her clutches and go to the kitchen for cold water, which I always keep at the ready in the fridge, in a spray bottle for flowers. Methodically, I spray down my wife: her face, particularly the temples, neck, arms, the wrists, and finally her feet. Her tremors slowly abate. And because I no longer have the strength to carry her back to her bed, I wrap her while still on the floor in a thick duvet reserved for guests, who never come to visit anyway.

One time I forgot to set my alarm. Something like that could never happen again. I awoke from a nightmare at 4:16 — I had dreamt of a volcano towering next to my bed, belching hot lava down on me. For a minute, I couldn't move. I was just a clod of lifeless dough the dream had flung into boiling water. Total silence reigned over the apartment; my wife hated the ticking of clocks.

I finally got up and went to the other bedroom. My wife wasn't there. An empty vodka bottle stood on the kitchen table, so she couldn't have gone far. Our apartment wasn't all that big, it didn't take long to search it. I opened the closet.

Nothing. The linen cupboard. Not here either. The pantry. No cigar. Back in the day Ema and I used to play like this. I even thought for a second my wife might jump me out of nowhere. Her shoes and coat were by the door, so she had to be somewhere inside the apartment. I heard a strange noise, something like applause, but it was just a shirt drying on the balcony, its empty sleeves slapping against the railing.

And then for maybe the sixth time I took a look inside the bathroom again, just in case. There she was, curled up in the bathtub, sleeping, her features marred by the hell of sobering up. I switched off the light, but her naked body continued to glow in the dark.

Mother and daughter finished eating and looked more than satisfied. I cleaned the knives and meticulously polished the steel with a special cloth, a task I never entrusted to anyone else. I was never satisfied until I saw the gleam of my shrunken face reflecting in a knife handle. Of course my face was a composite of countless features randomly collected, but despite this, or perhaps because of it, I found it beautiful.

I walked home and took the roundabout way along the seashore. In front of me or behind, I had to always have it within reach: the sea. And suddenly I realized why Ema's emails were so incomprehensible to me, why I read them with a degree of revulsion, though I should be glad for news about her and Mom and what's happening in my homeland: I could never find the sea in them. Her messages trudged through a primordial wasteland before the sea had even been formed.

I walked along the shore, raking the sand with a bamboo stick — it was pretty amazing what one could find. In my basement I kept a decent collection of objects the sea had left in my care. Even so, I printed out each new email from my sister, every single one, and deposited it in a cardboard box made specifically for this purpose. And, I realized, therein perhaps lay another reason why our relationship was shrouded in misunderstanding: I read them chronologically, as I received them, one after the other. Maybe they should've been read not *one after the other*, but *one over the other*, like the layers of an onion — her testimonies patiently assembled into the shape of the Sun and then disassembled again into the original void.

Something glistened at my feet. I cleared away the seaweed with my stick and spotted a buckle. I knelt down and dug out of the sand a fairly well-preserved woman's white cork sandal. Another bounty of the sea, another addition to my collection. And back home as I was setting my alarm to 3 a.m., I wondered where the other sandal had ended up.

•

Rybka was right. At the end of the narrow hallway was a window, and when Ema leaned out as much as the bars would allow, she could see, thirty, forty centimeters below, the athlete's enormous soles. He was doing a handstand, straight as an arrow, the realistically rendered band of his boxer shorts prominent in bronze above his butt.

The weird thing was that nobody had ever said a word about those feet. All the patients — given that alcoholism was classified as a disease under an F10 diagnosis, which was constantly being instilled and engrained in them and their family members by medical professionals, driven home by all the assignments and therapy sessions and open group sessions, a premise that was the perverse cornerstone of all treatment, a cornerstone that luckily was continually compromised by the wholly natural reactions of the nurses permanently annoyed that this notorious diagnosis required they care for women who instead of looking after their kids and families, like they did, rolled around in the gutter in their own puke, and for girls the age of their daughters who instead of going to school or learning a trade or helping out at home, no walk in the park, shoplifted and turned tricks to get money for dope, and now we're supposed to just serve them breakfast in bed and comfort them with kindness and strap them down so they won't do themselves any harm and won't get any bruises like when that posh lady beat us with her purse that we had to call her a taxi immediately to take her to Čelákovice so they won't complain to the head physician about us or send a letter of complaint straight to the Ministry of Health — all the patients in downstairs detox must have been convinced once they saw those soles, like she had just now, that they were experiencing some post-alcoholic, in Gizela's words, "wicked hallucination."

The nurse showed Ema her new bed and cubby where she was to put her things.

She turned to the woman in the turquoise velvet pajamas, it didn't look like anyone else was mentally present. "Hi, I'm Ema."

The woman didn't take her eyes off of her, her gaze fixed on her every move, but she didn't say a word. A translucent nymph lay in the bed next to her, eyes closed. The third bed was empty.

She lay down and opened her checkered notebook to reread Ash's entry: *I felt something remotely resembling anger . . . Having never been born, logically speaking, I couldn't die . . . I had long ago learned how people usually behave in a cemetery.*

"Druggie or alkie?" The turquoise one suddenly shouted when Ema was least expecting it.

"Junkie!" she replied as if to a drill command before burying her head back in the notebook.

The nymph opened her eyes and pleaded softly, "For heaven's sake, Vladěna, leave it . . ."

But Vladěna jumped out of bed and began orbiting Ema angrily in ever-shrinking concentric circles. "Junkie, eh? Some jilted doctor or unappreciated frigid intellectual who's just gonna throw her weight around? Who's always gonna have her nose in a book and act as if she's above it all? As if she knows more than us? As if she's got this whole fucking shitshow under control, only to write some deep article for the papers about the suffering of these alcoholic losers in here, who thanks to their own willpower and excellent therapists will be able to start a new life? God forbid the sow spits out a whole frickin' book! She makes me sick! Nuuuuurse!"

As an absurd gesture of self-preservation, Ema quickly put away her notebook and took off her glasses. She'd already had one baptism and didn't want to get into another brawl. She began to mentally browse through the lexicon of insults she'd learned in here, selecting which one to toss into the abusive mouth to shut it up, but she was at a complete loss. She would be pitifully polite until the day she dies. A sudden wave of nausea swept over her; nothing existential, just that regular morning physical queasiness children use as an excuse to avoid school. She simply saw herself through Vladěna's eyes and made herself sick as well.

She got the urge to stick a finger far down her throat, to fit the image as faithfully as possible. "You know what?" she replied with a saccharine, understanding smile, putting her glasses on again, "Here's a suggestion: do your best to ignore me, or else your aggression will escalate."

In the silence that followed, you could hear the nymph named Verunka biting her nails. "Come on, Vladěna, leave her alone . . ." she pleaded again in a scared, childlike voice. And the longer the silence persisted, the louder and more unbearable the clicking of her nails.

On the bed a couple steps away trembled a raving turquoise mountain. Verunka began to whine quietly like some oversized, battery-powered doll.

They kept their eyes locked on each other. Red spots appeared on Vladěna's cheeks. But Ema didn't want to engage in another staring contest as she had with Karolínka. She had stopped aspiring to immortality long ago. She no longer aspired to anything, and yet, in this moment of alertness, fearing an impending blow, she felt alive again for the first time since that interminable ambulance ride.

"Ignore you, eh?" Vladěna finally trilled, "ignore, escalate, and analyze!" That last word, which Ema hadn't uttered, rattled the mugs on the nightstands. Verunka crumpled into a cross-legged position and emitted a feeble wail, as if singing to herself.

Vladěna got up, her whole body clenched up like a fist, and she swayed unsteadily, barefoot by her bed. But instead of pouncing on Ema she suddenly staggered over to the sink and began to brush her teeth, gargling loudly. It was so unexpected that the nymph stopped biting her nails at once. Maybe it's a local pre-fight ritual, Ema thought. But Vladěna, lazily, almost as an afterthought, to save face, opened the door to the hallway and began to scream:

"Look, you can make me bunk with anyone you want, I can

handle anything, drooling old crones, even fuckin' deranged junkies, but this takes the cake! This deep-thinking cunt is only in here to mock us so she can run her mouth later with the other deep-thinking cunts about her experiences in here, well I won't put up with it! Look at her, Nurse, just look at that face! Exactly the type of woman who'd always push their pocket change on me outside the Anděl metro station at night after stumbling out of their office parties."

Rambo appeared in the doorway like a rampart, and Vladěna's yelling impotently bounced off of her. "Calm down, Novotná. Look, if you don't like it, we can bring in Medusa instead."

Ema had no clue who or what Medusa was, but the threat had a remarkable effect: Vladěna wordlessly returned to her bed and disappeared under the covers.

Marcelka had been right: they really did have a video player down here. That evening they all watched a film about ABBA starring Meryl Streep. The women set aside their magazines and knitting and began to clap, stomping their feet to the beat and yelling "money, money, money" as some of them took off their bathrobes and writhed in front of the TV, jiggling their enormous boobs, like on the dance floor of some bygone disco.

But that first night in downstairs detox, it surprisingly wasn't Vladěna who turned out to be the threat.

I fell asleep and suddenly heard a voice: "Look here, Mrs. Černá, don't fall asleep on us and give it a few good squeezes!" What nonsense, how could I possibly fall asleep amid this noisy swarm of hands? The watch on the nurse's wrist was thundering like a mountain storm. But was she a nurse? A woman all in black was sitting on the edge of the bed: she quickly forced a few drops out of the hypodermic needle and then jabbed it into my vein.

"Can you feel it?" she asked.

"Yes," Ema answered, "I guess so. I feel a big fist clutching my mind and slowly unclenching. I feel . . ."

"Enough." The black shadow leaned over me, a delicate, soft wing covering both me and my bed.

"When one thought has ceased," the woman continued, "and another has yet to emerge, when one image has disappeared and the next has yet to appear — is there not a blank space in between?"

"There is," Ema agreed in confusion.

"Extend it into infinity."

I opened my eyes. It was no longer the woman in black leaning over me. It was Verunka. Clutching a pillow to her chest, she slowly brought it closer to my face.

"You mustn't get mad," she whispered apologetically, "if I kill you during the night. I'm awfully sorry, but I have to kill you. It's not my fault I'm evil."

I jumped out of bed and ran into the hallway. The wall clock read 3:20 a.m. The hour when my brother would also awaken and get his spray bottle ready. Light was streaming out of the door left ajar to the nurses' station. My heart was in my throat. I reached the end of the hallway with the window overlooking the Garden. In the light of the streetlamp, the enormous feet shone white below me, as smooth, fake, and wicked as Verunka's face. I got down on all fours and turned into a rat. I scurried along the walls, under the table to the door locked with a hundred bolts, then back to the window again. I was sniffing for any crack I could slip through to get out. I warily avoided the door to the nurses' station and again set off on my pilgrimage, praying my claws wouldn't make any noise on the linoleum. I snooped every nook and cranny once more, and then collapsed in exhaustion at the foot of a bookcase. Layers of dust showered over me as one book toppled over and whacked me in the snout.

As I was panting for breath, a genuine rat hunger overcame me. I bit into the book's pages but had to spit it out. Another story about humans, over and over, just stories about humans. Stories about humans gave the rat terrible indigestion. It finally reached a page with only frogs, and tore into it with relish:

Once upon a time there was a frog that lived in a moldy well. One day, an ocean frog came to visit.

"Where do you come from?"

"From the great ocean," the frog replied.

"How big is this ocean of yours?"

"Very big."

"You reckon it's at least one fourth the size of my well?"

"Bigger."

"Bigger? Half the size?"

"Even bigger."

"Are you saying it's . . . It's as big as this well?"

"You're comparing the incomparable."

"Impossible! I've got to see it with my own eyes!"

They set out together. When the well frog spotted the ocean, it was such a shock that its head burst.

I was trying to keep my munching quiet, but a nurse must have heard me, because she stepped into the hallway. I quickly scrambled up onto a chair and pretended to be reading.

It was Karabinka, as everyone called her in here, a permanent, kindhearted expression etched on her face. She was a back-basket kind of person.

"Karabinka," I asked, "might the carpenter have left here a hole?"

"Eh? You've lost all self-control?"

Of course she was hard of hearing, no surprise there.

"No, I'm just asking where I could find an exit for rats."

"What's that? Your life's for the cats?"

"Good Lord, woman, just tell me how to get out clean?"

"Yep," she nodded, "dream follows dream follows dream . . ."

"Can't sleep, Mrs. Černá?"

"No."

"You know I can't give you anything for that, right?"

"I know."

We shared the silence. "Sometimes I can't sleep either," she simply said.

"But if you want to, you can take a pill for it."

For an awkward moment, she pondered how to reply.

"You're right. I can. What's that you're reading?"

I quickly concealed the half-eaten page. "I'm not even sure."

"You can stay here reading a bit longer, but then it's beddy-bye for you."

She really did say "beddy-bye."

"Nurse . . . It's Verunka . . . She frightens me."

"You're kidding!" she started to laugh. "That slip of a girl? After a dose of Subutex she does act up sometimes, that's true, and claims she's evil, but she's a veritable lamb."

Karabinka, beddy-bye, slip of a girl, lamb. It was starting to make me nauseous.

"Who is Medusa?"

Was I just imagining it, or did a shadow of fear really flash behind the nurse's eyes? She glanced around before making her voice real low: "Don't ever say that name aloud in here again! Ever!" She hastily bid me a good night and disappeared into the nurses' station.

I kept my eye on the long hand of the wall clock: for a while it stood still, and then, with a clatter, jumped two minutes ahead. Tick. Maybe Ash's wife had finally fallen asleep. And maybe so had the slip of a girl and the lamb. Sooner or later, even a rat gets its turn. Tock.

I wondered who this Medusa could be. I polished off the second part of the frog page and went to the bathroom.

A girl stood there, the hood of her hoodie over her head, blowing smoke into a hole in the wall. "Sorry," I said, but stayed put, fascinated by the hole.

"Fuck's sake, close the door, quick! The nurse'll smell it."

She pulled me in. Suddenly, we were stuck together in the cramped space, two strangers. We silently passed the cigarette between us, taking turns to blow the smoke each time into the hole. I began to examine it a little. About thirty by forty centimeters, the lower edge full of plaster and ash, twisting pipes on the inside. I tried to stick my head in, but no luck.

"The hell you doing?"

"Just trying something. Could be a way out of here."

"You're nuts!" she chuckled, "and where exactly d'you think you'd get to? You wanna end up back in upstairs detox? And the nurses' bathroom is below us."

I didn't have to ask, after a few days, it became clear to me who was druggie and who was alkie. And I was glad she didn't ask me either.

She sized me up from head to toe. "Well, maybe you'd actually manage to squeeze in there, you're like a spindly spider."

"I'm a rat, not a spider."

"That some kind of Chinese zodiac sign?"

"Who's this Medusa?"

"No idea. She supposed to be some alkie in here or something?"

I let it be. The girl lit another cigarette. In the light of the flame I saw brown eyes, two freshly shelled chestnuts glittering from underneath the hood. I wondered what would happen if I were to touch her face, just a graze of my fingertips. Stupid idea.

"Why aren't you sleeping?" she asked, "me, I can't. My father told me today he wants to have me declared legally incompetent. He's already filed the paperwork."

"That's awful . . ."

"The only awful thing about it is that he should've done it a long time ago."

We talked quietly. I talked about anything and everything that came to mind with ease. It was as if the clock in the hall had frozen and a multitude of events and people had been miraculously crammed into that one last "tock" and were now slowly rising through the hole with the smoke. And absorbed into the air, they disappeared one after the other — Dalibor disappeared, then Dita disappeared, my brother disappeared, and my mom disappeared, as did my dad, and eventually Rybka too floated away.

One more time, I tried to stick my head after them into that narrow darkness.

"You go first, close the door quickly and then knock if the coast is clear."

I quickly slipped out of the bathroom, gave the girl the signal as agreed, and snuck back into the room. Silence. The turquoise one and the nymph were both breathing in a regular rhythm. Outside the window the dark broke like a bar of chocolate into a new day. I suddenly had a terrible craving for it, so I opened my drawer and snapped off a piece.

In the gap between two images, sweetly dissolving on my tongue, a seesaw began to creak softly: one second I was up, then Rybka. The faces on the other end of the seesaw were changing, and after Rybka, Dita appeared: I could hear her yelling at me, "Take a deep breath, damn it!" and "You've got to really push off!" as if she wanted to dispel all my anxieties by that breathing in and pushing off; then it was my mom across from me, that silly hat of hers perched on her head, and she began to push off the ground with a surprisingly wild girlish energy, her hat almost toppling off, and after Mom came Rambo, who straddled the seesaw between her knees like a heavy motorcycle and began to emit motor sounds like kids make when playing with toy cars; and after Rambo it was Dalibor, my ex-husband, whose eyes, whenever they appeared above me, were full of reproach: "You should've connected them! Tied them together! How could you, Ema? I built us a castle and you spurned it, leaving our progeny to the mercy of many a danger"; I shut my eyes and pushed off as hard as I could, and when I opened them again, my brother Ash had replaced Dalibor sitting across from me on the seesaw, and he was clutching the seat tightly to keep his form, but with each hard landing a part of him diminished until he disintegrated altogether; after he disappeared, on the seat opposite me was Grandma, and behind her Grandad, behind Grandad the girl, behind the girl the dog, and behind the dog the cat. I didn't understand how they could all fit, as there were many others sitting behind the cat, one holding onto the other as Grandma yelled at me furiously, stop it already, stop it, do you hear? Can't you see you're robbing us of our vitality?

The clock ticked, and the minute hand jumped ahead. Everybody miraculously dissolved in that twitch of time, and only I remained, seesawing in my own mind, suspended in the space between two images. No faces were on the opposite end of the seesaw, but some kind of invisible force kept balancing my own movement. It held out its hand and gave me an egg with a surprise inside, and began to rock me one last time while a groan hissed through the wall: dream follows dream follows dream . . .

●

She kept seeing it in her mind's eye. Outside the window, the darkness was now rent and light was streaming through a crack with a similarly jagged edge. She had to make sure it was really there, that it continued to exist, that it was no mere delusion. Right this minute. Her feet touched the floor. The other two were breathing in a regular rhythm, as if having just experienced another day full of adventures at summer camp. The nymph was gently hugging her pillow which just an hour ago had been a murder weapon.

She took a few steps and froze. Her bare feet loudly smacked the linoleum. Under no circumstances could she wake them. She sent all her terrible desire, today she heard Dita's voice for almost a whole minute, straight to the soles of her feet.

Downstairs detox had a phone. Calls to loved ones were allowed from five to six, and by four-thirty a high-strung line was already forming at the door. A spot in line had to be fought for, and it was common to barter with cigarettes and phone cards and smuggled sleeping pills, and those at the end of the line had virtually no chance, because as soon as someone hung up the phone, the other one on the outside was calling back, five minutes per call, bawling and sobbing, pleading and imprecating, since each had to solve in five minutes what people need years to do. Each call was recorded by the nurse on duty, outgoing, incoming, from whom to whom, and how long. The phone was mounted on the wall directly across from the nurses' station and a nurse monitored closely who would replace the receiver in tears, reeling, entering into her medical record, family situation unresolved, revoking visitation rights is recommended. When it was finally her turn, having reached the summit, with the last ounce of her strength she stuck her flag into the ground and sunk into the snow.

"Can you hear me? It's a racket on your end! Rybka and I will visit you tomorrow, darling, I might arrive a bit later, I'll bike there, I figured out a decent route from Červený vrch to Bohnice." Not a flag. A flag is stupid. She'll bury a chocolate bar into the snow like Sherpas do, since the Himalayan gods are said to have a mean sweet tooth.

She had ears but couldn't hear. She had eyes, but instead of the snarling snake behind her, haphazardly sprouting arms and hair and grimaces and cries, she saw in front of her the plastic glasses of Andy Warhol, and behind the glasses the eyes of someone who hadn't slept for days. He had draped his leather jacket over her, she remembered, and when the redhead had opened the ambulance door, he'd commanded her: "Ruuun!"

"What? What did you say?"

"Dita . . ." She wanted to tell her she had managed to drag

herself to the summit, but had frozen up there, she'd frozen into an ice statue that didn't resemble her at all. She simply wanted to warn her, but her voice was gone, too.

"Alrighty, Her Highness has had her go, yeah?" Vladěna tore the phone out of her hand and hung it up.

Darling. Had she heard that right? Had Dita really said that? She'd never called her anything remotely like that in her life and had nothing but eternal disdain for terms of endearment. But if Dita really had allowed it to escape from her lips, it meant that even she had been imprisoned in a snowdrift, some strange, dirty pile of snow, which she hadn't chosen and into which she'd collapsed from total exhaustion.

She tried it once more: she sent her desire through her body all the way to the soles of her feet. And it worked! She floated ten, fifteen centimeters above the ground like it was nothing and, slowly swaying, weightlessly glided toward the door. It was so simple, and Ema became seriously indignant at herself because she couldn't understand why she hadn't done this ages ago, especially when she had lurched out of the ambulance and attempted to flee from the Garden. It was possible to move at any speed, and if back then she'd just shifted into top gear, the redhead wouldn't have stood a chance.

A dull purplish light flooded the hallway. She could hear the breathing of the two strangers behind her, she knew one was named Vladěna and the other Verunka, and surprisingly these names mattered for some odd reason, because both women slept suspended from their names as if from the last thread of an ominously torn spiderweb.

The door to the nurses' station was open a crack. Ema nervously wriggled her toes in the air like Dad used to do. What good would the absence of gravity do her, all this impressive floating, if the nurse caught her? She had to make sure, at any cost, that the place she needed to see again still existed and that her fingertips could still touch its jagged edges.

Thankfully, Karabinka was asleep, hanging helplessly from the armchair, the pale glow of the computer screen upon her face, and she looked like a large fat inflatable doll someone had dumped there. Ema quickly slipped to the bathroom and closed the door. She couldn't lock herself in, but that was a given. There it was. The hole cut out into the wall with the twisting pipes. She deeply exhaled the past twenty-four hours that had been lodged in her before quickly sticking her head into the darkness.

The pipes emitted a soft whisper like that bygone river split by the mirror wall on whose bank her father still sat on his fisherman's camp stool, parroting her gestures. A muffled thud, a sigh, a cry from sleep, a door slamming, a snore, the music playing during the credits of a TV show every now and then burst out of the homogeneous hum. The darkness, silence, and night were just an illusion: inside the house where she had stuck her head they were dissipating into a thousand unremitting murmurs.

In that moment, a toilet abruptly flushed somewhere above her. Instead of the sound of the water gradually abating, she realized it was growing louder and stronger, thundering. An ice-cold stream suddenly hit her face. As if the yanking of the flush chain above had burst a colossal dam, columns of water began to pour down the hole in the wall, that last possible route of escape. She was no longer standing nor floating. What difference did it make now? Using her last bit of strength, she grabbed a pipe in the hole; the tidal wave impassively washed over her, slammed open the door, and in an instant, flooded the entire ward. Ema looked over her shoulder: on the foaming crest of the wave, two metal bedframes launched by a whirl-pool were dancing right below the ceiling, clashing against each other like swords. Vladěna was probably screaming, but her screams, along with the water, mutely retreated back into her mouth. But where was Verunka? Pieces of furniture were whirling in vortexes all through the hallway, breaking and col-liding into walls, but all Ema heard was the barely perceptible original hum in the pipes.

She suddenly saw two lights approaching through the water, two pale, flittering fish. But those were . . . Verunka's eyes! The water made them look even emptier and duller than on dry land. They lightly grazed her and tenderly blinked at her like a doe before vanishing: "Tonight might be the night . . . Promise me you won't get mad!"

Ema sensed she wouldn't be able to hold on much longer. She still had a death grip on the pipes, her fingers encircling them like tentacles as her body helplessly flailed in the current, but she felt her strength waning.

Something enormous and white glided out of the nurses' station. A few bubbles emerged from a small crack in some-thing that might've been a face. "Holy Christ, what crap has upstairs detox pulled this time!" The large inflatable doll, Nurse Karabinka.

Another thwarted escape attempt. What now? She could try to fall asleep. But what if she's already asleep — what then?

"Well, with your being such a lightweight and those sticks for arms, you won't last long, dearie," she pitied herself, "and what good is it that you've been a rat, frog, and spider."

A faint "tock" came from somewhere in the hallway. The wall clock was contracting and expanding its translucent, medusa-like body as it continued obstinately to measure out liquid time.

Medusa . . .

And within that ticking, within that "now" briefer than a sharp inhale, when the waters of the past had receded and the waters of the future had yet to overwhelm her, Ema, to her astonishment, transformed. And it was so easy! She didn't even need a "drink me" bottle or to ingest mushrooms, she only needed not to miss that singular "now."

Her body, already so elongated and thin, grew even longer and thinner, her legs grew together into one, and her arms disappeared into her torso, like an airplane retracting its landing gear. Her new skin was now covered in a mesh of bluish luminescent lights, and Ema pushed off with all the might of her new body against the current through the opening in the wall.

The eel glided, undulating through the flooded bowels of the pavilion, higher and higher, lithely slipping past the pitfalls the narrow tunnel put in its way. The water was no longer water, becoming a sort of fifth element — pure, powerful joy. And as the eel choked on this joy, it forgot what it had been just a moment before, it entirely lost awareness of the intent that had created it. Ema Černá, that thread of a name wound inertly through the spiderweb of the world, again on the lam from rehab, along with her entire off-key orchestra of memory, dissolved like aspirin in the sea of the eel's joy without so much as a fizz.

Still — when the eel passed by the ceiling, it grew slightly uneasy. An uncanny sense of déjà vu caused its silvery body, fluorescing in the dark, to tremble. Out of the blue, pieces of soggy cardboard boxes began to batter its serpentine head, small sneering ceilings that for some reason the eel was unable to dodge; the glass lookout, resembling an enormous bottle with a castaway's message inside, loomed on the eel's left.

The eel suddenly felt as though it were being hemmed in from every side by an aquarium, a small insidious aquarium within the very heart of the flood. It quickly churned the water with its tail and shot skyward, higher and higher, leaving behind the billowing kelp of phrases in which it had been entangled: "Nurse, I'm . . . psychotic." — "So you're a junkie!" — "Loosen my chains, for heaven's sake!" — "And bam! They had me on Antabuse by week's end!" — "Ladies, come on, now, which of you's been smoking in here?" — "The paper is empty. It has no autonomous existence." — "God loves you, sisters. He is with you every step of the way!"

Through a chink between two roof tiles, the eel finally emerged above the pavilion. Ema would surely have been fearful over what she might encounter up there; she'd consider the extent of the catastrophe, if it had affected just the one pavilion or if the entire Garden was underwater, or even — God forbid! On the other hand, it goes without saying that from time to time natural and other kinds of disasters have occurred in myths and history, and they have to be faced with the cooperative assistance of all emergency response services and units and in addition — helter-skelter she stuffed the lifeless phrases into sacks instead of sand to build a dam.

But the eel remained mute, staggeringly mute in its liquid kingdom which now extended as far as the eye could see. Down in the depths below its belly, the rippling outlines of pavilions shuddered like the skeletons of long sunken ships, and the salty tongues of the waters licked the eel's body amid the quiet swishing of innumerable fins. A labyrinth of asphalt roads, avenues of trees which now already resembled their future petrified selves, the cross atop the Church of St. Wenceslas, vegetable gardens and greenhouses, the main building and stables on the hilltop above the Garden, all this vanished in the soft chiaroscuro beneath layers of sand, amid the swarms of plankton, and in the inflated, empty tents of mud.

Ema slowly awoke in the eel's body. "Dita, darling," she gasped, as if her gills had flared open only for a second, "I wanted to make a run for it again but it's all gone to shit. It's not my fault, I swear! Some moron in upstairs detox ripped off the flusher. Visiting hours are tomorrow, our first, we'll see each other after so long. But it won't be me, the person you'll be talking to and who you'll embrace. I've swallowed so many mountains of ice over the years that this is what I've become. If you could just see what I'm seeing now! Braids of seaweed and an orange coral mollusk, the lips of mussels opening and snapping shut, cuttlefish lost in their own ink cloud, sponges wildly sprouting in the dark depths — I so wish you could be here with me, dancing, don't laugh, I mean it! among the waves of eelish joy, on its crests, frothy like champagne. I can hear your griping: 'Cool it with the histrionics, you know how much I hate that, and anyway — did you forget I don't dance?' My love, that's because you can't see it from there. From the dry land where you stand — I know the surface must be some-where, the ceiling of the fifth element, above it only aridity — you can't see my new body. Remember how incredibly awkward I was on our first date? That would have all melted away if back then I'd been able to glide into the café in the form of an eel, in the form where I've finally found my refuge and feel at home, in the beautiful fish skin casting swarms of blue sparks into the darkness, all of it would've melted away and the waters beneath the ceiling vault would have covered us, closed over us like a huge, merciful accordion."

Ema dictated to the waves. Dita's face appeared in each one of them, briefly, before immediately, with a slight scoff, vanishing into the deep. A school of red mullet zipped by so golden that tears welled in her eyes, and right then something boomed behind her, a "tock" amplified a hundredfold, as if the minute hand of some galactic clock, massive and incandescent like a star, had jumped forward.

Jaws. They first clamped down on emptiness. The second time . . . the surface. Get to it and quick. But is it even still reachable from these depths? And does anything like the surface even still exist?

Blood began to stain the joy around her. Like the cuttlefish in its ink cloud before, Ema was now reeling helplessly in the murk of her own blood, and with each subsequent "tock" she lost another piece of herself. She no longer knew if she was fish or human, and, in the rhythm of the incessant chattering of teeth, she could've just as well been the dream of a mussel attached to a reef, or conversely, a mussel someone was dreaming.

A wave eventually hurled her, or what was left of her, ashore. Neither dead nor alive, she nestled in a tangle of seaweed with a single wish — for it to be just an ordinary bed in downstairs detox.

A man was approaching along the shore, raking through the sand with a bamboo stick. He reached down for Ema, turning over the oddity in his hands in disgust, but ultimately taking it home, adding it to his collection of "bounties of the sea."

•

"Roll caaaall!"

All the previous water abruptly retreated into a tiny cave she could barely fit into. She didn't mind, it was warm in there and nearby — at first she thought it was the goblin in the Garden banging its drum — she felt her mother's heartbeat.

She couldn't move, couldn't lift her eyelids. It was as if she had stolen into a stranger's body overnight, which, now that it was day, she was unable to control. Dita. Ema released a dove from the ark and it returned, four verdant letters in its beak.

"Where's Mrs. Černá? She's not still in bed, is she? Someone go get her!"

Half-asleep, I again held out my arm. Apart from her white horse and shakedowns, what became apparent later was that Rambo also loved drawing blood. I turned my eyes to the ceiling so I wouldn't have to look at the needle. Two barely perceptible parallel cracks ran along it, two tracks with invisible ties. A train was approaching from the corner above the window, a fairly small locomotive as if from a child's train set. Dad was leafing through a heavy tome, underlining words with a pencil, and Rybka's legs dangled in the air, still too short to reach the ground, her white sandals tossing back and forth. We were on our way to the chateau for the summer.

"Let's play the sound game!" Rybka begged to play our favorite family game. "Wanna win it for once!"

"You've already started," Dad said.

"How so?"

"Wanna win it for once — that's what you said, right?"

That inspired her: "Squids sneak in seaweed!"

Dad didn't even bat an eye: "Crazy quick quip, clever creature!"

A mother's heart and haversack heaved a hymn: I get to see you today. You and Rybka. You'll bring me chocolate along with a couple women's magazines where I proofread the recipes and labels for depilatory cream and hilarious advice on how to get a man, the girls will rip my arms off to get their hands on the crossword puzzle and funny quizzes, and Rybka will even bring me a new checkered notebook, since Ash partly scribbled in my old one and women from the room next door tore out the rest of the blank pages for tic-tac-toe. And as you'll lean over me to place it all on the table, I'll smell a blend of fragrances, damn near bowling me over: the perfume I once bought you, and the sun and wind of a brisk March day. How long have I been in here, anyway?

I won't have the shakes. Won't bite my nails. Talk over you. Cry. Laugh like a lunatic. Malign the nurses. Keep rushing to the toilet. I won't — In short, if the first thing I see now won't be Miss Turquoise, that is, Vladěna Tyrkysová, the visit will be a success.

"Your Highness, you're fucked, we're all waiting on you." A face full of craters shone above me like a mocking star, merrily wishing me all the worst for the coming day. And though Vladěna had concealed her turquoise essence with a snow-white shirt and pink leggings, the sight of her, those mounds of hatred directed at me from God knows where, shook me, imprisoned me with Xs from all sides and blocked every possible route to the two of you.

I scrutinized my arms and body with astonishment: they were wrinkled as if I'd spent all night in water.

I staggered into the hallway. The gaggle of women, usually chattering away since early morning, was now standing silently, mournfully, and orderly like a funeral procession, just

Karabinka stood there with her veil, crocheted out of goodness itself, dangling over her face. What happened? Was it because of me? The silence was hostile, thick and brown like the universal hospital gravy served at lunch.

"Finally!" Karabinka exclaimed. "Well, Mrs. Černá, that's minus two minus four."

I had no idea what those numbers meant, and got anxious she might ask me for the result.

"Point system," Marie whispered, the girl with whom I had shared a smoke last night, so long ago, in some ancient Stone Age, blowing smoke into the hole in the bathroom wall. I was forced to immediately hand over all the resident storylines and faces before they could touch my memory. They burned bright before vanishing in a flash, like eels, which I could transform into but never possess. You know what I'm talking about, brother of mine, and once I return, maybe you'll finally find the sea in my emails.

"Everyone's obsessed with the point system here. They spend every spare moment in front of the bulletin board and will burst into tears when they feel they don't have enough points. You earn points by serving food or scrubbing toilets or knitting scarves, or threading beads like your life depends on it, just to earn another two points for the product of the week, and when the princess . . ."

"What princess?"

"Were you born yesterday? Like I was saying, when the princess hands out roles for the following week on Sunday . . ."

"Roles?"

". . . it always causes an uproar like in an auction hall."

While Marie's voice was a hoarse whisper in my ear, I noticed everyone was here, assembled in that pale, plaintive crowd: Dana, who ate my portion of dumplings with such relish; round Marcelka with a golf ball for a heart; the White Queen, whom I didn't have the courage to unshackle, impeccably made-up and put-together as usual; fragile Verunka; and the bulimic saint Karamela . . . but someone was missing. I quickly scanned the crowd again: no, she wasn't here.

"Marie . . ." Marie turned to me her guileless eyes, shaded by her ever-present hoodie, and all at once grabbed my hand with terrible urgency — she held onto me and didn't let go, as if it were normal. I quickly looked around to see if anyone noticed. Vladěna. She was standing behind me. She was standing behind me, pressing the cold muzzle of her stare into the back of my neck.

"You filthy old dyke," she spat out. "Leave her alone, or . . ."

But a deafening roar unexpectedly drowned out the last of her words. Everyone turned in astonishment to face the open window: something out there was rumbling and thundering; the window shattered and glass crashed to the ground, the floor vibrating as if it were about to split open. I caught sight of the wall clock, spinning in a crazy dance. I saw the whirlwind tear off and unravel the thin veil on Karabinka's face. I saw the tableau vivant the sudden fury had transformed us into, a petrified sculptural group of frozen gestures and expressions, wide eyes, a sculpture resembling right then a grotesque monument to the victims of addiction.

Marie's hand, clammy and full of life just a while ago, had hardened into plaster.

"Damn," she exhaled, "this is intense. Sounds like the 'copter's gonna crash right into us, don't it?"

It really did seem as if it were about to land on the roof of the pavilion. Here in the hallway, too, the air was quivering like in the Sahara. The clock fell off the wall, the shark's teeth snapped one last time, and tiny droplets of time rolled across the linoleum floor like mercury out of a shattered thermometer.

"War!" Marcelka squealed hysterically. "War!" Dana hollered with joy. "Come now, ladies, calm down, it's merely . . ." But Verunka interrupted the White Queen with unsuspected vigor, rapture that was glittering in her eyes like a polished knife handle. "War," she unequivocally, unsentimentally proclaimed.

What the hell had happened? In a flash the plaster casts, stone sculpture, motionless throng transformed into a wild horde: and while a few of the women fell to the floor, obeying Karamela's appeal to, "Pray and repent, sisters, God shall forgive you!" most of them were stamping their feet and pounding their fists on the table, chanting "war, war!" raving like maniacs. Goodness was no match for Furies, O poor, helpless Karabinka! After all, not even the tank named Rambo would have been able to deal with such a spontaneous morning revolt.

In the general pandemonium, nobody noticed the roar of the helicopter gradually receding. And that Marie and I were still standing there, hand in hand, in our firm, impenetrable bubble of silence.

"War." Of course the monosyllable swathed itself in turquoise. Firm and impenetrable, you hear? It's not that farfetched to think the helicopter almost crashed into the pavilion just to neutralize your poison. But more likely it was piloted by my soldier, my own jealous sniper, who watched over and protected me from afar, who saw a stranger touching me, a girl I didn't even know.

I knew our meeting today wasn't going to go off without a

hitch. I knew you well enough and knew how you operated: shattered glass instead of awkward silences, war instead of empty consolations, a helicopter instead of a bicycle.

Finally, gym time. Marie immediately holed herself up in the corner, built herself a fort out of yoga mats, zipped up her hoodie like a sleeping bag, and went to sleep. I stood next to Marcelka, who in anticipation of morning exercise was merrily waving her arms. "Marcelka, where's Gizela?" No reply, she was pretending not to hear me. Who else but Mother Theresa would be leading us in exercises, for no less than six points. "Marcelka . . ."

"Sisters, please, settle down! I understand you're all still upset over the . . . because of . . . And that's why I'd like to propose, instead of our traditional warm-ups, we take a moment to pull ourselves together, a brief moment of meditation and contemplation." She turned on the CD player and at the sound of the first tone blown into a didgeridoo or whatever other shamanic piece of wood it might have been, a tone that didn't waver or modulate once the entire time, she folded herself gracefully into the basic yoga pose of Virasana. Following her, we obediently fell to the ground.

"Marcelka," I whispered again, and Marcelka slowly turned to face me, a sinister rigidness in her rotund torso, to give me the terrible, wordless answer.

"Bring your fingers together, connect your thumbs. With each inhale, we're breathing in hope, with each exhale, we expel the bad we've caused our loved ones."

So that's why the silent crowd out there in the hallway. Without protest, I obediently interlaced my fingers and connected my thumbs. Gizela. I see him drawing nearer to you across the deaf plain, your beau Tiny, swaggering closer, dressed in a black suit and white shirt. Beneath you, then, finally the dunes of warm soft sand you craved. You no longer have arms or legs, those roots and branches of the unessential, only the magnificent snakeskin, which suits you, with two beautiful snake fangs in the front of your mouth.

If I were to get up and walk to the basement window, I'd be able to touch the frozen winter dirt, sink my fingers into it, and shove a handful into my mouth. But why would I? I rocked back and forth, and this barely perceptible motion seemed to attract an unexpected dancer as outside the window a small plastic bag suddenly floated past, the wind flinging it skyward, so that I lost sight of it for a moment before it returned into the rectangle of the window. Mesmerized, I observed the elegant dance full of sudden lifts and pirouettes, and the transparent wing touched the windowpane and rustled to inaudible music, only to suddenly soar up in a spiral of wind, then just running along the ground for a while, curling up and now resembling a small envelope, and when it finally seemed to have flown off for good, it flattened itself against the window, as if laughing at me, playing with me, and that soul really did laugh at and play with me, that letter written for me and me alone.

A skirt now passed by the window. I could see a woman from the waist down only, the plastic bag had gotten tangled in her heels, she bent down for it and I caught a glimpse of her face, she freed the stabbed dancer and flung her away, and she disappeared from view. Soon after a white coat passed, then a black coat. Like an archaeologist, I tried to reconstruct the whole from a fragment. Two pairs of legs now paused in front of the window. Her hands were visibly trembling, his hung stiffly alongside his body. Tension rattled behind them like a tin can tied to a string.

And now that the world was accessible to me from the waist down only, its darker, centauric nature, I wondered whether I'd be able to recognize my loved ones by their legs alone. And if they were to be standing on the other side of the window would their other, unseen half belong to me.

A little girl stopped outside. She pressed the palms of her hands against the glass, gaping at us. We were in the middle of trying to replicate the snake asanas as directed by Karamela, during the monotonous drone of wind instruments, only Marcelka was stubbornly doing aerobics on her own. The little girl started to laugh maniacally, stomping her tiny feet and tugging on someone's hand, someone who couldn't see what she could. I waved to her, for a while we waved and made faces at each other, exchanging grimaces and gestures. Marie, burrowed in her nest, joined in.

"Looks like the lesbos are having a field day."

It had completely slipped my mind. Vladěna was breathing down my neck. Where else? It wouldn't have surprised me in the least if she had grabbed me by the hair and smashed my head into the ground. Instead, I heard Dana's detached, raspy, assertive alto, unexpected support from the upper realms: "Stop picking on her! Didn't you hear how she kicked Mother Theresa's ass in upstairs detox?"

Silence spread behind me. So overly reverential, coming from Miss Turquoise, it made me want to retch. Dita, just seven hours and twenty-five minutes to go before the magnificent gates to this sewer open, this forgotten aquarium covered in slime, and you can sail in to see me. I'll never tell you what embarrassing, pathetic act, what insipid moment of passion finally managed to land me a VIP ticket to this place.

So, my acceptance into the order was a success and I'd be

the one taking charge of things from now on. Ema got up, asana or not, and turned off the CD player. She quickly rifled through the CDs until she found something that perhaps could revive the half-dead gym class. She cranked it up to the max.

You like it when the day covers you in ash . . . belted out Monika Načeva. The specters, gradually roused by the change of song, began to slowly get up from their yoga mats. *Yeah, you like day's end with the din of collecting trash . . .* Mother Theresa began to protest, *and like a death camp your soul splayed on a plate . . .* , but to my surprise, feebly. "Now that's good," someone yelled, "can you turn it up?" *I carry inside me a slave, made myself an inmate . . .* Then the refrain kicked in. We all erupted in dancing, starting to whirl around ridiculously across the gym, and suddenly it didn't matter at all that some of us were eighteen and others sixty-five, Marie was gyrating as if at a rave and Marcelka bravely stepped a polka to the strains of the saxophone, but Ema didn't dance: she climbed onto the stationary bike and pedaled.

She pedaled like her life depended on it, barely noticing the half-century of her life whizzing past. In the passing scenery, she caught glimpses of countless brief images, moments, and places, but they were alternating so quickly that only a few remained lodged in her consciousness: Dad rummaging through a pile of her old toys; Rybka defiantly running away from home and repentantly returning; and finally, in the distance to her left, a majestically glittering castle, the fortress built by Dalibor for his ungrateful wife.

Spider on a stationary bike. They were all laughing their heads off, the dolts. So I seamlessly and unwillingly took on the role of buffoon, as their laughter dubbed me the jester of this hapless court.

Blank sheets of sketch paper in front of us, boxes full of colored pencils, crayons, and chalk on the table. Like in kindergarten. The task given to us during today's therapy session was to draw what "the woman within" meant to us. While irate Dana, "fucking bullshit," was busy covering her paper with lewd imagery morphing into the abstract, Marcelka's paper was blooming into a lush garden with puppies, kids, and a little house, a satellite dish sticking up from the roof, a pool beside the house, round, of course, for which she used up an entire stick of blue chalk.

"What time is it?" The wall clock, my resident angel with an incessant tick in its limbs had bitten the dust during the morning air raid.

"That's the tenth time you've asked. It's the visits, isn't it?" Marie chewed on her pencil over her blank paper. "Total bullshit. The assignment, I mean. Help me out here."

"What about an eel?"

"Pretty sure the topic wasn't the eel within, dummy." She gave it a try anyway. "Damn . . . That looks like . . . but Dana's the one doodling dicks!"

In the corner of the hallway, a handyman was refitting the panes of the broken window, another casualty of the war, his ears red. Another nail in the coffin. As if it weren't enough to have the White Queen hovering around him incessantly. "My, my, it's a joy to watch a craftsman like you at work! You've got extraordinarily deft fingers, and your approach to the work!"

With admirable, spectacular disdain, Mother Theresa ignored all this embarrassing conduct and shallow talk. Her astral body was surely now traveling in realms where the stink of disinfectant, UBG, and the feet of the new patient sticking out behind the table like a mute heap of rags did not exist.

She was covering her drawing with her hand; I noticed she was using a yellow crayon and nothing else.

"Hey there, Miss Irena, come join us!" Marcelka attempted to save the handyman. "You've only drawn two stick figures so far!"

"Stick figures? What do you mean, stick figures?" the Lady objected, affronted. "Those are my two sons! One is studying macromolecular biology at Harvard and the other is a lecturer in twentieth-century history at the University of . . ."

"You could've given birth to two popes for all I care," Marcelka interrupted her with unexpected coarseness, "but in here, they're just two stick figures."

Vladěna dumped a pile of T-shirts on the table. "Get a load of this. Is he a total idiot or what? This is what he thinks I should be wearing in here." She began to hold the T-shirts up to her body, one after the other. Jack Daniels. Jägermeister. Finlandia Vodka. Tequila. Fernet Stock. All showy promo stuff.

"It would seem your partner," the White Queen said, gazing sadly at the handyman she'd allowed herself to get lured away from, "has a sense of humor."

"Has shit for brains, more like. He works for the Božkov liquor company."

"I've got an idea," the clown said and wrote two words on her sheet of paper: ŽENÁM MANÉŽ, "women's arena," a palindrome. "Pick out the nicest shirt with a pretty bottle and a logo that's visible from a distance, I'll wear it for tomorrow's ward rounds." And the jester shook her head until the little bells jingled amid the skeptical silence; so what if the throne at whose feet she made faces was disappearing into the heights, far above all the ceilings she'd never be able to see.

"You wouldn't."

"I would."

"That's even more demerit points."

Tactfully, I disregarded the meaningless argument.

"The head nurse is gonna lose her shit," Marie said dreamily as she took a red pencil and colored in the clown's nose.

Mother Theresa, wholly baffled by us all, let her guard down for a brief moment, allowing me to glimpse what she'd been hiding: a well-executed, relatively realistic, completely golden Virgin Mary, wires sprouting out of her head to support her halo, as round as Marcelka's swimming pool. God knows why, but I was moved by the drawing and felt sick at the thought of her poor Madonna being disassembled, wire by wire, in the coming therapy session.

Therapy. Talk, talk without end. Streams of utterances, a river of words. Talking and sometimes listening, as if these were the only two elevators available to get down the shaft. Babble and prattle, to omit through talking and futilely conceal, because the therapist is well aware of what lies beneath your verbal garbage dump and when the moment is right to pull down your pants in front of the others. To recollect and associate, to reflect and repent, to confide, to reveal, to tearfully pull out splinters long rotted, to unconsciously accept the set rules, with dull obedience to color in the lines that have been pre-drawn for us by others, over and over again. And to take a moment to genuinely give thought to why Marcelka forgot to add her husband to the garage in her drawing, why Dana's paper is studded with dicks, and why Marie has covered her paper with neat rows of teardrops.

"It looks like a wall," the head physician said. Some people pay good money for this, Ema thought with astonishment, and observed with horror the way Miss Irena drank in the doctor's every word, gaping up at him devoutly from her lowly position.

"Yes, a wall," she nodded, since the floor had been opened to free discussion of the drawings. "I think Marie has raised a wall between herself and reality. She's worried if she'll be able to face it without drugs." She was improving position. The White Queen.

"It's not a wall, they're teardrops. I just like drawing them. It calms me down."

But right now, Marie didn't look all that calm, fidgeting in her chair, tapping her foot uncontrollably against the floor. Quickly, I tried to figure out how to help her out before all those impeccably rendered teardrops actually burst out of her.

"A smile," said Karmela pensively. "One arc next to another, the whole paper full of smiles would surely have the same calming effect, but you chose teardrops."

"Yeah well," Dana piped up, "it's no joke when your pa's dead set on gettin' ya declared legally incompetent."

I suddenly had the feeling that therapy was making everyone in here absolutely bonkers, so I bellowed at Marie, as if we were in some Zen koan: "What time is it?" She flinched before automatically placing the clock dial before my eyes. Her leg stopped jittering.

"I was just listening to Bob Marley while drawing, is all. No woman, no cry. That's all there is to it."

In that moment, as we were sitting in a circle on the floor of the gym, someone paused right outside our window. Holding a valise of some sort, God knows what, it looked as if he were just standing there and watching us, which made no sense: how could he possibly see us with his darker, blind half from the waist down? Suddenly I realized that the valise . . . It was a woman who was standing in front of the window holding a carrier with a cat. It was the cat observing us, its eyes flitting around the arena of women, over the human beings sitting in a circle, perched there like diamonds in the aureole of the yellow Virgin Mary in the drawing lying on the floor in front of them. It was the cat observing us; two layers of bars separated us, and the animal stuck its muzzle through its own bars.

The head physician lifted the clown off the ground. Don't let it get to you.

"A mask."

"Yeah. She put it on when she had to come to terms with her divergent sexuality."

"An evasion of responsibility."

"A desire to remain a child, not to grow up."

I was impressed. The girls quickly understood what was expected of them.

"Is the red nose a slip-on, or red from booze?" Marie tried to return the favor for my asking her for the time, but nobody laughed. And then came a move that simply caught me off guard in this irresponsible childish game of masks. The head physician turned the clown upside down and handed it to me.

"Do you realize you've completely failed as a mother?" I grabbed onto the window, but the woman with the cat was no longer there. "Your daughter calls us daily, she's worried about you, she has to take care of everything out there, she has no time to live her own life, because now she's living yours. You've made her your surrogate mother."

Attractive, charismatic, omniscient. I stared at the clown, dumbstruck. He was doing a handstand just like the athlete statue in front of the pavilion. My brain swung into gear as if someone had let hoops run downhill, a mass of haywire haloes bumping along the cobblestones into the abyss. But something else was reeling in me: Rybka had been practicing the "Turkish March" on the piano one day. She must've been about ten, eleven . . . I was sitting next to her, and after the tenth time she played F instead of F sharp, I lost my temper and slapped her in the face. She hadn't been expecting that at all, and neither had I, for that matter, and she sat there on the revolving piano stool, spinning from the slap, and spun around and around, whizzing past me silently, helplessly, uncomprehendingly, her feet in the air, for what felt like an eternity.

"But I've failed in other roles as well," I pleaded. Yet the doctor was implacable and refused to bestow any part of the blame on anyone else. How could I've done this to you? Cast you into this cycle of mortality, imprisoned you within the drum the goblin of the world is cheerfully banging? I should've known that once I sent you spinning, you'd be spinning forever, and there would be no force that could stop you.

I wanted to drown in Marcelka's blue swimming pool. "Don't do that, a bloated corpse would ruin her picture." I was smoking with Marie again in the bathroom and I didn't give a damn if the nurse caught me, minus fifty minus twenty for all I cared, the ages of me and Rybka. The hole we were blowing the smoke into couldn't have been the same one as at night. This one was empty like the back basket of that half-deaf old hag, and it led nowhere.

"Why aren't you asking me what time it is?"

In ancient days, when my brother Ash was empty, emptier than a hollowed-out nutshell of nothingness, he decided to outfit the nut with the likenesses of others; day and night he would wander the streets and ask random passersby for the time. Every so often a reply, a gesture, facial expression, or tone of voice would fall into his nutshell, which he then appropriated. But maybe he did it simply because he felt lonely.

It wasn't blood coursing through that other small head inside my head but the time that remained until visiting hours. Why would I need to ask?

A scrum formed in front of the mirror. Everybody wanted to look beautiful, or at least conceal what they could, the awful fatigue and helplessness that had, like a resident parasite, sucked out and ravaged their faces. They traded tops and color-matched outfits, goofing around like little girls plundering their mother's wardrobe.

"Come, now, Miss Ema," the White Queen scolded me. "Don't just lie there like a rag doll! You'll soon be reunited with your better half! What do you say to this little outfit? It would look exquisite on you!"

A master switch. To be able to flip it and turn off the lights in one ward room after the other, to peel reality layer by layer like an onion and be allowed to assemble it anew. To extinguish the Garden, the city, the world, to slam the door shut and set out on a journey, walk, strut, stride, pant up a hill, flee, march through the countryside, a horizon beyond the horizon and so on over and over, a well springing from the earth, your saliva, life. To burrow into a vulture's feathers and to circle with it through the wild air over the foot of Mount Kailash.

Despite all warnings and prohibitions I burned your snakeskin: if I touch you, you'll vanish into oblivion, as if you had never existed. "Ema . . ." Come in a Viking mask. "Ema!" Show up in the doorway holding warriors' shields. Arrive as a cliff, flow in transformed into a raging river full of ice, the cracking deafening, emerge on the surface, smack in the middle of the room, in diving suits, or at least in green raincoats.

"At least brush your hair, dummy." Everything was a blur, as if I'd taken off my glasses, as if everything was taking place underwater. Marie was handing me a hairbrush. Oh, right, I should acquaint myself with the hairbrush. I turned it over in my hands in awe, this pretty wooden brush, a tiny life raft in a place where all bridges have been torn down. Dutifully, I combed my hair and borrowed an awful clown shirt from Miss Irena; it must've been covered with all the flags of the world, as if custom-made for the performance to follow.

We all crowded into the open doorway, because we weren't allowed to wait in the hall leading to the main entrance. "They're here!" someone exclaimed excitedly, and the acrobats, bear trainers, and tightrope walkers began to spill into the arena. The first to appear was a little round man, hiding from the curious gazes of so many women behind an enormous bouquet. Marcelka couldn't take it and ran to meet him.

"Get back!" It sounded as if the thunderous voice came from the very heavens. Rambo, the circus director, stood in the orchestra pit above, so that all human and animal acts were in her purview and nothing in the sawdust ring would escape her notice.

But more and more visitors were already streaming into the ward to the tinny sounds of a brass band, the nurses on duty were recording their names and who they were visiting, handsome young men with roses, aging equestriennes with wrinkles concealed underneath layers of makeup, fathers and children, mothers and Lipizzaners, lovers, trombone-wielding bears, and whole squads of relatives laden with coolers full of homemade comfort food.

An elegant lady of indeterminate age appeared. Two young identical boys clung to either side of her. The lady stopped in the middle of the corridor. "Blanka, over here! Blanka!" she called my way. I didn't understand. There was no woman here by that name. Suddenly I noticed that Karamela was standing right next to me in the doorway. Mother Theresa. Of course, Blanka Vodseďálková must be her real name then! And she has twins! Weird.

Something happened right then that none of the onlookers could have predicted. When the boys spotted their mother, instead of running to her, they began to wail in unison and run toward the exit. We all stood frozen in place. I've never seen anyone turn pale in real life, but the life drained from Karmela's face, as if she had lost liters of blood. She was rooted to the spot with the impeccable posture of a ballerina, and I again pictured her wolfing down everyone's leftovers, dumping bread baskets left over from breakfast into the oversized pockets of her bathrobe when she thought nobody was watching. God knows why I wondered just then if she'd finished writing her essay on suffering.

Maybe she's not there anymore . . . I was hoping but I was wrong: Rambo had seen everything from above. A smile on her face, she raised her arm like a bludgeon and the moment she swung it the orchestra fell silent, the conversations stopped, and the horses let out a final whinny.

I'd seen enough of this circus. I returned to our room — to Verunka, dangerously clutching a pillow, her parents leaning and shedding tears over her, just what I was missing — and I lay down on my bed and closed my eyes. A drum thundered in my temples, as though I were inside it.

It arrived ahead of you. It preceded you. The fragrance.

The perfume I once bought you, and the sun and wind of a brisk March day.

"Mom!" From a terrible distance, I heard an absolutely flawless rendition of the "Turkish March." "Get this — the nurse searched my backpack and confiscated Mr. Mouse, said you're not allowed to have stuffed animals!"

Even old Mr. Mouse, whom I had operated upon back in the day, removing his stuffing, and whom you'd played with as a kid, used to be one of my many stash spots. What if they're still there, sewed up inside? At this point I couldn't care less. And as I finally held you in my arms, I got an urge to whisper something in your ear for you to pass on, something silly, which the mishearing and mispronouncing would gradually transform into truth, for me and for you and for everyone, especially for Dita at the end of the line.

Darling. Maybe I really had misheard you on the phone. Like Dr. Veselá, you stiffly stared ahead at a point ten centimeters above my head, clutching a chocolate shield in your hands — I've truly never seen such a humongous chocolate bar — and your wrinkles, parentheses I so adored, containing my chaos, were turning right before my eyes into the alphabetic characters of an unknown language. One, two, three . . . Worse still, I was unable to count your fingers. It seemed as though you had six fingers on your left hand, I kept counting them again and again in a panic, because I was well aware that all it took was one extra finger for us both to plunge into a dream and turn to dust. I had also gotten lodged in the crevasse of your silence — up until now you hadn't uttered a single word — and in a desperate attempt to extricate myself from it, I began to make one blunder after another, everything I'd forbidden myself to do that very morning: I got the shakes, I bit my nails. Cried and laughed like a lunatic. Talked over Rybka and didn't let her finish. Maligned the nurses, wallowed in self-pity, showed off, swore like a sailor, and there was no end to it, and it was all Vladěna's fault, because she was the first one I saw this morning, Vladěna, now weeping with her face turned to the wall, because her beau, who had sent her those promo T-shirts, hadn't shown, it was gushing out of me like porridge out of the magic pot, like Mom's spinach that time long ago, and when they were already knee-deep in spinach, Dita suddenly discarded her shield. "What's happened to you? This isn't you anymore."

Only now did she look me in the eye. Then she got up and with resolute steps, my heart clenched at the sight of her delicate, girlish back betraying her, she walked to the door. "I'll wait for you outside," she said to Rybka and left. Heading North, I suddenly thought, God knows why.

"Go to her. I . . ." Rybka ran after Dita and didn't return.

Silence. My heart escaped my body and slipped into my new checkered notebook like it were a herbarium. I couldn't scream, I couldn't go after you, I couldn't do anything at all. I stashed the chocolate you brought me into the pocket of Mother Theresa's bathrobe, thrown over the armrest of a chair in the hallway, and began to examine the flags on my midriff: the Congo, Jamaica, Cameroon, Honduras, Papua New Guinea, Nepal, and the cedar of Lebanon with torn buttonhole.

Suddenly, the wind — I didn't understand how it got here since the window was shut — lifted my ridiculous shirt like a sail, and the masts, cursed for long hours and days into immobility, creaked and I shoved off from shore.

•

I stood with Mom at the Anděl intersection, waiting for the light to turn green. She held onto me, digging her fingernails anxiously into my arm like a small child frightened by the huge world thundering around us. She tensely waited for the pedestrian icon to flash and then scuttled by my side while recounting to me the intricate relationships of some TV show. I was giving her crap for watching such garbage and myself for chiding her at all, but we could hardly hear each other in the din anyway. We were out to buy her a hat, the same type worn by one of the characters in the TV show. People were streaming around us and past us, someone forced a flyer into our hands, a well-known politician was delivering a speech from a makeshift podium, and on a crate next to him someone with a mic was invoking the apocalypse. It grated on my nerves, and to top it off, I didn't know the first thing about hats.

People poured out of the No. 9 tram that had just pulled up to the stop. I was scared that someone was going to knock my mom down, that the current would sweep her away, she was nothing but a wisp, a shadow of an old woman, so petite, ancient, and helpless, so like a spider I spun a web out of my fear, one delicate and soft as the duvet with which I covered Mom.

At that moment, I spotted her. The tall, gaunt woman, dressed head to toe in black. She was a good head taller than everyone else as she made her way through the crowd . . . No way. She walked as if no one but her were on that frenzied intersection, as if she were trekking through a wasteland where nobody could cross her path. And so it was — the space suddenly cleared of people, the speakers fell silent, and the shrill music swiftly coiled into silence.

"Wait here, I'll be right back." I left my confused mother standing in front of a tobacconist and rushed off after the woman. She had a small carrier in hand. I could hear the soles of her boots tapping against the cobblestones, and pushed my way through the crowd after them. She was heading toward the five-star shopping mall. Yes, it had to be her. It was she who had once given me an egg with a surprise inside, another egg, ad infinitum. It was she who had returned the yarmulke that had fallen from our balcony. And it is she who knows those three words in that unfamiliar language which I have to learn and never forget.

The glass doors slid open for her and closed behind her. I hurried after her, but try as I might, the doors just wouldn't open for me. I stomped on the cursed doormat in rage, trying to trigger all the sensors and banging on the glass, but it was no use. The doors had stopped being doors, because they didn't open, and the glass had stopped being glass, because it couldn't be broken. The woman with the cat simply vanished from my sight somewhere within those inaccessible, five-star bowels.

I walked back to Mom. "Where on earth did you go? I was getting worried you'd leave me here!"

"I thought I saw Mrs. Schwarzová."

"Mrs. Schwarzová? Doesn't ring a bell."

"Our neighbor. She once brought us the yarmulke that had dropped from our balcony."

"A yarmulke? I don't remember us having one of those, certainly couldn't have been your grandad's . . ."

We took the tram to the Malostranská stop and walked back home, passing Abbé Dobrovský and the largest plane tree in the world, the pier at the museum with the giant flood-defying chair and the row of yellow penguins glowing into the night, through the city, shimmering anciently in the air like a memory that wasn't even ours, through the backdrop of a leaflet in which the two of us no longer had a place.

On the way, Mom kept taking off and putting on her new hat, which looked like an old-timey aviator helmet, turning it over in her hands and examining it with childlike joy. I took the keys from her hand and unlocked the door to our building. It was in this hall that I had once stood with Dalibor in an embrace, unable to let go. Mom and I got into the elevator and I pressed five. It took me a moment before I realized we had passed the floor and were rising higher and higher, and that Mom wasn't worried at all, as she still fidgeted with her hat and quietly sang something, and the elevator now soundlessly broke through the roof of the building, going straight up, soaring, as mother and daughter clung to each other in the tiny space, as we flew through the clouds over the city, where around us stars began to explode and contract again.

I latched onto the pitch, now we were flying and singing a duet. I knew the motion would never stop and this was the only way we would stay together forever, I just had to make sure to keep singing and to stay awake. But the syllables in my mouth began to get mangled and my eyelids started to droop against my will. I was mad at myself for singing off-key because I was so sleepy. I was mad at my mom, who was spinning her hat around and singing cheerfully without a care in the world, and I was mad that the woman with her cat and those three words had now escaped me forever and that down in the hall Dalibor's embrace would never again be waiting for me.

A crack appeared in the elevator wall. I yanked Mom to the opposite corner, but cracks began to spread all along the elevator's walls as if it were an old, crumbling fresco lit up by the sun. Before I could catch hold of Mom, a whirlwind seized her like a sheet of paper torn out of an ancient diary and vanished with her into the darkness, hat and all. I began to plummet down a smooth and cheerily colorful chute, carved out by gravity and my anger, and the stars went out one by one and I slid through darkness thick and warm as pudding and somewhere a million light years from here the lost flying saucer of Mom's new hat spun helplessly, and try as I might I kept nodding off and jolting awake again and eons passed and the years went by and in the meantime somebody tore down the cities below me, and somebody else built new ones, and as one by one the differences between me and the darkness began to be imperceptible and just when my memory was about to fail me for good, I suddenly shot out of the chute and crashed into moss.

I wasn't alone. A man in uniform stood in front of a bunker, waving us goodbye. Dita and I hit the road. According to our map, Strašmania, the land of the all-possible, lay just beyond this forest. This time, I already knew what I would choose.

•

We were supposed to meet at 8:30 p.m. at the parking lot in front of IKEA. It was 8:42 and Ema was nowhere to be seen. It didn't surprise me; she was always late. This time I decided to give her an earful — not because her unpunctuality bothered me, but because it's what was expected from the one waiting, who was well within his rights to express disapproval. I mulled over what I would say. I stood leaning against a wall, the ventilator of a warehouse softly purring in my ear. If I squinted, I could picture the sea spreading out from the tips of my shoes.

"Help me," she had said into the phone, "help me find Rybka, please. I think I know where she is, in that old factory hall in Podolí, where the Society for the Preservation of Darkness supposedly is based, but I . . . I went there once, there were metal hooks on steel cables hanging from the ceiling, glinting, and in the light of an open firepit, women in rags, totally sloshed, were sprawled over the concrete floor. We have to get her out of there while there's still time!" I wasn't sure if I could believe anything she was saying. "I'm afraid to go there by myself. I know that tonight, like every night, at 3:20 a.m. . . . you have to be by her side, spray bottle ready, and that . . . Look, I've never asked you for anything, until now, dear Ash — deny your wife this one single night and give it to yourself, to me, to Rybka."

I didn't say anything for a long time. I couldn't decide which of my stolen reactions to summon up. Each time it was random but never easy. "Fine. But tomorrow, Anatole . . ."

"We'll find Rybka and then all three of us will go to my friends' party, it's already been decided, and tomorrow, just like any other day, you'll don your chef's hat and once again conjure bliss out of empty pots! And I'll go back to rehab, because I promised I'd finish the treatment. I swear! Just this one night."

She finally showed up. My intended diatribe abruptly petered out before it even began. It completely dissolved in the shadows that made up the jigsaw of her face and in her absolutely outrageous, cheerful shirt covered with the flags of the world like some old children's encyclopedia. Not compassion,

152

not pity, not a stomach in knots, just astonishment as my sister, that unfamiliar, old, childish, ridiculous woman came toward me across the parking lot, battered by her escape out of my boxes like a trapped animal. There was a time when she would slip into the hollowed-out nutshell of nothingness after me and casually shut the shell behind her. The farther I got from her the closer she was, like that time among the gravestones, "Here lies Váša Šála," where we had staggered from one gravestone to another, from distinct likenesses to abstract jumbles of lines, where we had traveled through those oval-framed portraits across the land of the dead.

I was feeling down. I'd help her find Rybka but would skip the party, because having no opinions, there was nothing for me there.

"Let's get going, no time to waste," she said, stepping toward my car. "Just like a mouse might accidentally get baked in a loaf of bread, my life had become stuck in a single month, February. In a loaf of bread still frozen that no one has the strength to break in half."

I thought what she said weird, given the hot summer night air quivering in the parking lot. "Get in," I said, pointing to a shopping cart.

She didn't bat an eye as she climbed into it. I grabbed hold of the handle, her shirt billowed like a sail, and off we went.

"Hey, something's sticking out of your pocket, maybe it's the metaphysical essence of the box," she said mockingly.

I pulled out a wad of balled-up paper. It was a receipt with the ingredients to a quite sophisticated recipe scribbled on one side and a doodle of branches on the other. I handed the drawing to Ema. "In appreciation of the dessert, a customer explained fractals to me. He drew a branch, then another one growing out of it, and more branches springing out of each other until they covered the whole paper."

She turned the drawing this way and that and said: "It looks like a genealogical tree. There's an ancestor hanging from every twig . . . Look! Here's Dad! I don't understand how I could feel alone in this marvelous forest. A glitch in the matrix."

My sweaty palms were slipping along the cart handle. A desperate yell burst from the maw of an open window and I was hoping it would alter our direction, break our path, and divert us from the futile search, that in a moment we would enter a stranger's apartment and maybe prevent a murder, that we would find ourselves in some other, more merciful contingency.

Alter. Break. Divert, prevent, and to find ourselves. Words were growing out of each other, ramifying into a complex iron structure, a solid scaffolding with which I tried to buttress the ceiling; I spewed out words and chopped them fine and condensed them and flung them into boiling oil, because I felt that if I were to fall silent for a single second, the unhewn blocks of my sister's transformations would collapse on top of me and the overflowing dumpsters of her cursed Garden would bury me alive. And right when I began to elaborate some sort of confused thought on cannibalism, I suddenly noticed that the tip of an enormous needle was sticking out of her heart, through the blue stripe of a flag, and through the eye of the needle time was flowing in all directions.

As soon as Rybka's found I'm going home. The future was teeming in that eye like worms under an overturned rock, and I quickly flipped it back. Tomorrow, then. Not today, not yet. Tonight's mission was to bring home a lost child and return

Ema to between the walls covered in neat rows of teardrops, far away from the reach of our common blood.

At times I could hardly budge the shopping cart, while at other times it felt as though it were floating and pulling and dragging me along so swiftly that I was barely able to hold on as I hurtled after it like a water skier behind a motorboat. A child sat in the middle of the sidewalk, drawing a circle around herself with chalk. She didn't even look up as I skirted it precariously. We passed by the sidewalk tables of restaurants and bars, a cluster of foreigners crowding a hotdog stand, a homeless man, his toothless mouth grinning right through us . . . And even though the cart was rattling and clamoring on the cobblestones so violently it was a wonder it didn't fall apart, and even though Ema was jumping and jostling around in it and waving her arms this way and that to command the vessel's trajectory, now full steam ahead, now to the left, and even though I had just a moment ago nearly crashed the cart into a car, everybody's indifferent and unsurprised stares shot right through us as if we were nothing but a volatile, random cluster of particles in the beam of a street lamp, as if we were nothing but . . .

In that moment, we both had the same realization. "Petr . . ."

Ema became subdued. With all her might she pressed her palms into the bottom of the shopping cart, and when she held them up to me, they were etched with the pattern of the mesh.

"What if . . . it's just a dream?"

I didn't respond as I mindlessly pushed forward with the absurdity that was growing out of my hands and was a part of me.

The lights and noise faded, the streets disappeared, and darkness tore into the city behind me. Though the dark scar to our left allegedly was Botič Creek, I wouldn't put it past us to be lost.

"How could I've possibly gotten out of the Garden? After all, I'm an involuntary commitment. And you wouldn't come to visit no matter how much I begged you to. You didn't even show up for Dad's funeral."

I noticed a soft, persistent clicking noise. She was biting her nails, and I saw red. Did it matter if the chiding and the clicking were real, or came to me in a dream? And as if she knew what I was thinking, she said: "It doesn't really matter."

And then in the desolate light of stars from which a hot, gooey, shapeless sludge gushed over us, she began to count her fingers like a little kid. Seemingly satisfied with the result and no longer caring where we were going, as if she'd completely forgotten about Rybka, she began to rummage in curiosity through the grocery bags. Grocery bags? I was positive the cart had been empty when she'd hopped in . . .

"Don't sweat the party, Bro," she said, pulling a leek and bunch of onions out of a bag, that party of hers was the furthest thing from my mind, she was now brandishing an eggplant in my face and drumming on canned olives and juggling tomatoes so that the darkness in front of me turned red, and — "What good is meaningful conversation about the harm caused by neoliberalism and the pitfalls of consumerism, what good are opinions! They're slipped on like flip-flops only to be kicked off just as easily. But you, brother of mine . . ." — she paused and I, resigned, waited for what would eventually emerge out of her ramblings — "you are the king of the senses."

Right. She had forgotten all about Rybka. Like that one time we were at the fair. Ema didn't walk past a single shooting gallery without showing us what a good shot she was. And she was. Rybka's arms were soon overflowing with paper roses giving off a godawful, cloying odor, sticks of cotton candy, and stuffed animals that produced a breezy tune whenever their bellies were pressed. And while the mother forged her way through the crowd and one touching memory after another poured out of her mouth, she completely forgot about her own child, her personal little caddie, that dainty Sherpa sinking beneath the load of her mother's sentimentality.

The squeals of animals ebbed behind us until the booming loudspeakers swallowed them for good. "Ema . . ." Once she got started, it was impossible to stop her. On top of that, she had just come to the opinion — what good are opinions, she said! — that we were actually twins who due to some biological anomaly had been born a year apart.

Rybka was crouched on the steps leading to the Loch Ness ride in a scattered pile of knick-knacks, crowds of strangers stomping up and down past her; shreds of paper roses clung to her cheeks, and she was so terrified she wasn't even crying. Her mother's roses had likely poisoned her.

I wanted to throw it back in Ema's face, but at that moment we careened down the steep bank into the streambed and I don't know how I kept my grip on the cart. I got stuck ankle-deep in the mud.

"See, I told you we were close to the Botič!" she said triumphantly.

"We're not close to the Botič, we're *in* the Botič." I bent down and brought up a handful of mud. It was green.

"It's spinach. I was kind of expecting this. It's proof we're going the right way. And also," she added apologetically, "that I haven't forgotten about Rybka."

If I could still push the cart through the spinach for another 100, 150 meters, she said, we'd reach a canal about a kilometer long through which the Botič flows into the Vltava. And then — "And then just a little farther on we'll clamber up the river-bank, you know, Dad used to go fishing on the opposite bank, and we'll climb over three mountains, a mountain of sawdust, a mountain of gravel, another mountain of something else, and then we're there."

"Make sure the baguettes don't get soggy," I muttered, unable to help myself, but proceeded to lean into the dead load with all my might, forcing it laboriously through the sludge, which was now everywhere, in the sky and on the ground alike.

The stars above us surprisingly still glowed faintly, as if they were affixed with wire to invisible skewers and were just wait-ing for Ema to shoot them down. I brought my palms right up to my face to examine three large blisters. Two were empty of pus, but the third one had a swirl like snow in a snow globe I once got from Dad and carefully kept hidden lest my sister confiscate it, and in that third blister a swirl of tiny women in short nighties milled about chaotically beneath the firm trans-lucent skin like in some miniature aquarium.

My watch showed 3:11. In nine minutes, all hell will break loose which, for the first time in a long seventeen years, I will not be there to witness. What will my wife do when she real-izes she's belching lava by an empty bed? Who's going to clean up her puke, methodically spray her temples, neck, arms, and wrists with cold water? What invisible body will her claws sink into, what immaterial concept will she drag beneath the sur-face? I have already come across so many bodies and so many concepts in the alluvium, so many bounties of the sea have washed up at my feet. The admonishments sank into the spinach as if I'd emptied my pockets of crumbs.

How much easier it was to push this absurd cart through the green mire! I wanted to ask Ema, I'm sure she'd be happy to advise, if it'd be possible to impose a lifetime involuntary commitment on my wife, but when I looked into the cart, a shard of mirror caught my eye. It must've cracked and fractured from the jolting and now, instead of phenomena — a physicist might explain this optical illusion to me one day after dessert — it was reflecting only their latent likeness: a toddler would see the old man he'd grow up to be, a skull would see the head of the newborn that had once pushed its way into the world, and what I saw in it was the oddly completed image of a familiar woman who was and wasn't me, the image of my year-younger twin sister.

"I must've nodded off there for a minute," the mirror piped up, "and this is indisputable proof that we're not dreaming this rescue mission to save Rybka, because I couldn't possibly be having a dream within a dream. I ran out of the chateau where we used to spend our summers into the garden. Trimmed boxwood hedges crisscrossed the grounds in a right-angled grid, and to this day the smell . . ."

"For the love of — get to the point. I've been trudging through this muck like a burlak for ages, and that canal you promised is nowhere in sight."

"My name of course was Alice, not Ema, and I was wearing gym shoes and a white T-shirt and those blue gym shorts that were always so itchy. I'm sure you remember that used to be the mandatory gym outfit for girls in school. And as I ran into the garden and along the boxwood hedges, I was astonished to see that it wasn't just me there, that a myriad of identical little girls were running through the garden in every direction."

I became flustered. Somewhere along the way I must've inadvertently steered the cart out of the streambed, because its wheels were no longer slipping through muck whose green had crept up to my knees, but were now clattering on a sandy surface.

"Every Alice headed somewhere different, a different adventure awaiting each one."

"How many were there?" Horrified, I expected her to say a hundred.

"Don't know, maybe ten, eleven. The first Alice, for instance, fell into the fountain and drowned."

Excellent. If it was going to go this fast, we'd be getting this dream-within-a-dream out of the way in short order. "Shouldn't you start chucking out the tomatoes, if any are left, so we'll be able to find our way back again?"

She paid me no mind. She was there with the girls, swirling in her words like those tiny women in my translucent blister, she was in the garden where the individual paths branched out into different eventualities.

"The second girl sat down on a bench next to a man who was writing something. 'What are you writing?' she asked. 'I'm translating *The Grandmother* by Božena Němcová into Chinese,' he replied. He handed her a sheet of paper and taught her two characters, one signifying water and the other air. I would've liked to believe this experience was the catalyst for her later interest in Sinology, but in reality, the man was a pedophile who dragged her off into the notorious chateau ravine."

"And what happened to the other Alices?"

"The third Alice planted herself in front of the crumbling sandstone statue of Neptune and stood there until 1992, when she wasted and withered away in a hospice underneath an incredibly low ceiling, never seen a ceiling that low in my life. I went to visit her once. The doctors claimed she'd suffered memory loss, that she didn't remember anything at all, but the time I was there she lifted her arm and pointed to the ceiling with her fingers spread and twisted in the likeness of Neptune's raised trident and said: 'Our garden is still here.' Remember? When it rained, the spiderwebs in the hedges glistened with a host of metallic flies. And the next girl, Alice or Ema, what difference does it make, it was still just me, cloned by some unintentional transmutation induced by the chateau, the next girl ran down to the pond where children weren't allowed to go. With the help of two boys from town, she built herself a raft out of bamboo and pieces of wood and decided to sail to France where she would find happiness. She sailed to France, entered an apartment, found happiness, and vanished."

"She didn't find happiness and she didn't vanish. She's curled up in the bathtub, sleeping. At least I hope so. What about you?"

"Well, it's a bit embarrassing. When I saw everyone scatter, I didn't have anyone left to play with. So I . . . I returned to the dining room and sat at the table where Dad was in the middle of discussing something with some very important man. The professor was unstoppable, and I had no clue what he was talking about. Bored, I was fiddling with the saltshaker on the table, and the saltshaker had on a Viking mask and a crystal warrior shield, it transformed into the diving suit of an underwater explorer and became a cliff a tectonic shift had rid of stasis — when all of a sudden, I simply refused to accept any responsibility for it, the saltshaker slammed into a cup of coffee that tipped over right onto the professor's lap. Something happened that I was hardly expecting: as if something inside the professor had also shattered, he ceased his lecture mid-sentence and in a voice altogether different to the one he'd been using, in a voice hideously transformed into an exasperated girl's falsetto, he began to shriek: 'Out! Get this little girl out of here at once! I don't ever want to see her again!' He bolted up from his seat, coffee streaming from his blazer, raised his arm over the table, and slapped me in the face. I was dumbstruck — not so much from the slap but rather his abrupt transformation. It's as if the professor had split in two, into two completely different beings. But truth be told . . ."

"Was that the legendary Professor M.? I didn't know he went around slapping kids."

"But truth be told, it wasn't the last time I heard his, 'I don't ever want to see you again, girlie!' over the next forty years . . . Just the form of address changed."

My body was soggy and lifeless like an old sock puppet full of holes. The only thing pushing me forward robotically was her pulling me onto her hand and controlling my movements. What more did she want? My pity? My empathy? My tender attachment to her random memories? Someone had cleaved Ema and my wife, initially a single being, into two: one half found herself alone for the first time in seventeen years, staggering through the hell of sobriety, howling like an animal and burrowing her head into the pillow, while the other half had been searching for her daughter for the better part of the past seventeen years, even though they'd been walking together hand-in-hand this entire time, clinging to each other within their circle of trust and safety, indestructible by nothing and no one.

No longer muck or sludge or spinach, it was a poison that oozed through me and rose up to my eyes, and higher, and I grabbed my sister by her shoulders as she perched on an ancient litter borne by slaves, on that Asian palanquin adorned with towering sheaves of asparagus and pyramids of avocados and all the delicacies in the world instead of garlands and flowers and dragon sculptures; I gripped her firmly and hurled the poison in her face: "Oh, so that famous professor really slapped you, huh? Interesting! You should take it up with your therapist — it might just so happen that the cup of coffee that tipped over onto the lap of the structuralist is one of the causes of your addiction propensity."

But no matter what I said, no matter if I tried ridicule or compassion, the words immediately spilled out of the ripped bag like dried fruit, drily trampled into the sand by my mud-covered boots. Into the sand? There could be no more doubt that we had long since left the streambed behind and were now headed God knows where, increasing the distance between us and that derelict factory somewhere near the Vltava, where, according to Ema, foul-smelling bonfires were currently blazing, which Rybka leaped over wildly, back and forth, until she was burned up to the waist, until her legs transformed into blackened stumps, while in my mind she was still cheerfully wiggling her chubby legs in the baby carrier on my back that time in the cemetery; when she jumped for the last time, mid-leap above the flames she caught her old school pencil case, all tattered and charred, and I froze in terror at the thought that she'd open it and skim her schedule to the end of the day.

In that moment, simply because my only accomplice was the sea, the immense wall of a wave rose out of nowhere and advanced, extinguishing and leveling everything in its path: the pencil case and the fire, the cemetery and garden, all the floors that were also someone's ceilings, and all the ceilings that were also someone's floors, my sister and my wife and the whole Society for the Preservation of Darkness, even the darkness itself.

Sand, maybe gravel. It really did seem as if we were now just going around in circles on a running track. Sand or gravel or even clay, it really seemed as if the ground beneath my sister's majestic IKEA cart had turned red. The needle sticking out of her heart pierced the darkness, and to my utter horror, a radiance trickling in through the pinpricks illuminated an endless tennis court, or whatever the hell it was, extending in all its bloody glory to the horizon.

But . . . but she'd told me she had a compass! With the supreme confidence of someone sporting the flags of the world on her shirt, directly on her body, and who therefore must know how to get to Tierra del Fuego, let alone Podolí, she ordered me around, throwing out navigation commands and setting the course while I, knighted by her a mere moment ago as "the king of the senses," like a deaf and blind coachman, believed we were at the Hostivař Reservoir on our way through the creek meander in Záběhlice, past Tyršův Hill down Pod Seřadištěm Street, through Grébovka and all the way to Vyšehrad, where we were finally supposed to come across that purported canal . . .

All I had to do was stop the sea from deafening everything, all I had to do was stop raking through the sand with a bamboo stick and finally focus my sight: instead of a head, the quivering omelet of a compass bobbled on my sister's thin, scrawny neck, the broken magnetic needle, wrinkle-like, flickering helplessly on the pivot, disoriented.

Just then, a figure stepped out of the darkness ahead. It grabbed the cart from the other end and we struggled over it for a while, as if we couldn't agree to whom the cart's peculiar contents actually belonged. The unexpected appearance of another person, whoever it was — a hobo, vagabond, scumbag, mugger, deadbeat, thug, bum, or murderer — filled me with a dizzying hope: I don't want him to stand opposite me; I'll ask him to stand behind me, even reward him with the caviar and champagne lying next to Ema, if only he won't stand opposite me, if only he stands behind me, if only he'll wrap his arm around my shoulders or waist and help me with my burden and go fetch his buddies, one embracing the other, and once the row of all this wretched human detritus, pushed all the way here to these sandy outskirts, thins out, Grandad will appear out of nowhere, bustle over to us and hug the last in line tightly, and Grandma behind him, and they will all help me pull out the cart, which had sprouted roots into the ground, they will all enable me to extricate myself from the cocoon of the curtains, tear the crusted glue off my skin and become one of them.

But reality took on an altogether different, unexpected form: the man clutching the other end of the cart didn't resemble a vagabond at all. Carefully and meticulously, he inspected the contents of the cart, every item, every limb, product, commodity. He was extraordinarily short, hardly taller than the cart itself and, as far as I could discern in the twilight, dressed in a rather elegant suit. My experience as a chef had taught me a little about formal fashion, so I was able to tell that this was a traditional evening tuxedo with lapels covered in a glossy fabric. And yet there was something cartoonish about the overall impression. It might have been his disquieting stature and his tuxedo which, inherited from a giant by the looks of it, was billowing around him in the foehn like Ema's cursed shirt.

I could've said anything in that moment, I could've said, for instance, "the sky is full of clouds, rushing wildly in the opposite direction," or "burrow into a vulture's feathers and circle with it through the wild air over the foot of Mount Kailash," or "What's happened to you? This isn't you anymore!" But in the end, I only managed to say, "What do you want?"

The little man peered at me through coke-bottle glasses. I'd never seen such thick lenses before. They hovered so close to me, I felt as if I'd go tumbling down two frozen wells at any moment. His throat, chin, cheeks, and entire head were covered in soft, snow-white rabbit fur. God knows why right then I remembered the shed and the wind driving in flurries of snow through the open door. Once, during New Year's Eve of 1989, when I was chopping wood in a shed for the first and last time in my life, an animal appeared in the doorway, and the ax split a piece of wood and one of the halves hit a rabbit right between its eyes. Or was it a dog? I can't remember, it was such a long time ago . . .

"Sorry . . . almost didn't see you there . . . They got rid of all lighting in this VFS a while ago."

"VFS?"

"That's right. You've evidently come a long way and gotten lost, haven't you? You currently find yourselves . . ." he gave a meaningful pause, his velvet vest expanding with pride, "in the Valley of the Five Senses. During the day you'd be able to see the entire landscape covered with the remnants of red rock, which used to be mined here. My God," he suddenly exclaimed as if laughing at me, "but that was ages ago . . . Here and there you can still stumble upon the ruins of a mining tower or the skeleton of a derelict factory."

With a sweeping gesture of his fingers, resembling paintbrushes sticking out of a velvet sleeve, he etched a line through the entire wasteland, steppe, desert, or wherever it was we found ourselves, all the way to the dusky horizon, vanishing somewhere in the unseeable distance.

"Did you say factory?" Ema perked up, as if she could possibly have any idea what this creature was talking about. Her back, arms, calves, everything was marked by the mesh imprinted into her skin, as if she were just the impression of the cage in which she rode.

"Yes. I used to work here in a factory for eyesight, but due to a certain . . . how to put this . . . due to a certain miscalculation of the research department . . ." With an air of resigned sadness, he tapped the thick lenses of his glasses, "I've been on disability pension for the past sixty-two years."

"What are you going on about, buddy?" I snapped at him. "We're in Prague, somewhere on the outskirts, in fact I'm pretty sure we just crossed tram tracks a minute ago . . . We were just in the creek meander in Záběhlice and passed Grébovka, and we'll be under Vyšehrad soon . . ."

The man was no longer wrestling with me for the cart but walking by my side with the self-assuredness of a dandy. His coke-bottle glasses had now transformed into two headlamps, and we could see several meters ahead of us.

"Yes, I used to work here as an engineer, but that doesn't matter right now . . . It's somewhere around here that I must've lost . . ." Suddenly a squeal erupted out of his throat that froze the blood in my veins. "You see that tower? See that tower on our left?"

I didn't see it and didn't want to see anything anymore either. Except for maybe: the giant freezer I would open tomorrow morning in which I would find the only thing that mattered, the elements I would assemble again into a comprehensible version of the world.

"In this desolate wasteland, it's the only structure to have retained its original appearance: take note of its completely intact, gold-plated, onion-shaped dome . . ."

"What does *valley of the senses* mean? Didn't you mean to say," Ema said in amusement, "*valley of sense?* Maybe the extra 's' slipped in there by mistake."

The white rabbit fur started to ripple all over his head, maybe from the heat quivering in the air, or it was just the way he laughed.

"Oh, not at all, you inquisitive treasure," he really called her that, "by *sense*, I in no way mean signification or thought content, but the organs one uses to perceive the outer world."

I drew in a lungful of suffocatingly hot air. If I was still certain of anything on this confusing expedition, it was of the absolute, colossal, ruinous absence of the sea.

Out of that absence, out of that stiff air, suddenly arose a stench. I wondered where such a stink might be coming from, most certainly not the pristine engineer, and I bent my head over the cart. Ema long ago chucked out her white cork sandals somewhere along the way, and her feet were now sticking out through the bars. The heels of her socks were darned with a trellis stitch, so no, it wasn't smelly socks, it was the Roquefort melting in the sweltering heat. A trellis stitch! The last time I'd seen one was forty years ago. I was completely flabbergasted by this little detail, and it threw me back into childhood, where Rybka wasn't yet crouched on the steps leading to the Loch Ness ride in the alluvia of poison roses and sticky cotton candy, where there was no need to look for her because she simply did not exist yet.

"Oh, if only I weren't so old, weak, and useless, how I would love to devote all my remaining energy to restoring that tower, making it into . . . an eternal reminder of a wasted planet, a vanished homeland — does this word still exist in our vocabulary without its nationalistic connotations? — nothing but a respectable mausoleum of time lost."

As if he had suddenly remembered he might be running late for something, he reached into the breast pocket of his tuxedo and pulled out a watch, the dial the size of a tart, known colloquially as an onion, hanging from his pocket on a chain.

"Blast it! The hour between dog and wolf has flown by! It appears that I've definitely missed a very important tea party. At this point, the only things left on the spattered tabletop will be . . ."

"Toothpicks and needles," Ema burst out laughing.

And then something strange happened: as they were both laughing as if they'd just made the joke of the century, Ema, with a bit of legerdemain, removed the needle from her heart and handed it to the engineer, who thanked her with a courteous bow and stuck the needle, as if it were some rare gold pin, through his glossy lapel, peering at the unexpected ornament through his thick glasses with pleasure, and he brought his snow-white rabbit head to my sister's ear.

With growing revulsion I could hear the man intimately whisper to her: "I believe you asked me what it was I lost here."

Though they were talking right next to me and though I was straining my ears as much as I could, their conversation filtered in as nothing more than a sort of tattered web of sounds, their voices winding and crisscrossing and intertwining indistinctly like fibers, creating a pontoon to an island to which I was denied access. How she had pleaded into the phone, begging me to help her find her daughter! And now she's cooking up some inane circus-level scheme with a rabbit instead.

Just then, Ema stuck her arm into a shopping bag and handed the engineer an onion. He gave a whoop and pressed it in his hand, as if he'd just discovered a manual for determining the next course of action in a combat game.

"Onion. Like that watch you've got on a chain in your breast pocket, their hands twitching crazily and confused like my compass needle. Onion, like the dome of the tower over there, the only one still preserved, the tower you want to make into a museum of time, and you can peel this onion layer by layer until you get to the primordial energy that created it."

I recalled what she told me when we'd met in the IKEA parking lot: my life had become stuck in a single month alone, February, like in a loaf of bread. My sister's name was February and she hovered above me in the sky like a caricature of a mirage.

"Be so sweet as to scram!" I cracked my whip of sibilants at the rabbit. Surprisingly he vanished so suddenly and completely, it was as if the darkness surrounding us were just the black inside of a magician's top hat. I could just make out a squeaky, mournful rodent squeal coming from the bottom of the hat: "That book . . . If you happen to come across it, oh, if you were to one day write it yourself . . . Well, you know what it resembles."

And now something strange happened. As soon as the rabbit vanished, so did Ema. I began to rummage through the contents of the shopping cart in desperation, where the hell had she gone, picking up herrings and oysters, my fingers getting tangled in the gills and stuck in cans, the crimson of canned tomatoes dripping off me, and as I was brandishing a pair of green bell-pepper mittens, I couldn't quite believe the variety of delicacies my sister had wanted to please the party-goers with, whose sole sustenance was opinions, and they were vegetarians to boot — I at once took the Styrofoam tray with offal reddening under plastic wrap.

I finally found her. She was crouching in the corner of the cart, small and scabby like a pineapple, stiff, green leaves topping her head.

Come what may, I kept moving through this endless "valley of the senses," and all I knew was that the *sense* of this pilgrimage wasn't signification or thought content, that it was simply meant to be this way, since my will, which I'd never been able to muster anyway, was dancing in front of me like sand in strange and wonderful patterns.

At that moment, a dazzling white bolt of lightning tore through the sky. I was expecting it to fade and sink back into the darkness, but it stayed unmoving, quivering in the sky like a trickle of saliva. Suddenly, nothing around me resembled anything like a landscape, like a valley, let alone Podolí; nothing even remotely resembled anything at all. *Absolute nothingness.* I stood helplessly with the cart in the very center of this nothingness, at the core of this void, mockingly illuminated by saliva. It was impossible to describe this pure absence of everything; in the emptiness, my face twisted into a circle, into a snake biting its own tail, into a flaming hoop through which I would hopefully, finally, be able to jump, and into the world to join others.

And still it seemed as if within this *nothingness* something now and then trembled, drawn taut like a string, an embryo or premonition of sight, hearing, touch, taste . . . the five senses, ready to create forms, shapes, and colors, as if I'd rumbled with my shopping cart into someone's untainted, nondualistic mind.

"Śūnyatā . . ." the string twanged, and another responded, "śūnyatā . . ." and I couldn't not join. My thumb skimmed over the string, just barely, adding a tone to the singing emptiness, and I immediately felt how Petr Ash was melting like butter forgotten in the sun, how all my borrowed and stolen voices and gestures and expressions were seeping into the voidness, being absorbed by it. Once and for all, the vessel shattered, and the space within and without became one.

Only then did I notice the token lodged inside the slot of the shopping cart. I pried it out and flung it into the nothingness, as if I were playing pétanque, and it too twanged against the strings and dissolved in the enormous frying pan of non-duality.

I had a sinking feeling as my professional eyes began to examine the trays of meat scattered all around Ema. The labels with the product details were missing from the backs of the wrappers. I carefully ripped off the plastic wrap and sniffed the soft, dark reddish meat. And as if it were my very first sensory perception, I proceeded to familiarize myself with it by touch, smell, sight, and if that weren't enough, I raised the body parts to my ear in the hopes of hearing an answer: "Have we found her yet, Brother? Please tell me I'll get to hold her in my arms soon . . ."

The strings were now wildly snapping, one by one. One of

them lashed me across the face as I tore off the last plastic wrap.

It's good you're so minuscule, transformed, and oblivious in the corner of the shopping cart. I turned my back to you and clenched your daughter's heart in my hand.

•

". . . I'll allow myself the luxury of sincerity and openness, even though you'll probably hate me for it. No one should ever again relieve you of accountability, no matter how much you attempt to downplay it, while you point to all the idiots who try to reform the world and the psyche. By the way, I'm talking about accountability for us both. Is that something you even still care about? I just don't know . . . A mountain of lies — how long have you been piling the dirty snow between us — has clouded and tainted all our acts and words, even the most loving ones that I want to believe are genuine . . . Once you find the strength to actually hear what I'm saying, once you hear my voice on that clattering, egocentric merry-go-round of yours, once you really start listening to what others are telling you, only then will you be able to rid yourself of addiction. And calling addiction a disease is an oversimplification, only for total losers."

"What's happened to you? This isn't you anymore." She walked to the door. The back of her shirt bore the words in English "Nice person, wrong planet." She turned to Rybka. "I'll wait for you outside," she said, gripping the door handle. Instead of a hallway, the open door revealed a long-forgotten road full of snowdrifts. I wanted to fall down on all fours and gobble them all down, but I couldn't move. As Dita receded in the distance, as she turned and yelled, "I'm heading North!" perhaps so that I could find her in another lifetime, her hand with a thousand fingers kept a tenuous grip on the door handle.

A gust of wind — I didn't understand from where since the window was closed — violently rocked the hammock strung up between two paintings and swept a tangle of syllables off the table. "Your words: only the wind blowing, touching lightly and then it's gone. But I choose to believe that behind the rigid grimace is still a person, set apart from the inhuman masses. If only I could hug you, if only you could hug me — when it happens, we'll exhale in relief and sweep away this oppressive time into the muck. I hope.   Dita"

•

Ema and Marie were standing by the window, pressing their cheeks against the glass. Today the Garden was concealed in a glass of milk, and anything could be imagined in its place.

"Down in the fog," Ema said, "are moments stumbling around when I got off the tram one stop earlier, forgot to say hello, came late, failed to spot a wrinkle, failed to hear a chord, plugged the silence with words, failed to unlock Irena's shackles, lost my daughter at a fair, arranged to meet my brother at IKEA and failed to show up, moments stumbling around, lost in the fog, unable to find the way out. Also moments when someone lulled me to sleep with a look, not the other way around, and forgot to wake me up."

"We have a cabin by the Berounka, right next to the river," Marie said, "the river's right outside the window."

Ema thumbed Dita's letter in her pocket. The letter was

folded into a square. The square resembled a tiny box. In the tiny box made up of Dita's words, Ema and Marie were standing by the window, pressing their cheeks against the glass.

"Outside the window is pineapple pizza the size of a wagon wheel."

"Outside the window is the endless Sahara."

"Outside the window is a bubble bath."

"Outside the window is a bathroom you can lock."

"Outside the window is silence. Absolute silence. And the winds be blowing, the winds be blowing . . ."

"Outside . . ." Marie was about to continue, but suddenly paused, and turned her face from the glass; while one of her faces, cracked and made of glass, turned toward Ema, the other one, calm and mild like a cutout of landscape, remained hanging on the window.

"Dad came to see me."

"Did he change his mind about the competence thing?"

"We didn't talk about it. He told me . . ." Marie stopped talking, taking down one of the White Queen's crocheted dolls from the window latch and beginning to pick it apart as eons passed. "He has cancer." A rip and the doll disappeared, only grimy yarn remained, spooled on a finger. Marie cracked the window open and chucked it into the fog.

"Unravel more," Ema urged her.

"You'd love that, wouldn't you?" Marie chuckled. "This building, Dr. Veselá, Rambo!" She pulled her hood over Ema's head as well. Now it covered the both of them. The hood is in the tiny box made from the letter and the letter is being tossed at the end of a glassmaker's blowpipe in an incandescent, undulating bubble of glass. The glass cools, solidifying into a tumbler. A glass of milk that Ema had broken once, but which today contained the entire Garden. Anything could be imagined in its place.

"It's my fault. Ten years of putting up with my crap. You don't wanna know how I made money to pay for smack."

"I don't want to know. Beyond the glass . . ."

". . . my dad is teaching me how to drive his old Jawa 250 behind our cabin."

Like a flatboat on the Berounka, the hood now gently sways in the milk, in the waves of fog, in the liquid yarn. Ema cuts a tiny round hole in it. Expecting the ceiling, she is instead met by the sight of a billion stars. Swarming and glittering like children's fingernails, they whirl at the end of a glassmaker's blowpipe in an incandescent, undulating bubble of glass.

"One time — don't worry, you can hear this one," Marie laughed, pressing her cheek back against the windowpane, "this one time I desperately needed to get hold of some dough, so I stepped into the first shop I saw. It had a bunch of super weird shit for sale, I had no idea what kind of store it was. Along one wall was a massive aquarium with a long, thin fish swimming back and forth inside of it."

"Probably an eel."

"I dunno, but it looked exactly like the sales girl hovering close by."

Someone had just brought a glass to their lips. Pavilion No. 8, drowning in white, rose from its foundations and slid into someone's mouth. A hand emerged out of the fog and handed Ema an egg with a surprise inside: another egg inside the egg and so on, one fitting into the next, and it wasn't until the very last molecule that Marie's blue hood appeared and trapped stars sparkled in the glass.

"I grabbed the first thing I could get my hands on and made a run for it. At least that's what I tried to do, the thing I had nicked was some sort of suit, super heavy."

"A heavy suit?"

"Yeah, that rubber kind divers wear."

"Wetsuit."

"Yeah. Wetsuit. They caught me within a couple meters of the shop and now I'm on probation because of it. You wouldn't believe how expensive a wetsuit is."

Shouting reached them from a distance, the torso of a surname; Ema caught only the "-ová," momentarily jangling as if stuck in a harp, before bouncing off the windowpane and disappearing again.

She looked into the Garden and spotted her in a rift of fog, she saw her, she saw little Marie, stumbling along the sidewalk with the wetsuit, while all around her, tires rustled soundlessly, while grinning puppets, offering a more suitable world, gave her a wide berth, she dragged the rubber wetsuit in the glare of window displays, an inviolable circle around her, lugging it behind her, that hermetically sealed sack of a decade in which she lived and didn't, like her own waterproof shadow which had grown attached to her, like her ailing father.

One eye of the building was observing her, an enormous eyepatch of ads covered the other. The plump woman standing on the corner didn't even bother to don her mask. The botched theft, the thwarted robbery, the mass of rubber now come alive derisively shoved Marie in front of itself deeper and deeper into the city, shimmering anciently in the air like a memory, into the panorama from a leaflet she had no place in and that she was sure to have pinched somewhere, too. Countless lips formed into an "oh" and gasped out an "ah" just before the city descended on her and twisted her arm behind her back.

They're both covered by the hood, but Marie was still teetering on the sidewalk in front of the intersection, because it's not her, it's the wetsuit pulling her along, dragging her, limp and empty, through the streets, while it's pumped full of her life like a giant parasite.

"You hear that?"

"I can hear Mother Theresa. Laughing. She's been laughing like that for three days straight."

"No, they're calling for someone. They keep repeating Schwarzová, Schwarzová, Schwarzová . . ."

"There's nobody here by that name as far as I know. Wake up, dummy, they're calling for you to go get weighed."

The fog below parted. For a second, she saw . . . No. In the milk, in the waves of fog, in the liquid yarn, it could've been anybody.

She stepped into the hallway and truly: like an icy draft, Karmela's laughter was howling through the entire ward. The White Queen sat ramrod straight at the table, her low-cut cleavage jutting out as she flailed her arms wildly, willing her nail polish to dry. It looked as though she were conducting the pitiful laughter.

"Mrs. Černá, up you go, on the scales! And then it's off to the head nurse with you. She'll get you started on your treatment plan. Congratulations!" Two rows of white teeth seemingly with no end dazzled her; they stretched into infinity and only there did they intersect triumphantly. A crossword puzzle lay in front of her, looking like a miniature chessboard from a distance.

"Congratulations . . . Congratulations, Mrs. Černá," she

kept repeating as she fanned out a deck of cards in her hand, card games were not allowed in the ward; she could only see the backs of the cards as the White Queen began to describe the handful of trump cards in colorful detail: "Congratulations for having to keep a journal, mandatory daily entries a minimum of ten lines, and imagine — with an actual pen! Because, lest you forget, we are on an island — no microchips, no cellphones, no internet — its idealized outline extends around the entire Garden; should your daily entry manage to sound sufficiently positive, your therapist will reward you with a gold star; and I further congratulate you that you will dance spontaneously when told to do so, and you will be allowed to smoke during those few scant minutes of free time in your packed all-day schedule of various activities, like at summer camp, in the basement smoking room bearing the sign NO SMOKING OUTSIDE THE DESIGNATED TIME AND AREA; there, in that cramped space, you will for the first time in your life feel a genuine sense of human fellowship, if only for the fact that in the thick, suffocating smoke it will no longer be clear where you end and where others begin; you will merge into one just as you will become one with the rules and become a fanatic collector of points! You laugh, Mrs. Černá? Well, don't; I am not exaggerating! Even you will chase after them, just like all the others, regardless of race, age, education, and religious belief; one day the nurse will catch you smooching Kurt Cobain, who you've cut out of a magazine and taped to the wall, which, by the way, is forbidden. Minus two minus four will fill you with profound despair and a sense of guilt. Those stairs leading to the gym, where you like to observe the passersby outside the window so much, where you like to observe the world from the waist down, its centauric nature, trying to reconstruct, like an archaeologist, the whole from a fragment, well the stairs that lead to the gym, that barred mass confessional, you'll be taking two at a time; you'll throw up a bit and feel better; what of it that Rambo, that lily-white monster, ominously sprawling from one end of your unconscious to the other like an iceberg, bursts into the rooms and conducts a shakedown from time to time, what of it if she takes the little you have and dumps it into a pile, confiscating what's prohibited, two ibuprofen tablets and shampoo containing alcohol which you could guzzle in a moment of weakness, anti-aging moisturizer containing alcohol which you could scarf down in a moment of weakness, and then she scans these dregs with eyes ablaze and they burst into flame and the white fire at the base of the iceberg turns all your letters to ash, you know them by heart anyway, and not only them but Vladěna's promo T-shirts too, as well as the fairy tales by the Brothers Grimm, which you read out loud to each other before lights out, and maybe that's why the night, like a spinner, then presses its huge thumbs into your temples, the cold barrel of a revolver; you do receive compensation for the minor damages — you are allowed to watch a biopic about Johnny Cash; ten minutes in and there's no doubt that washing down benzodiazepines with liquor is not healthy; and there's one more recompense by Rambo in store, yes, Miss Ema, just for you! she will accompany you on your first walk outside; the sun will blind you, the bursting buds of the chestnut trees will terrify you, your legs will buckle like two thin wooden stilts that don't belong to you; you'll ask the clock: 'How long has it been since the two white sandals were floating above me in the February sky? How long have I been in here?' and the clock, with its wide lips, mouth, and vocal cords like any other, will answer, 'A second. A thousand years. You were never anywhere else, or maybe only now is it about to happen;' it's spring, you look intently at the asphalt, it lessens the pain, but even the asphalt is extremely unusual; nevertheless, all of it — a candy wrapper, an engine starting, a scream, a piece of slag, a rusted screw — pulsates with a terrible energy that's melting down individual elements into a homogeneous mass, into a blend of colors, sounds, and motions, free of your perception; your sad posse shuffling along is being passed by roller skates, an ambulance, a patient from another pavilion is pressing his face into the wire mesh of the fence, grotesquely sneering, sticking his tongue through the mesh and shouting 'Blot! Blot! Blot!' over and over again, perhaps it's because his surname means 'blot' and he wants to introduce himself; paths cross, diverge, become denser, the Garden turns into a labyrinth, the Garden becomes a labyrinth; Rambo's arms now resemble tin signposts, she knows the way, at home in the labyrinth; several bravehearted women hide at the tail end of the procession, smoking discreetly, cigarettes hidden by their palms; half-squatting, they blow the smoke down onto the asphalt; you overhear the quiet exchange of recipes between two of them: 'Anal tampons, ever try it?' — 'No, that's a new one.' — 'It's easy, quick, and doesn't damage the liver. All you need is a few drops of vodka, you slip it in, and voila. And the money you save! If you're careful, you can make a flask last you over six months'; you walk past a blossoming hawthorn and bury your face in it; the spring day no longer terrifies you, on the contrary, having thrown the stilts aside, within you it deftly shimmies in a spiral and skips on a high bar; you walk through an open gate and find yourself on a farm; a cage is right in front of you, an ape not unlike an old man squats lethargically inside; the women are glued to the bars, as if wanting to take the wretched, mangy lump into their arms, they stick their arms through the bars while screeching and yowling in such an inhuman way that the despondent animal, completely baffled by this group of crazies and alkies who year after year without respite have continued to rattle his abode, desperately darts toward them, teeth bared and eyes sunken to the very depths of rage, relentless in his own howling, and he begins to pound his long limbs against the bars; you turn your back on the scene, but Rambo is already dragging your disgruntled posse past a cage of cats and a cage of dogs to the stud farm; Marcelka turns to the ruler of the labyrinth with an obsequious request, 'Nurse, I heard you and your husband bought a horse — could you show it to us?'; something remotely resembling a pleased smile flickers across Rambo's face, otherwise barren and uniform like a steppe; wordlessly, she signals to the group and you follow her into a gloomy stable; the air is heavy, the spirits in the shrine stink, donning the heads of horses; the buzzing of flies, rustles and sighs, the gritting of teeth, but the nurse is already bringing out her very own Šemík, that fabled horse, to show him off, glistening in the sun; the women are in awe; the women voice their awe; the women voice their awe and admiration and the smile is now a permanent fixture of the steppe, etched into it like a conjured, life-giving river; the proud owner is patting her horse on its back and neck with a large but gentle paw, pulling at its bridle, and a reverential circle forms around her and the animal — understandably, the women don't dare throw themselves at the horse or even babble at it like they had at the ape, and good thing too, as it turns out the horse bears the name Tsarevich; the escalating cries of admiration are lashing the stallion across its massive backside, its impressive roundness eliciting an alarming euphoria in Marcelka: 'My God, Nurse, what a pair you two make! Can we see how you look sitting on top of him?'; the others, apart from a few exceptions — Miss Marie and, naturally, Miss Ema — join in: shakedown forgotten, the labyrinth domesticated; with surprising grace, the nurse swings up into the saddle and freezes in place; her audience is dumbstruck; for a long time Rambo is completely inert, as is the horse, infected by her statuesqueness; the circle and the Garden, the steppe and the hawthorn drown in the silence, as if all of it has disappeared at the same time beneath the water's surface, as if the whole scene has collapsed into another element; and perhaps the silence would have been, as they say, absolute, were it not for the unending bellowing of the enraged ape that has reached your ears; in your dream, Mrs. Černá, Rambo was straddling the seesaw, pushing off wildly; you can still see her securing the Lady to the bed with practiced moves so tightly the White Queen's wrists are rubbed raw come morning; but the monument she is currently personifying with her Tsarevich is devoid of motion or expressions; a white monster has sprouted out of the white horse, merging with it into a single entity, hollow plaster just knock; Marie turns away and bends at the waist; it's not clear if she's vomiting or stifling a fit of laughter; all this awaits you once you get started on your treatment plan, all this and so much more: you'll become a potter, a basket weaver, or, should you prefer, a spinner with a thumb as large as a crowbar, all under the roof of the Occupational Therapy Center; in the Church of St. Wenceslas where the architect Václav Roštlapil managed so admirably to combine Romanesque elements with playful Art Nouveau, you'll have the opportunity to hear the Word of God during your bibliotherapy sessions; the pastor's lips may be soft and sweet like jam but his gaze is like refined steel, cutting into whoever it lands on; you sit in a circle, of course, in the center of a cushion glitters a rainbow sphere, a marble representing a pearl; one circle pierces another, the first pierces a second, the second a third, they bang into place, until the long chain lies in the Garden like a snake that lovingly coils around all the pavilions, one squeeze turning them into rubble; one of you opens your heart to the Lord; the heart is like a tent, like a wigwam, like a tepee, it's like a snow-white igloo in whose bowels Rambo's white steed neighs and pounds its hoof; something white flashes in the pastor's hand, perhaps a sugar cube for the horse; he tosses it into the heart that has just opened, he will fling the pearl as a reward into the heart of just one of you; but now he opens the Bible, even you sitting in the circle have tomes like large black cats heavy in your laps; an almighty bass erupts from the marmalade lips, so powerful it makes Mother Theresa, coveting the rainbow marble in a daydream, blink rapidly like a doll shaken by an enraged toddler. '. . . As he neared Damascus on his journey . . .' Miss Helga, turn to page 875, we're all on page 875!, 'suddenly a light from heaven flashed around him. He fell to the ground and heard a voice say to him, Saul, Saul, why do you persecute me? — Who are you, Lord? Saul asked. — I am Jesus [. . .] go into the city, and you will be told what you must do [. . .] So they led him by the hand into Damascus. For three days he was blind, and did not eat or drink anything'; the voice solemnly falls silent; Miss Helga's eyes look as if they're about to pop out of her sockets, perhaps under the impression of Saul's miraculous transformation into Paul; a gust of wind carries the sound of a rooster crowing three times from vegetable gardens somewhere into the deathly silence, completely out of context since it's from page 804; the pastor encourages you to explain what actually happened on the road to Damascus and what impression the parable made on you; he completely ignores Karmela's eagerly waving hand, the only thing moving in the frozen space of the room, and pins his gaze on Vladěna; Vladěna says nothing; you fear that once she opens her mouth, stuffed with chewing gum, you'll hear the cock's crow for the fourth time; while the others have witnessed a miracle, she was busy arguing with her partner in her head, a stack of useless promo T-shirts the only thing she has left of him; the pastor attacks; Vladěna stares hatefully at the marble, heavy and blue like a planet; she finally blurts out, 'Not gonna lie, it's super weird what happened to him. Must've been one helluva bender.' Apart from the pastor, it's obvious to everyone who's being referred to; no longer just the lips, but the pastor's entire face is now red, as if someone has smeared jam over it, two knives jutting out of his eyes; he averts them from Vladěna with disgust, piercing Helga with hope: 'And you, how do you understand the story?' — 'It depicts, with astonishing precision, the telltale signs of an epileptic fit,' she says coldly as an introduction to her roughly twenty-minute disquisition, which the pastor attempts to interrupt unsuccessfully; Miss Helga is a neurologist; Miss Helga's eyes look as if they're about to pop out of her sockets, not because of the Bible but because of her long-term, excessive use of psychopharmaceuticals; the miracle slowly evaporates from the Petri dish of science, the city walls of Damascus disappear from the scene like set pieces being carried off; the symptoms of epilepsy stir up the rare interest of the entire circle, many an alcoholic present having experienced them before, and set in motion a lively discussion; the women bombard Helga with questions, shouting over each other and flinging their arms around so vehemently someone accidentally tees off the rainbow marble like a golf ball, the marble, which is a pearl, which is a planet, rolls into a corner somewhere forgotten by all but Mother Theresa, who falls to her hands and knees and begins her search, the pastor is shouting, the pastor is screaming, veins like ropes popping out on his thick neck, but the women are already off the leash, soaring, the pastor's Solingen steel sinking helplessly through the mayhem as if cutting through fog, or milk, or liquid yarn, the tomes disappear from the women's laps and the women breezily float through the room, resembling sheets of paper freed of their paperweight, finally Mother Theresa tracks down the pearl and hands it to the pastor, but he's utterly consumed by his attempt to subdue the riotous mass and paying no heed to symbols, he bangs his Bible against the table; he suddenly raises himself up in all his bodybuilder glory and in a voice that turns cities to dust roars, 'Piles of shit!'; and as if the words were a bucket of ice water he's dumped on them, the women immediately fall silent and stare at the enraged pastor in awe, all of them now as goggle-eyed as Miss Helga; Mother Theresa is blubbering loudly, the pastor cannot stop shaking, 'How dare you . . . how can you even, you, you . . . you with backs bent under piles of shit!'; having returned surreptitiously to the cushion, the Earth stops spinning, the lone pearl has frozen in place within the depths of the universe; the bibliotherapy session is over; all this awaits you once you get started on your treatment plan, Mrs. Černá, all this and so much more . . ."

The White Queen was lightly chewing on her pencil, engrossed in inscribing neat, block letters into the little boxes of the crossword in front of her, and it didn't seem as if she had anything to do with Ema's immediate future.

"Why, Mrs. Černá," she glanced up, "you're staring at me as if I were still trying to feed the chair! Run along and go get weighed! By the way, would you happen to know 'a member of a mythical race who did no work and subsisted solely on the lotus plant,' nine letters? Starts with an 'l.'"

Ema was on the way to the nurses' station when someone suddenly pinched the back of her neck with two fingers. "Wait a sec, I got an idea," Dana whispered and ran off.

Ema closed her eyes. Behind her eyelids, Rybka flickered in a colorful spectrum; she was in the middle of trying to burrito herself with a sheet of Christmas wrapping paper — how old could she have been? two? — and with an expression so radiant it hurt Ema's eyelids, she kept repeating, "Thank-you-Angel, thank-you-Angel, thank-you-Angel, than—"

Dana was back with two filled 1.5 liter PET bottles, which she proceeded to stuff into the back of Ema's jeans, which were hanging off of her, pulling her hoodie over them, looking supremely satisfied. "Okay, now you can go."

Ema strode into the nurses' station, stiff as a board, and stepped onto the scales. And as she stood there, nothing but an inanimate lump of clay, nothing but a sleeping golem with an empty cavity in the middle of its forehead, I slipped into her quickly, as if she were only a stolen wetsuit.

Onscreen, a beautiful woman in an all-white outfit was falling into someone's arms — no surprise there, given the height of her heels, but I didn't see who was catching her, since Karabinka was eclipsing the right side of the screen. Instead of falling into someone's arms, she might've been falling under the wheels of a car or out of a plane, into a swamp or into thick, green muck.

"My, my, Mrs. Černá, I must say, I'm proud of you! You've gained three kilos in just one week!"

I swallowed the mood stabilizer, stuck my tongue out at Karabinka, as was the custom here, so no one could hide the pill beneath her tongue, and clumsily backed out of the nurses' station. I crashed into Dana. She barricaded my way and barked out, "You owe me!" A mean, defiant smile split her face in two, as if someone had taken a razor to her face. "My old man's been in the slammer for two years. They're allowing him a conjugal visit tomorrow. Lend me five hundred and get me outta here."

"Are you out of your mind?" Dita: maybe it wasn't me anymore, but this sharp-edged, gaping grimace of a face wasn't Dana anymore either. With each jerk of the minute hand on the wall clock, nearing the head of the unsuspecting Lady like the blade of a pendulum, all our masks were showing more and more cracks, and utterly unfamiliar, empty, hostile faces were peering through, disintegrating into a tangle of lines like those oval-framed portraits of the dead in the cemetery.

I wanted to get back to Marie, back into the hood of her hoodie, but the hallway was suddenly crowded. New cots, packed together like sardines, had appeared. I didn't understand how the head nurse had managed to process so many incoming patients in such a short amount of time, as I was being weighed. Some women, likely doped up with Subutex, were snoring loudly, others were crouching on the cots, hugging their naked knees to their chests, track marks down their arms, rocking back and forth, back and forth, like rocking horses, others clad in the flimsy barely thigh-high local attire were squashed in the narrow spaces between the beds, wildly arguing about something, shouting over each other as if they were hawkers at a bazaar, at times in languages I didn't recognize. There was nowhere to avert my eyes, they were everywhere:

mouths twisted into "ohs" and "ahs," cussing and imploring pleas, curses and prayers in deferral of death, ashen faces smoothed of features, thighs, white and thick like the under-bellies of fish.

My gaze turned to the window with the view of the athlete's feet, but there was no window, and there was no wall: instead, the hallway segued into an open space outside, hospital beds dotting it all the way to the horizon. As far as the eye could see, thousands of women were on their backs in the crumpled bedsheets, waiting, the young and the old, resignedly motion-less or defiantly wandering their white territory while their corporeal vessels abandoned them, as if someone had stolen their bodies from them like a piece of baggage, for in the Pali language, the word for baggage and body is identical, the mumbling and the mute, in bubbles of silence or in screaming booby-trapped pits, besieged by the beehive opening of rela-tives and loneliness, covered in sweat or shivering with cold, up to their chins in memories or stuck in the present moment, abusing the nurses or slipping crumpled banknotes into their coat pockets, waking up or falling asleep, dying or returning to life, the needles of time on their nightstands, crutches in the form of photos on their phones, they were on their backs in the bedsheets and all of them, whether they faced their illness head on or avoided it their whole life as if it were an embar-rassing relative, were waiting, I didn't know what for, but the waiting trembled through the landscape like enormous swarms of insects, binding the beds together with a blue mesh of veins; maybe they were waiting for night to fall, for their dinner to be brought in, for the loss of memory, for their foreheads to touch the ceiling, sinking under the weight of a thousand pairs of eyes staring at it.

"Mom!" I shouted. For a while nothing, then the air on my face warped into a barely perceptible, warm whisper. "Ema, Emička, rise and shine! You have to go to school."

I tried to move, but the hallway with the landscape had grown straight through me. I shouted again . . . All of a sudden, everything went silent, even the snores of the sleepers, and the women turned to me. Somewhere in the distance, far away in this land full of beds transformed into a single endless pavilion, an old woman took her dentures out of a glass of water, put them in, tentatively snapped her teeth a few times, and in that sudden silence, I could hear it all the way to here.

A girl, her face full of piercings, sidled up to me, the one who had exhaled spinach in my face ages ago when I had been admitted, along with those impossible to remember, mysterious three words, and barked at me like Dana first had: "You owe me!"

"But I don't have anything here, just a letter from Dita . . ."

I pulled the folded letter from my pocket. But when I unfolded it, a single sentence was squatting inside like a moth: "A shameful fate painted over muck."

I felt as if this sentence unquestionably contained all the others; it had swallowed the rest and made them part of the whole, becoming the swirling snowflakes inside the snow globe that for years my brother had kept hidden from me. Even this sentence soon disappeared as the letter began to disintegrate in my hands, first into a tree, then the mother of the logger, and finally into non-paper elements.

Nobody paid any attention to the letter. Exclamations of "You owe me!" began to bombard me from every direction, hands extended in supplication. The girl glued herself to me, her sticky tentacles encircling me in a tight grip. "Look, day after tomorrow, I have to hand in a three-page résumé. I'm stretching out my handwriting like a schoolkid and triple-spacing like crazy, but I still don't have more than a paragraph. We all have to write it, otherwise they won't ever let us out of here. These others," she tossed her head with disdain, "screw 'em. Give it to me!"

"But — give you what, for Chrissake?"

"Your past, of course! We don't have ours anymore."

"Give it to me!" — "No, give it to *me!*" One after the other began to beg and plead, shoving and shouting over each other. Those who had been bedridden until now tore the IVs out of their veins and began to rave on the beds. A bag-of-bones woman, her ribs jutting out through her nightie, extended her hand to me and opened her fist. "See? I don't want it for free. Give it to *me!*"

A large, dappled bean lay in her hand, translucent and cracked like a leaf. "All you need to do, honey, is plant it in the ground beneath your feet. It'll sprout before you know it and the offshoots will climb up your body and in no time it'll grow all around you, so thick nobody'll be able to stick a bottle through it, not even a teeny shot glass!"

"But I'm a pillhead!" I shouted and threw myself in a panic into the rising waves, into that terrible sea of bodies, reeking noxiously, I thrashed around and dug my nails into God knows whose flesh until I finally found myself, breathless, at the door, the completely ordinary door with its completely ordinary door handle. I quickly reached for it, as if it were a lifebuoy, and barged inside.

In the room stood a woman in front of a mirror, brushing out her wet, gray hair that came down to her waist. Her gray strands teemed and writhed along the edge of the sink like grass snakes. She looked like Dita from a twenty-year-old photo of her, where she's standing in front of a row of targets, her finger on the trigger of a pistol aimed right at the camera. The resemblance was so uncanny I couldn't move, as if I were positively expecting that long-ago gunshot to ring out now, right now, in this moment, to put an end to the animalistic pandemonium behind me, the odor of women and the stench of gravy, the résumés and sessions of nonverbal communication, the bartering and begging for a spot in line, to earn extra points, and shoot the unlockable doors to shreds and riddle with bullets the doors to which only others had the keys.

"Get in here, quick! And close the door. Judging by how much they're acting up in there, the women have gone off the rails today. Karabinka is no match for them."

I quickly slammed the door behind me and pressed my back to it. No gunshot rang out, though: it was clear this woman had nothing to do with Dita, apart from her likeness, that she didn't care whatsoever about this land, feral with screaming women and dotted with hospital beds. For just a brief moment, she tore herself away from her hair enveloping her like a beautiful, impregnable nest and pointed her hairbrush at me, not like a weapon, but a teacher's pointer. As she was blatantly and dispassionately scrutinizing me from head to toe like some sort of specimen, she began to reel off: "Height approximately 175 centimeters, thin, age around fifty, countenance: terrified. She entered the room," she glanced at her watch, "on March 28, 2010, at 2:46 p.m."

Great. Just what I was missing. I figured it might be a good idea to go back into the hallway, or to at least crack the door open two fingers and hand the *jezinkas*, those wild women of the woods, what they wanted from me. I was about to reach for the door handle, but discovered I couldn't. In both hands I was holding —

And then I saw us, Dalibor, in the mirror above the sink full of grass snakes. Your straw hat, sunglasses, stubbled chin, sunburned nose. We're sitting side by side on the cliff above the bay, still on the lookout for our swimmer, that tiny dot lost in the vast blue of the sea. The moment lasts, it hasn't passed, is here with me, in this room in this moment just like all the others, and I get a second chance.

I'm clutching a sandal in each hand. I hear you saying, "Don't throw them away. But if you really have to, tie them together." I won't throw them away. Not this time. We'll make our way down from the cliff, I'll pack the old shoes into my suitcase, and we'll fly home.

For a very brief moment, that nebulous "home," that altogether different future remained in the mirror, as if someone had breathed on it. I quickly shoved the sandals under my shirt.

"I don't like you," I told the woman. "You or your hair."

She didn't seem offended as she carried on with her report. "Concealing shoes beneath shirt. Conduct: suspicious."

She suddenly flashed me a warm smile and held out her hairbrush to me, transformed into an olive branch. "But Mrs. . . . Mrs. Černá, I believe that's your name, isn't it . . . I'm simply trying to memorize every single detail, you understand? Every little tidbit of information is incredibly important! Everyone knows me in here, and nobody makes a big deal over it. All sorts of things could happen, theft, for instance . . . Once, someone's luxury lingerie disappeared . . . Anything's possible in here . . . or, God forbid, murder! Where would they be without my testimony?"

The wishing game. What do I look forward to most once I get out of here? Silence. Absolute silence. But for now, until a stranger will wake up on a pew in some church with the snow falling through the domeless roof, a stranger whom I come to in his dream, I have to persevere. The screaming behind me, the daytime and nighttime racket, the words without end.

"But you didn't just come in here for the hell of it, for my luscious hair, did you?" the woman laughed. "You must be here for Mrs. Vodseďálková."

I had completely forgotten about her. Karmela. Her laughter, that icy draft, howling through the ward for the past three days, now drowned out by the strange, thunderous landscape behind me. I looked up at the ceiling.

Karmela was hanging there, her back pressed up to the ceiling as if it were an enormous strip of flypaper, her lanky limbs dangling in the air, limp and lifeless. She was hanging there, laughing and laughing, and her mouth, made huge by the incessant laughter, swallowed up the rest of her face, her whole being disappearing in that dreadful cackle, as did her sons and asanas and essay, as did her monstrous, insuppressible, endless hunger.

It might've been the chocolate, I suddenly realized, that humongous chocolate bar Dita had left for me, the one she'd used to shield herself from me — I had slipped it into Karmela's bathrobe later — that might have been what turned her into this grimace, this grin.

I went out into the hallway. "Left the room at 2:52 p.m.," I could hear behind me. It was empty apart from Miss Irena, still solving her crossword at the table.

"Lo-to-phage," I enunciated with care, slowly, syllable by syllable.

"Say what?" she looked up, surprised.

"A member of a mythical race who did not work and subsisted solely on the lotus plant, nine letters. I remembered."

Outside the window, reality remains hidden in a glass of milk. I could imagine anything in its place, but why would I? Just one of the athlete's enormous big toes is sticking out of the fog, resolutely pointed skyward. Dana at the window. I know what she's going to say. What she's going to yell at me. You owe me, get me outta here. To go see her old man in the slammer in Mírov. Why not?

"Why not?" I said aloud.

She was standing there, seething, her thick, fat legs akimbo and anchored to the linoleum like two immovable columns, the whites of her eyes red with rage, a lack of sleep, and a monster dose of Antabuse.

As soon as I recalled a certain receipt, it all went surprisingly smoothly. That one time, perhaps in a dream that wasn't even mine, Ash had shown me a crumpled receipt, lines scribbled all over it. Fractals. The same Dana who had stood up for me not that long ago in the gym was now shooting daggers at me, her eyes piercing me; ". . . or, God forbid, murder!" nothing lasted in here, nothing counted, I knew that now: each one of us here was like the scenic countryside along the train tracks, a sequence of stills that burned brightly and immediately disappeared. Perhaps the Rapunzelian woman was right, perhaps it was necessary to capture every single detail, for instance, the quiver running down Dana's body at this very moment, or a single teardrop in Marie's wall of tears drawing, and that plastic bag, that translucent wing twirling to inaudible music and ascending on a whirlwind several days ago outside the gym window. As potential testimony, but more likely just because.

Dana suddenly staggered on those two enormous columns of hers like a behemoth. She began to tremble, lifting her bare arms and gaping at them as if they didn't belong to her. Suddenly, the skin above her elbow split open and a sprout emerged, resembling a stump, or a branch. She moved it around to see if she could control its movement. But then, another twig shot out of the branch, and a new one out of that one, ad infinitum, it was impossible to keep track of it all anymore, her entire body began to expand and intertwine and ramify and undulate, transformed by some terrible effervescent force into the snarl of a proliferating tree, a living shrub, where only the two huge glowing whites of Dana's eyes remained.

I rushed over to the window and opened it. "Hurry up, Otesánek, the coast is clear."

The massive branch-creature crackled as it moved. The first of its sprigs extended through the bars of the window and latched onto the plaster of the pavilion's facade. The half-plant, half-creature tearing through the fog with its wooden, bark-covered limbs, slowly and laboriously lurched its way toward freedom.

"What's the hold up?" The head nurse. I quickly closed the window. It had totally slipped my mind that I was supposed to be starting my treatment plan. From one floor to the next, from one space to another; by now I knew it by heart and could reel it off in reverse, as it was the same backward and forward: I'll burst through the ceiling and find myself in a larger place, again and again, ad infinitum, like in that dream my brother had transformed into reality with cardboard and glue. Simply because I didn't know how to turn into a tree like Dana.

"Marie's already packed your bag for you. Mrs. Černá, really — bit of a slowpoke today, aren't you?"

The blue hood gently swayed in the liquid yarn, like a flat-boat on the Berounka. One hood for the both of us. I wanted to say goodbye to Marie, but didn't see her anywhere. Maybe she pulled on the wetsuit and like a diver fell backward into the water headfirst in search of the eel.

"No more monkey business! They're gonna set you straight in there," the head nurse exclaimed, grabbing me by the elbow with her clawed fingers as her other hand unlocked certain doors and locked others, as the elevator rumbled down the shaft, as a serving cart rattled past and some girl was banging on a piece of sheet metal or shard of a bell screaming "ther-a-pee, ther-a-pee," it's a wonder her vocal cords didn't give out, and the din drowned out the rest of the nurse's words.

"You really acted out like an angsty teen at times, Mrs. Černá. That ends now. No more pranks, no more T-shirts with liquor logos during ward rounds and, most importantly, if I can give you some advice — no more dreams."

I've been here before. In front of the nurses' station, this is where I squirmed helplessly in my socks, having barely had enough time to slurp up and swallow clouds one last time. And here, here is where the stench of spinach pushed me down the stairs like a murderer and I hurtled into our long-gone kitchen, landing right at my mother's feet. A month ago, a second ago, three breaths ago, before our time, during the Pliocene. Select all that apply. Maybe none of it's happened yet. Or it's all about to happen.

Underneath the wall-mounted telephone lies a stack of journals, mandatory daily entries a minimum of ten lines, a gold star for demonstrable progress. This time, the canteen is empty, the tables — one of them, facing the others, must be the princess's dominion — are littered with knitting needles, hair clips, scrunchies, colored pencils, postcards, shells, tinfoil: details that, like spiders, instantly scamper off into every corner. And here's the kitchen pass-through with its roller blind. Suddenly, the blind shoots up and a face appears in the opening, hidden beneath a layer of powder. The woman is sporting a Bosch baseball cap and holding electric hand tools, and she stares at me. I lean against the counter. She immediately gets it.

"What'll you have?" she asks.

"Two Mojitos and a Cubist cream puff," I answer.

"What's that? We don't have that."

"You do. Over there. The square one."

She turns around, bustling around for a minute before handing me two plates, grinning from ear to ear, the lines in her empty palms running deep.

"This it?"

"It is."

"You wanted two, aren't you alone?"

"No. I'm not alone."

Next to the canteen is a spacious room with chairs lining the walls. In the center of it lies a bedsheet congregating a bunch of cute crafts objects, the products of the week. Plus two points — better than nothing.

And then I see it. That baseball cap should've been a dead giveaway. The reproduction ran the entire length of the wall — who on earth decided to put it here, of all places? — an enormous painting of the Garden, a mockery of symmetry, a monstrous cosmos split into a triptych, pulsating wildly as if it had sprung into existence just a second ago.

I come closer. Everybody is there: the damned riders saddling hogs, galloping past clusters of dead birds raining down into a well; the devil-pope, devouring naked bodies only to defecate them, the infernal band and the goblin with its drum and scorpions and salamanders, the two earlobes joined by a needle, a knife blade protruding from their midst, the man crucified on a harp, and here, here a tree-human, like Dana before.

I doubt I'm able to do it, but it surprisingly goes off without a hitch. I climb up onto a chair, enter the painting, and the wings of the triptych close on me like two halves of a giant clam.

•

Hi Mom,

You won't believe this! Uncle Ash and I have started emailing each other. He said he packed my childhood drawings of tadpole people in a bag when he left home that time. I actually don't really know him that well. Some of the stuff he writes is legit weird, like about that one time he wheeled you around Prague in a shopping cart. And like in his last email he wrote about an onion. He sent me some of your old photos, too, the two of you are so alike it's crazy, like twins, I swear. He said I could come stay with him if I wanted, could work in the same restaurant as he does and stay at his place, his wife is in rehab for the long haul, so he says. I'm really thinking about doing it. You don't even know what sort of shit I've been going through this year, I haven't told you to keep you from worrying. I need a change of scenery and I've also realized I just really, really miss the sea.

Keep earning those points, obey the princess, and come home soon.

Your Rybka

•

The little girl ran out of the chateau into the garden. She could still hear that old professor's shrill falsetto in her ears, the one she'd spilled coffee on, her left cheek still red from the retaliatory slap, but she didn't care about that anymore. The sand crunched beneath her sandals and she was surrounded by trimmed boxwood hedges, crisscrossing the vast, fragrant labyrinth of that summer. In the hedges, spiderwebs glistened with yesterday's rain and a host of half-dead, half-alive metallic flies, resembling snap fasteners.

Neptune, imprisoned in a scaffolding, was already hailing her from afar with his prongless trident. She passed him by, pattering across the grounds past the fountain and found herself in an alley of trees. A translator was sitting on a bench, bent over his notebook. Yesterday, he'd taught her two Chinese characters, one signifying water and the other air, but today she steered clear of him. Eyes in the tree bark watched her, and every so often the trees laboriously extricated their roots from the earth and lumbered across the wide path, back and forth, stiffly, like the castle guard.

"The cat held onto the dog, the dog onto the girl, the girl onto the grandad, the grandad onto the grandma and they pulled and pulled and . . ."

She didn't know why she was telling the story, but as they stood there in a row, one holding onto the other, as more and more of them appeared and as the line grew, winding all the way to the horizon, she didn't even register the sound of tires behind her, so lazy and silent as if they had all the time in the world, that quiet car creeping toward her down the lane.

And then out of the blue, quite close by, someone began to

spin a ratchet. "You-too, you-too, you-too!" In her imagination, she suddenly pictured a small Eskimo floating away on an iceberg, God knows why. Just where had she heard that same drumming and rattling before, so loud she'd had to cover her ears?

A guy in a white tank top, redheaded as all hell, leans against an ambulance, a wooden toy in his hand spins around and around and rattles and rattles as the other guy yawns behind the wheel. But someone else is here, too: having emerged out of time, he hears the ticking of your fear within his body, the alley of trees stretching like a palm line of his hand.

"Are you Ema Podobová?"

What's next, little girl? The ratchet continues to spin as grit soundlessly, patiently falls from Neptune.

"You must've mistaken me for somebody else."

You're not lying. Your name in the redhead's mouth doesn't belong to you. And maybe they've really mistaken you for somebody else, somebody who both resembles and doesn't resemble you: you in forty-three years.

You stifled a scream. Nobody was there. The translator was no longer sitting on the bench, Mom and Brother were definitely still asleep, Dad was cleaning off the professor's suit jacket while apologizing, and the uprooted trees had shambled off to God knows where.

The ratchet fell silent. You weren't even sure how, but you found yourself inside. The ambulance drove off. Since the redhead had strapped you to the stretcher, you couldn't move. You focused on the back of his neck where a naked lady was dancing and sipping a glass of something green. Above you, clouds were rushing by in the opposite direction in that vast, endless expanse and you couldn't tell — as if you were at sea — whether you were getting closer or drifting away.

"No matter what, it's gonna be one hell of a trip. Want to play the broken telephone game with me?"

He didn't answer. He thought you need more than two to play. Bullshit. I could play it alone.

So you started to mumble, mutter, whisper, prattle, and babble until the word "owl" came out. In a flash, you were covered in feathers and you slipped out of your bindings, flying out of the ambulance through the cracked-open window.

The wind sweeps you up into a pirouette, as if sketching the Chinese sign for air with your new body above the alley of trees. You are light, just a motley of ridiculous wings and feathers and nothing, just roughly, hastily approximated wind, and you begin to twirl and dance like that plastic bag outside that future barred window, still hidden behind the walls of time. You rise up in a whirlwind spiral, gliding along for a while before hurtling down suddenly to a fruit stand, barely missing the embrace of a sliced open watermelon beneath a fan of wasps. You soar off and circle the chateau, which has suddenly emerged before you like a rosy cliff of quivering blots and shapes. You circle it once, twice, and the air, having become pure, powerful joy, breathes into you incomprehensible words, words you've heard before, straight into your bloodstream: "Body and temple, like the universe and boxes of all sorts . . . These are all contained spaces. Only I am able to cut them open, to allow you the chance to breathe and soar."

Petr stood at the open window in his pajama jacket and examined in the light what he'd kept secret, hidden from you: the transparent snow globe. If he weren't holding it, if he were to set it aside, if that artificial, hollow planet hadn't gotten stuck directly in between him and you, he'd be able to see his sister, that night creature soaring somewhat awkwardly through the blinding blaze of day.

A German shepherd rattling its chain, a horse lifting its head to the sky, a frog on its tree-stump throne, even those flies glittering in spiderwebs — they were human beings who had been transformed, just like she had transformed into an owl in the ambulance, to escape danger and to reanimate the world, flittering randomly and bereft of order beyond the glass.

"We'll head South," she decided. It was nothing but nice-sounding syllables, something ordered by the hero in the book she was reading yesterday before bed, just one sound out of a myriad of untranslatable sounds surrounding her that someone had emptied of meaning.

And so the owl flew aimlessly over hills and valleys, silos and headlands, billboards and pine groves, meadows and the town of Tábor, with its rotunda tower and moat — you couldn't be wrong, you'd been here once on a field trip before school vacation with your gym teacher, who'd pressed his lips into an evil line when you botched a cartwheel — the town hall and far below you Jan Hus on the square, pressing his Bible to his chest and gazing upward, enraptured by your wings paddling through the sky.

And there, high above the Jordán Reservoir, with the setting August sun flopping around on the water's surface like a gigantic shiny fish, it happened: word by word, the motion of your wings tore from you the ability to speak, speech disappeared and along with it so did you; nothing remained of the child you once were but a rustle, a flap, a handful of feathers.

Vietnamese market stalls soon appeared below me, women rummaging, rattling hangers of multicolored blouses billowing in the gusts of time that flung me through the air from garden to garden and drove me out of my childhood all the way here. A serpentine row of shoes was winding down the sidewalk out of sight around the corner; dusk began to try them on, one pair after another. A neon sign, HEUTE SECHS GIRLS, glowed hot pink like a highlighter on the facade of a building on Božena Němcová Street. Two or three more flaps of my wings until I finally touched down on a tall, twenty-five-year-old spruce, which I knew because Dita had planted it the year her son was born. My wings, which I could barely move anymore, hung limply beside my body like two broken paddles.

To sleep, to fall asleep, to switch off the mind beneath the veil of branches — dreamless, flightless, no pills, no metamorphoses — to sleep for twenty-four hours and then wake up, pull up the blinds, go to work and for a lunch of halušky with Rybka and to wait in the evening for the sound of the key in the door and Dita, and to laugh and make love all night long. Just moving within the safe belly of the world I am innately a part of, just to prick my finger with a needle and sleep for ages until the gardens, those that are desolate and those inhabited by goblins, are overgrown once and for all by the tangle of vines of the terrible and merciful everyday.

I was just about to lose myself in it when a sudden noise jarred me awake. I forced my eyes wide open. In the light of the moon, the stars, and the lanterns hanging off two apple trees, the lawn beneath me was swarming with a merry company. A few girls were perched on a long, wooden bench at a picnic table, leaning toward each other, whispering, bursting into giggles occasionally as if they were playing the broken telephone game. A house rose out of the darkness behind them — I'd never seen it looking like this before — and its angular silhouette quivered almost imperceptibly, rounding into the shape of some unfamiliar, incongruous phenomenon, possibly a honeycomb or an onion.

A young man in a rainbow beanie stood over the grill, though it was a hot night, and with a blank look on his face, he kept mindlessly poking the meat with a skewer. From time to time, his greasy fingers would push up his large white glasses that kept sliding down his nose, no longer able to see a thing. Another two guys — I curled up in the spruce needles, became one with them so nobody would notice me — were excitedly shuffling around directly beneath me and arguing, brandishing barbecue sticks like rapiers. "Nonsense. You haven't taken into account that if we were to consider both through the prism of genetics . . ."

The other one cut him off. "Genetics, seriously? Don't make me laugh! I mean, while special content can be altered in extensive ways without confusing our instincts and resulting in flawed conduct, the slightest of changes to the structure itself will only lead to confusion!"

The girls were prying corks out of bottles, and one landed all the way underneath my nose. And then I saw her. Dita. Kneeling in front of the fire, she was chucking old gnarled cherry branches into the pit, the flames blazing in her eyes and over her whole face, which the firelight had smoothed of all wrinkles, the line between her and the fire dissolved.

A girl came out of the woodshed with an armful of logs. Though she was hidden behind the stack, I was sure it was her. "Adéla!" someone yelled at her, but she ignored it, it seemed as though she were ignoring everything and everybody here, the conversations, the moon, the wine, even the fire. She set down the wood and knelt by Dita's side.

A pang shot through my heart. I felt a sudden, fierce yearning for Dita to notice me, to invite me to join the cheerful company of her students, to recognize me in my new body, in my new form, which was now strangely constricting me like a hostile force, as if a too tight coat had fused with my skin.

"Dita, it's me, Ema! Don't you recognize me?" Instead of my voice and words, which my flight across the Jordán had torn out of me, nothing but a croaky coo erupted from my beak.

A little pooch hurtled out of the darkness and began to tremble right underneath the spruce tree, barking so loudly it almost choked. I answered it to call you, and since I no longer had tears nor a human voice, I had to go about it like an owl: so I hooted and honked and hollered, I cawed and cooed and croaked, crossly, I crocheted a coniferous cape, a cosmic cloak like this August night sky, just so I could solemnly lay it at your feet as a gift from my travels and a plea for forgiveness.

The girls sitting at the picnic table had fallen silent.

"What the hell are those sounds?"

"Some bird, right?"

"Probably a raven."

"Oh, Professor," one of the girls exclaimed, "would you recite 'The Raven' for us, you're always so good at it!" She must've been failing Czech class that semester and was now obnoxiously sucking up.

"I noticed the BB gun in your garage. We could give the intruder a bit of a scare, shake things up a bit."

The sensitive girls were appalled at the idea and berated their classmate. "You'd seriously shoot a bird that's flown here right out of a poem?!"

Everyone rose and slowly began to approach the tree. The

spruce, not much older than they, was grabbing at the stars with its branches, pulling them down. Dita couldn't resist, though her hands were full, holding a plate of grilled meat, and she actually began to recite the poem, and she really was good at it.

"'Leave no black plume as a token of that lie thy soul hath spoken!

Leave my loneliness unbroken! — quit the bust above my door!

Take thy beak from out my heart, and take thy form from off my door!'

Quoth the Raven 'Nevermore.'"

"Up there, look! That's no raven, it's an owl!"

"And it's got two faces."

The melancholic young man in the rainbow beanie stood only a couple feet away from me, scrutinizing my limp feathers, my neckless head, turning from side to side, uneasy with all the sudden attention, and the white plumage around my round eyes, not unlike his glasses.

"Three," he stressed.

The others turned to him, curious.

"O, what a marvel it appeared to me,

When I beheld three faces on his head!

The one in front, and that vermilion was;

Two were the others, that were joined with this

Above the middle part of either shoulder,

And they were joined together at the crest . . ."

A deep silence settled over them, the only sounds the crackle of burning cherrywood along with the muted din of dance music coming from the nearby brothel HEUTE SECHS GIRLS.

"I wonder if anyone knows," Dita asked excitedly, "what Kamil was just reciting?"

Silence. Some of the youth were a bit wobbly on their feet, evidently worn out by the excess of poetry and wine.

"Dante's *Inferno*, Canto 34."

I suddenly spread my wings, wanting to embrace Dita, but she jumped back in fright, and as she did, the meat from her plate went flying and ended up on Adéla's shirt, standing nearby. Chaos ensued. Dita kept apologizing, someone chuckled, some of the girls began to writhe strangely, at first I thought they were dancing, but they were just shooing mosquitoes, and someone began to vehemently persuade the others to check out the neighboring sechs girls.

And then, with a barely perceptible, slightly ironic smirk on her face, Adéla suddenly pulled the grease-stained shirt over her head. She was wearing nothing underneath. Everyone froze. The moon floodlit her naked body, her pale breasts, and the owl, now forgotten for good, closed its eyes, crushing its sense of sight within, followed by the other senses, one after the other.

To sleep, to fall asleep; yet to be born; to switch off the mind beneath the coniferous veil and return home, and to manage it all on one's own, because no metamorphosis could help me avoid what dances out there, grotesque and radiant, randomly and bereft of order, beyond the glass.

I bought a ticket to Prague. I ordered Kofola on tap in the station pub, which looked as if it hadn't changed one bit over these past fifty years I've been on this earth. At ground level, the scenery along the train tracks, the hills and valleys, silos and headlands, looked completely different. As did the hallway in our old Smíchov apartment building, both familiar and unfamiliar, like a dreamscape transcending any understandable dimensions, as if I were returning to this place out of some bygone age, palpable only in geographical layers, or at least after a vacation.

Maybe Mom was going to reproach me for leaving her all alone that one time in front of the tobacconist at Anděl; that I had slept and slept and slept through the moments she recounted and remembered and sung of Russian romance, waiting for me in vain to join her in a duet, and the moments I'd been floating in the ether and gliding through the waters like an eel instead of safeguarding her sleep.

"Which floor?" A robust woman stood in the elevator with me, in her arms a plastic shopping bag brimming with groceries, sweat trickling down her face and onto the neckline of her shirt. And — as her gaze locked with mine in a staring contest, as if she were challenging me to a rematch after four decades — I was astonished to recognize Karolínka in her.

There wasn't a hint of reproach in Mom's expression when she opened the door to let me in, stepping back into the hall. All those familiar, commonplace items around us grimaced animatedly, some malicious force deforming them beyond recognition.

"I'm glad you came. They brought your dad back from the hospital this morning. He wants to die at home."

•

He was there. The loon wrapped head to toe in a swath of shawl clambered out of some godforsaken, forgotten fissure of time and again planted himself on a bench, wildly cheering someone on. "Go, go, go! You can do it!" he yelled, flapping his arms, and he suddenly began to furiously unravel his cocoon, tearing off the shawl as if he were a reanimated mummy, and then spread it out where there was *absolute nothingness*, unfurling it in the very center of this nothingness, at the core of this void like a path soft and derelict and boggy, along which I continue onward even if it were to curve into a circle and bite its own tail.

•

I wanted to grab her and shake her, to breathe back into her face, transformed by grief into the face of a stranger, that meandering memory of hers. "Mom! Get a grip, for heaven's sake! Dad passed away more than ten years ago!" But a flash illuminated what I should've grasped from the start: a cliff towered in my mother's place in the hall, a jagged rock where time stood still. Like an ocean wave, that age-old "you-too" rhythm, that progression of time, no longer continuous and unidirectional, had been wearing down the rock for so long it had turned it into an indestructible matrix. I ran the pads of my fingers over its surface like a blind woman. They were all there, all the events woven into each other, an enormous onion of one image layered atop another, like an erupted volcano, and if each of these events had become petrified, if even Dad's dying had become fossilized, it could never end, and I'd have to relive it over and over again.

"Hi, Dad."

He was lying in bed in my childhood room, the lampshade still covered in colored stickers and a poster of an Indian on the wall, a quatrain scribbled underneath his moccasins:

Our pal, the Indian,

likes to wear his moccasins.

He takes them off at the door,

so not to soil his mother's floor.

Why is that poster in here? It's ridiculous. It's supposed to hang by the front door. Everything's different, it's all wrong.

Dad said nothing but didn't take his eyes off me. I wasn't sure if I was supposed to stay silent, too, or start chatting away, telling him how Rybka was doing and how work was going, where I was planning to go on vacation, and get this, this one girl stole a wetsuit and this one pastor almost had a stroke in bibliotherapy, and if I were recounting things still yet to happen, so what, I could also read to him political commentary from the newspaper or passages from *The Tibetan Book of the Dead*, I could . . .

I had no idea what I was supposed to do, because nobody had ever discussed dying with me. And as the person in front of me flew through space and receded like a star, all I had to offer him was a wheelchair.

"O nobly born! Listen well to what will occur at the moment when the senses and the elements begin to dissolve. With every thought of fear or terror or awe for all set aside, may you recognize whatever visions appear, as the reflections of your own consciousness; the radiance of thine own true nature."

When Dad's intent gaze began to cause fragments to become the whole and vice versa, I went to stand by the window. Below, trams were whizzing past and in the park across the street I saw that old familiar wilting willow with a hollow in its trunk, which you couldn't whisper a secret into for all the noise, but where you could fit a small enough box, holding the infinitely folded letter from Dita. But even the view from the window was now struck by light, streaming in from an unfamiliar land behind Dad's eyes. Here, too, were objects struck by this light just as in the hall, by that incomprehensible radiance, that revolt; a flowerpot that sprouted a fin glided out through the window; in place of the keyhole, the door had the mouth of an orating dictator; drawers, a grimace for the bottom, shot out of desks and marched across the room on spindly legs; syringes and vials with medicine began to writhe like pale, animated maggots; sleeves of pajamas and nightgowns knotted together and with prostheses jutting out of shirttails stomped a round dance at the foot of Dad's bed; and all these rebels against humankind, all these objects, now transformed beyond recognition, all these pranks and courteous gestures, were ominously running riot through the room, while the only thing inert and not participating was my father, burrowed beneath his blankets.

"Mom, what's this map doing here?" It was spread open on the rug, and I hadn't noticed it until now.

"Dad wanted to find a certain street," she whispered. "Said it's called Ve Studni, but I couldn't find it. It doesn't exist."

I don't know why, but I lay down onto the map next to Dad's bed, somewhere between Hrdlořezy and Smíchov, and immediately fell asleep.

I don't know how long I slept on the map, jolting awake and dozing off, again and again. At times it was no larger than a tiny round pill, stashed in a mint container, other times it expanded into an enormous tarp that could cover a thousand cities.

Suddenly, I heard Dad's voice: "I want . . . Once . . . What's the word . . ."

It almost seemed he had started playing the sound game

with me. He was enunciating each word clearly, with care, like a child that wants to please the adults.

"I don't want to be buried . . . I want ashes."

The hands on the blankets no longer belonged to him. What was now forcing its way out of one space into another, knocking a hole through the ceiling only to encounter another one, no longer resembled him or any other reality that I recognized.

I tried to get up. A section of Košíře tore off the map and clung to my back as if Petr's glue hadn't dried yet.

"Are you even listening to me? I said I don't want it."

But he suddenly switched to the tone he would always use when ordering in a restaurant from a baffled server, "Or just chop me into pieces and feed me to the vultures at the foot of Mount Kailash, like the locals do."

A wasp nosedived into a glass of something viscous and syrupy. I quickly covered the glass with a saucer. Day and night, night and day, I held vigil over its struggle. Oh, just look, just see, you rebels come to life, you pale maggots of things, mad procession of objects! Soon, like this wasp, your dance will end and you'll be immobilized forever in the goo.

A tram pulled up to the stop below. To my surprise the people spilling out of it all somehow seemed familiar, giving off an air of summer and confidence and amiability, like that girl over there in a miniskirt and T-shirt with a gigantic headshot of Kurt Cobain, a poster tube tucked under her arm, which must've contained a rolled-up drawing demonstrating her indisputable talent. I could imagine, quite vividly, inviting her for a Mojito or a Sex on the Beach, and what's in my heart would in no time be on my tongue: "I don't know if you've been informed, but coffins come in two varieties, celluloid with a zinc bottom or metal with a leakproof lining. The cremation itself takes approximately ninety minutes. We primarily use an eco-friendly, computerized procedure as well, and it ensures that no carbon dioxide, the main greenhouse gas, nor the toxic mercury in tooth fillings are released into the atmosphere. It also frequently happens that pacemakers are not removed from the mortal remains and subsequently the battery explodes in the furnace."

I went to get a straight razor and washbasin to shave Dad's face. Like the Fates, sitting at our kitchen table, underneath which I'd mobilized my bean army once upon a time, were three impressively well-maintained and positive-minded ladies, as if they'd rushed over here straight from the pews or an aerobics class. "Life goes on," the fattest of them proclaimed, the one next to her quickly adding, "The pain . . . it'll pass." It seemed as if they'd divvied up consolation into three equal portions like a cake, and when the last one finally blurted out, "Time is a great healer," I couldn't help myself and slammed the door so loud that only shards remained of their platitudes.

"Dad." I positioned the washbasin under his chin. He was eying me with interest when he suddenly asked, "And who are you?"

I searched his gaze for the telltale signs of irony, of facetiousness, but an overgrown, unfamiliar child was lying in front of me, one that was seeing me for the very first time. I froze. Like my mother before, his question had transformed me into a rock where time stood still.

"It's me. Ema," I spluttered, "your daughter."

He wagged his finger at me, "Now now, Nurse, don't be silly! I don't have a daughter. Only a son. His name is Petr.

Not the sharpest tool in the shed, true . . . Resented school, spent his days peeking into Mom's pots in the kitchen. He trained to become a chef."

Nobody had ever discussed with me what it's like when a loved one no longer recognizes you. The universe simply contracted into the hollow trunk of that willow tree and abruptly became the sum total of a passing of time I no longer wanted nor could be a part of.

I turned my back to my dad. His shaven stubble was floating in the washbasin, flitting around in a sort of symmetrical dance like protozoa underneath a microscope. Though the Indian on the poster was clad in ridiculous slippers, almost as awful as the ones my mom had given me for Christmas, he had his bowstring drawn tight and aimed directly at my father.

And I suddenly heard the barely perceptible sound of clicking in the room. Someone else, other than the Indian, my dad, and I, was also in here. I looked around. In the dusk-drenched corner, a gaunt woman was seated on a kneeling chair, dressed head to toe in black and absorbed in her task of darning a sock, stretched out on a wooden mushroom. When the needle came into contact with the mushroom, the soft click echoed through the light my father's mind was transforming into, as if the sweep hand of a clock somewhere had jumped ahead.

"Thank you for coming."

The gentle rapping of the needle must've set off the sudden avalanche within me, held back all those days and nights, and I knelt down next to the woman and hugged her knees and right there, on the floor by her stockinged legs full of runs, the tide of sleep began lapping at my feet, washing up mangled shards of grievances onto the shore. "I change out the bedpan and shave him and even give him his shots — me, who's terrified of needles! — and then he goes and says he's only ever had a son! He'll depart, disappear, ditch me, he'll clear out and hightail it out of here, leaving me here with nothing but useless consonance rattling around in his urn. But what about me, today, tomorrow, in ten years' time? Just a worthless eel and owl fleeing from garden to garden, forever doomed to searching for a way out. Dream follows dream follow dream, and Petr . . ."

But Mrs. Schwarzová abruptly cut me off. "Stop complaining. And stop your whining and accusing, it's unbecoming. Remember, nobody likes a girl who's a tattletale, especially one who doesn't eat her spinach."

I wanted to ask her to finally translate those three words in that unknown language for me, I wanted to ask, just to keep talking, how her cat was doing, but just as somewhere in the future, the motion of my wings tore from me the ability to speak, now death had molded the syllables into a mere muddy, stuttering clod. "Why bother . . . with the socks, I mean . . . Nobody sews nowadays, nobody mends or darns, if that's the right word . . . just throw them out and buy new ones."

The room was plunged into darkness. The willow outside the window now resembled the long, thin shadow cast by Mrs. Schwarzová. No sooner did the light of the streetlamp touch the tree, along with all the things and people in the street below, than they vanished like the elements of my father's dissolving consciousness down the gullet of that mysterious radiance. I no longer heard the clicking of the needle nor her soft reply coming from the corner of the room, "The dead do, Mrs. Černá. The dead still darn socks."

The Fates had long departed, and Mom was napping on the couch in the living room. And as if the darning mushroom had turned into a drum and the needle into a drumstick, as if an orchestra were tuning up for a symphony, a deafening, thunderous rhythm suddenly staccatoed through the apartment.

"Stop it, you hear? He's not going to need those socks anymore!"

My own shouting jolted me awake. The bedside lamp covered in cheerful stickers was on. Dad was sitting on the edge of the bed, bare feet planted on the floor, and was rummaging through a dusty old trunk full of toys.

"Dad, what're you . . ." I quickly corrected myself. "Sir, don't walk around barefoot in here, exposed needles might be lying around."

"Nurse, this trunk," he mumbled apologetically, "was underneath the bed . . ."

I looked at the alarm clock. It was exactly 3:20 a.m., the time my brother fights his wife's demons. I began to pull toys out of the trunk and handed them to my dad, one after another, just like he'd once done for me. And suddenly there was nothing left to nourish any questions, and Mrs. Schwarzová had disappeared, too, nothing, not fatigue, not helplessness, not death. Battered wooden blocks, the disemboweled Mr. Mouse with his botched surgery, a pichenotte board, and nuts and bolts from the Merkur construction set were floating into the hands of the dying man through the enormous eye of a needle, and he caught them, gripping them in his hands before releasing them, just like his mind had been doing a while ago with his memories, holding them up close to his myopic eyes and touching them and setting them aside on the duvet, and I watched as those objects were assembled into an endless, tender caravan, paving a way for him out of time itself.

He thumbed a layer of dust off the roof of a railway car, pressed his face to its windows, and peered inside. It was an exact replica of an actual train, the narrow corridor leading into a tiny compartment complete with sliding door, and I could see what he saw and watched in awe as Rybka and I squirmed in our seats, my dad handing us cookies and sandwiches wrapped in cellophane; it was snowing heavily and the river the train was now passing was rolling from side to side like a colossal white dream-being, on its bank a fisherman made of snowflakes sat on his camp stool. And Dad broke a cookie in half and the ice floe on the river snapped and cracked and thunderously floated off with some unfathomable, mysterious cargo, and that impenetrable stubborn geometric screen of snowflakes transformed our train compartment into a transparent globe, the snow swirled by the jolting of the train, the clatter of the railroad ties, and Dad's voice: "Look out! Tunnel!"

He began to tickle Rybka in the darkness; she kicked her legs, flip flops on her feet, still too short to reach the ground, and when we emerged from the tunnel, they both acted as if nothing had happened. The conductor, puny as a LEGO figure, began yelling at us for leaving wrappers and crumbs all over the floor, and I looked out of the window and jumped back in alarm. Something strange was obstructing my view, and it wasn't snow. Pressing against the window was a dark lake, a bottomless well, inside which the remaining elements of the world were dissolving.

Dad finally tore his eyes away from the train car and placed it on the duvet. We rummaged around in the trunk for a bit longer, dusty toys lying all around us, on the carpet, on the bed. This torso with one long, thin arm must've belonged to a

Barbie I'd filched from Karolínka, and this small jester's lute . . . "Śūnyatā . . ." a string twanged, and another responded, "śūnyatā . . ." and then at once the third one, because that's as many as the lute had, snapped and lashed me across the face.

I looked at Dad. A whirlwind shook him, slamming into him at the top of a chute, which twisted down into a steep, endless maze. And my father hurtled for an eternity and a second and his mind exploded into the emptiness like a holiday fireworks display, and he clenched his fist.

I heard three final exhales in rapid succession, the three final phonemes of our game. I knelt down by the bed and closed the trunk.

Two undertakers waited at the front door, standing on the doormat underneath which I had once, and then later over and over again like in a freeze-frame, searched for a pill for oblivion, standing there, rigid and alert, like two-dimensional plywood mannequins, looming like silhouettes at a shooting range, wearing dark suits a size too small, white socks sticking out of their pant legs, just like my dead dad on the bed.

A coffin was set in the corridor behind them. It evidently was neither celluloid with a zinc bottom nor metal with a leak-proof lining. This one looked shapeless and shoddy, as if it were one of my brother's cardboard creations slapped together at the last minute.

I was taken aback by how big it was. I'd have thought that coffin makers take into account the width of doors. They do. It surprised me how easily it fit through our door.

Mom and I slipped Dad's favorite pair of Oxfords onto his feet, the ones he always wore, under the pretense of business meetings, to Café Louvre to observe the aquarium with water turtles hatefully snapping at each other's heads. And then I forced open Dad's clenched fist. It looked as if he were hiding something in it. Three tiny hex nuts from the Merkur construction set lay in the center of his palm. I quickly shoved them, so the undertakers wouldn't notice, into Dad's pocket, those three minuscule nothings, practically invisible like snowflakes, their core motif repeating in endless variations, that Dad took with him on his journey.

•

Oh, where were you then, brother of mine, where in that moment in time? What were you in the middle of cooking in your pots, simmering with your fervent prayer, wrapped up in itself? Whose facial expression did you steal this time, in this moment of three rusted hex nuts, before peeling it off like plastic wrap? I see your reflection in the polished handles of your knives, I see you wandering the streets, asking random passersby for the time so you could steal their voices as well, and I see you embracing your naked wife, glowing with anxiety in the empty bathtub. Have you taken up residence on some stranger's ceiling, or are you relishing the sight of your collection of bounties of the sea? I ask like an ocean wave that has brought them to your shore, I ask you again and again and will never cease asking, each time differently and yet identically: Oh, brother of mine, where were you in that moment in time?

•

The door slammed, Rambo's bundle of keys rattling in her fist on the other side. I took a deep breath, as if I wanted once and for all to inhale and ingest all the details I had left behind in there, along with those yet to surround me, which I would step into like into a swarm of mosquitoes.

A tote bag full of dirty laundry and my notebook of tic-tac-toe scribbles over one shoulder, my knapsack over the other — it almost looked as if I were returning home from some half-assed summer camp, nothing but stupid scavenger hunts and a baptism in a cesspool. From afar, all the way from the farm, or so it seemed at least, I heard the ape's furious howl.

Above me was a sky bluer than ever before, not a single cloud in sight, with only a smattering of crisscrossing contrails. And before I set out on the road of the loon's shawl, ready to lead me, docile and reconciled, out of the Garden, I sat down on the bench where he had once been hopping and turned on my phone after three months. It began beeping awfully, emitting whiny sounds for a while like the gluttonous dog that ate the cake in that fairy tale by Josef Čapek.

"Dear Ema! I hope you're feeling better . . . Unfortunately . . . In accordance with the provisions stipulated in the Labor Code . . . per § 52 cl. C . . . On grounds of redundancy . . ."

Fired, then. Something I should've expected, that a women's magazine and a debilitated owl don't go together well. In my head, the White Queen began to promenade along one of my synapses, back and forth, her crimson lipstick lifting into a smile. "Congratulations, Mrs. Černá! I really must offer my sincere congratulations!" she kept repeating behind the familiar fan of cards, whose faces only she could see. "Congratulations for being asked to provide the decisive facts, such as your record of social security payments, on the basis of which you will be registered as a job applicant and will begin receiving unemployment benefits. You will occasionally be required to show up at the employment agency where you will take a number and with the other socially maladjusted stare at the TV screen, where a professional auto body man is merrily tightening a screw and a professional chambermaid is even more merrily and responsibly prancing across the hotel carpet with a vacuum cleaner. You might feel a moment of despondency; it's hot and stuffy in here and everyone's absent-mindedly crumpling their number tickets in their sweaty palms, and nobody here will give you a gold star, not even for filling out the dozenth form, and if that weren't enough, two wooden earlobes joined by a needle are squatting next to you on the bench, ten sharp acrylic nails jutting out of them, and the ceiling is under your feet, as if a Ferris wheel had turned you upside down; but everything will change once your individualized plan is formulated under client number 8212! A young woman bearing the expression of a tortured saint will hand you two available job postings: in Světví, yes, the name of the town is really 'world knows,' there's an opening for a skilled furrier and in Harrachov a snowboard instructor; it just won't do to mire yourself in the muddy Botič, to enter a painting, or to get lost in any old galactic gutter, gaping beyond the farthest outskirts of your hometown; after all, it's only two tram stops from the employment agency to the welfare office; God knows why, Mrs. Černá, but I do, forgive me, hold it against you because it doesn't make a good impression, you keep lugging that knapsack wherever you go, at least you're not visiting these offices in your slippers, that absurdly tacky, ultimate capitulation courtesy of Vietnamese market stalls. A woman turns to you in the tram, she looks familiar, as if a mirror were growing out of her bloated neck instead of a head, and she holds out her hand, palm side up; I have nothing, you say, through clenched teeth, I'm literally on my way to hand in my welfare application! I don't want to worry you, I mean, you can always appeal the rejection of your application per § 77 Art. 2, and rejected it will be, within fifteen days of the decision; but you will suddenly feel ashamed: 'You there,' you address the woman in a gentle voice, 'did you happen to see a different kind of world pass by here?' — 'Eh? The goblin plays by ear?' — 'No, you don't understand. I just mean that, sometimes, when all hope is gone . . .' — 'My words exactly. Humans are the devil's spawn.' The Earth will stop spinning, the lone star will freeze in place within the depths of the universe; all this awaits you, Mrs. Černá, all this and so much more . . ."

I stopped listening to her. I was worried sick about Rybka. She was on a train, currently on her way to the seaside, and though her legs could reach the ground for a while now, I was afraid she'd find nothing but the sandy valley of the five senses extending endlessly beneath her feet and, instead of my brother, just an oval-framed portrait, his likeness disintegrating into a tangle of lines.

I looked back. Something beyond all understanding began to near Pavilion No. 8 from behind, over the ground and through the sky, that painfully vivid, solid blue. It looked like an enormous rosy cloud that some threatened animal had discharged to conceal itself, but it was actually something altogether different: the surrounding air was quivering with heat like during a fire; it was a medusa, a jellyfish that engulfed the entire building along with the nearby, endlessly sprawling landscape filled with hospital beds and eclipsed with its body all the barred windows and leeched onto the pavilion and concealed it within its tentacled grip, crushing it in its embrace.

When it pushed off from where the pavilion had stood for more than eighty years, nothing remained in its place.

And yet deep down I knew that someone had rescued them from the ruins, that someone had yanked them out of that hellscape one by one at the last second before it detonated, transplanting them faster than a fleeting thought out of that threatened locked-down space to safety: I spotted the round-ness of Marcelka, kneeling at a flowerbed in front of her beau-tiful new house, the azure eye of a swimming pool straight out of a catalogue at her back, also the White Queen, Irena, hands finally free of cards, a Louis Vuitton handbag hanging from her arm as she preened in an outfit by a top Czech fashion designer at a fancy banquet, a glass of water in hand, elegant gentlemen with extraordinarily sensitive fingers orbiting her, and just as I resurrected her, as soon as I managed to roll aside the stone barring the entrance to the cave tomb where she had been rotting until now in her thigh-high nightie, Marie thun-dered out of it on that old Jawa 250, hurtling to God knows where while clinging onto her dad like a tick; and then the others also emerged, Tree-Dana and Vladěna and the fragile nymph, the lamb who wanted to suffocate me with a pillow, and Gizela with Tiny, who immediately got lost amid the dancing crowds at a Shakira concert, and finally Blanka Vodseďálková alias Karmela, Mother Theresa pointed her camera at her twins on the seesaw, "Take a deep breath, damn it!" and, "You gotta push off more!" and they pushed off from the ground with all their might, disappearing in the sky and reappearing on the ground until the camera went off and everything was plunged into darkness.

I got off the tram and wasn't even surprised by the towering church in place of the newsstand with the fatso and Bistro

Pivoňka. Nobody was inside, not even that sleeping man whom I hadn't been able to wake up that one time, just in the distance, where the enormous, pierced feet of Christ loomed over it all, something kept intermittently howling and falling silent: a woman in a headscarf, babushka style, was pushing a vacuum cleaner, hoovering the altar carpets.

This time, no snow was falling onto the floor. As expected, the Gothic ribbed vault towered over everything. The saints were clutching crucifixes, animals, and Bibles to their bosoms. Please turn to page 66. "All that night the Lord drove the sea back with a strong east wind —" Mrs. Černá, are you paying attention?! You're still on the road to Damascus! ". . . and turned it into dry land. The waters were divided, and the Israelites went through the sea on dry ground . . ."

I didn't want the woman with the vacuum cleaner to notice me, so I treaded lightly, crouched and silent, on the dry ground, walls of water to the left and right of me. I ascended the wooden, spiral staircase to the pulpit, taking the stairs two at a time. That tiny door was at the very top, so tiny it couldn't possibly be intended for a human being. Nearly kneeling, as if I'd taken up praying at the last minute after witnessing those parted waters, I was just about to grasp the door handle when someone abruptly yanked the door open from the other side. I fell through it.

"Welcome aboard our Boeing 737." Mrs. Schwarzová, for the first time not dressed head to toe in black but in the chic uniform of a flight attendant, handed me the tabloid *Blesk*. I collapsed into a seat and began to leaf through it. One story caught my eye: "A woman from the Icelandic town of Hlynur can recall every single event in her life from the past 25 years. She is even able to remember exactly what she was doing, with whom she met, and what she had for lunch on any given day."

Suddenly, I heard laughter and an odd rustling sound somewhere behind me, as if someone were tearing apart cardboard boxes, or as if a diminutive person were pushing their way into the world through a sheet of Christmas wrapping, giggling like crazy. The tiny door was here for them.

I turned around. Rybka. I wanted to call out to her, to explain so many things and clarify so many others, but I had no words left, something inside me had snapped for good, like the three strings of that old jester's lute.

She was sitting next to my brother Ash as they looked through her drawings of tadpole people, and with their heads leaning against one another, as though one were growing out of the other, nothing but rustling and laughter.

And Mom was sitting over there! She was drowning in her seat and examining us all with worry, scrutinizing us one by one to see if we were dressed warmly enough for the trip, if Rybka wasn't laughing too loud, and if Dad didn't forget to pack some of his medication.

In that moment, Mrs. Schwarzová rose to her full height in the aisle and with a blank expression and robotic motions began to pantomime the safety demonstration for us, all those steps needed to activate one's lifejacket. Our eyes were locked on her, only Dad kept his face pressed against the plane window, observing with a hungry curiosity, like that one time with the toy train, the unpredictable trajectories of the laden luggage carts crisscrossing the tarmac.

"There's an order to it," he mumbled to himself, "I just have to figure it out. It's an incredibly complex, yet highly efficient system."

226

"Dad," I whispered tentatively as the engines began to rumble and the airplane taxied to the runway, "where are we going actually?"

He gave me a look of disbelief, his expression almost one of awe mixed with disgust, like that time he'd been tutoring me in geography and I couldn't for the life of me remember the capitals of the Baltic states.

"Come on, you know. You have to know. Why are you asking?"

Of course I remembered: Vilnius, Riga, Tallinn. And for a while, I kept repeating those three words like an incantation, like a mantra, like the only prayer I knew by heart, and of course I knew where we were headed: to Strašmania, the land of the all-possible.

Like that bygone plastic bag, the plane rose above the city in meanders and pirouettes, above the cityscape shrunken to the size of a crossword puzzle, and as we flew through the clouds into the blue, soaring above all the ceilings of the world, all the defined phenomena and apparitions, all the individual entities, transformed into an infinite flow, into waves of the identical, into the dazzling surf of non-elements and dance figures.

NOTES

79   *City on the Kama* . . . : a song composed by Lev Alexandrovich Schwarz : Город на Каме / Где — не знаем сами / Город на Каме / Матушке-реке.

80   *Take a sheet of paper* . . . : The passage is a paraphrase of Thich Nhat Hanh's sermon on "Interbeing," based on the Czech translation.

92   *the time of mobilization:* in the spring of 1938 Czechoslovakia mobilized reserves in anticipation of an attack from Nazi Germany that never materialized. The border regions are still dotted with concrete bunkers from that time.

100   *I ride around* . . . : the four lines are taken from the Radůza song "Dědek s cibulí" ["Graybeard with an Onion"].

103   *O nobly born* . . . : from *The Tibetan Book of the Dead.*

136   *You like it when the day covers you in ash* . . . : the italicized lines come from the song "Udržuj svou ledničku plnou" ["Keep Your Fridge Full"] by Monika Načeva with original text by Jáchym Topol.

149   *Abbé Dobrovský:* The Josef Dobrovský Monument at the edge of Kampa Park, right across from the plane tree planted by the Kolowrats in 1813.

196   *Otesánek:* A folk tale by Karel Jaromír Erben, it was made into a film of the same name (known in English as *Little Otik*, or *Greedy Guts*) by Jan and Eva Švankmajer.

ZUZANA BRABCOVÁ (1959–2015) was born in Prague to the literary historians Jiří Brabec, a signatory of Charter 77, and Zina Trochová. Denied by the Communist regime the opportunity to study at university, she worked as a librarian, hospital attendant, and a cleaning lady. After the regime fell in 1989, she had a short stint at the Ministry of Interior before serving as an editor at Prague publishing houses. Her first novel, *Far from the Tree*, came out abroad in samizdat in 1987, and was awarded the very first Jiří Orten Prize, and officially published in Prague a few years later. In 2000, she published *The Year of Pearls*, a groundbreaking novel for Czech society about coming out as lesbian. Her novel *Ceilings* appeared in 2012, receiving the Magnesia Litera Award for Prose Book of the Year, and it was followed by the short novel *Aviaries* in 2016, completed just before her untimely death and winning the Josef Škvorecký Award for best work of fiction.

TEREZA VEVERKA NOVICKÁ was born in California to Czech parents who had fled Communist Czechoslovakia. She grew up in San Francisco before moving to the Czech Republic in 2000 and completing her MA in American Literature at Charles University in Prague. She has translated a number of Czech and Slovak poets into English, including Ondřej Buddeus, Sylva Fischerová, Nóra Ružičková, Olga Pek, and Jan Škrob. She is the co-translator of *The Absolute Gravedigger* and *Woman in the Plural* by Vítězslav Nezval, and translator of *Aviaries* by Zuzana Brabcová and the monograph *Ludvík Šváb: Tidy Up After I Die*.

CEILINGS

Zuzana Brabcová

Translated by Tereza Veverka Novická
from the original Czech *Stropy*,
published in 2012 by Druhé Město, Brno

Design by Silk Mountain
Set in Janson Pro
Frontispiece by Rybka Ivanko Brabcová
Cover image by Unica Zürn, *Untitled*, 1965,
reproduced by permission of Brinkmann & Bose Verlag

First edition 2025

TWISTED SPOON PRESS
P.O. Box 21 — Preslova 12
150 00 Prague 5, Czech Republic
twistedspoonpress@gmail.com
www.twistedspoon.com

Printed and bound in the Czech Republic by Protisk

Distributed to the trade by
SCB DISTRIBUTORS
www.scbdistributors.com

CENTRAL BOOKS
www.centralbooks.com